ELMORE LEONARD
STICK

"A writer with a deadly accurate ear and a lovely rhythm . . . A little beauty of a story . . . a hot, fast read with pungent characters and a particular code of honor as one of its central tenets. Above all, it feels real."
Los Angeles Times

"Cream of the crime writing crop . . . Leonard's dialogue and descriptions are so good that they . . . keep the reader glued to the pages."
Chicago Sun–Times

"The hottest thriller writer in the U.S."
Time

"Brilliant . . . Wonderful . . . Perfectly executed . . . *Stick* is the kind of book you spend days quoting to your friends."
Detroit News

"No one writes better dialogue. No one conveys society's seedier or marginal characters more convincingly . . . Leonard's sardonic view of the world proves immensely entertaining, and not a little thought-provoking."
Detroit Free Press

"A surprise on every page . . . Elmore Leonard keeps you guessing."
Boston Globe

Books by Elmore Leonard

And in Hardcover

Tishomingo Blues

ELMORE LEONARD

STICK

HarperTorch
An Imprint of HarperCollinsPublishers

❦

HARPERTORCH
An Imprint of HarperCollins*Publishers*
10 East 53rd Street
New York, New York 10022-5299

First HarperTorch paperback printing: August 2002
First HarperCollins trade paperback printing: November 1998
First William Morrow hardcover printing: February 1983

HarperCollins ®, HarperTorch™, and ❦™ are trademarks of Harper-Collins Publishers Inc.

Printed in the United States of America

Visit HarperTorch on the World Wide Web at www.harpercollins.com

10   9   8   7   6   5   4   3   2   1

For Joan, always

_____

1

STICK SAID HE WASN'T GOING if they had to pick up anything. Rainy said no, there wasn't any product in the deal; all they had to do was drop a bag. Stick said, "And the guy's giving you five grand?"

"It makes him feel important," Rainy said, "it's how it's done. Listen, this's the big time, man, I'm taking you uptown."

Rainy told Stick he didn't even have to say a word unless the guy Chucky asked him something. Which he probably would, Chucky liked to talk. He was a you-all, he talked real nice and easy, real slooow, slower than you, Rainy said. Stick said he could hardly wait to meet the guy, thinking: Rainy and Chucky . . . like they were hanging around the playground.

You go out to Hialeah, Calder, Rainy said, everybody out there, the cocktail waitresses, everybody, they call him just Chucky. But you go down on Southwest Eighth Street, around in there, or some places down in South Miami where they used to know him on the street, anybody down there they still call him Chucky Buck, Rainy said. It was like his street name before he moved up to his top floor condominium. Yeah, Chucky Buck. Now, he went to his country club, any place like that, he used his real name again, Chucky Gorman. He was about forty but tried to act young. Big guy. Not real fat, but he had a weird shape for a guy, like a woman. Maybe he was even kind of a weird person, some people thought he was a switch-hitter. But a nice guy. You could jive with him, say anything you want, Chucky never got bummed or nothing.

Rainy's real name was Rene Moya: light-skinned Puerto Rican and something like one-eighth Haitian from his mother's side. He drove van loads of marijuana from Miami up the Interstate to Toledo and Detroit. He weighed a hundred and thirty and wore a neat little waiter mustache.

Stick's name was Ernest Stickley, Jr. He was forty-two years old, born in Norman, Oklahoma, but raised in Detroit where his dad had come to work at Ford Rouge. Stick looked like he was from another time: dustbowl farmer turned hobo. He was at a low point in his life.

He and Rainy had met in Jackson, Michigan, when both of them were staying at 4000 Cooper Street, gateway to the world's largest walled prison: Stick doing seven to twenty for armed robbery; Rainy three to four, possession with intent to deliver, after they told him, "You walk you talk," which meant probation, and he turned them down, hung in and did the full three. Rainy got out a few months before Stick's release date. He told Stick to come down to Miami and get some sunshine, some fresh air, man, meet some chicks. Stick said he was going down there anyway to see his little girl; he hadn't seen her since she was seven.

What they were doing now was not recreation; it was to make a buck.

Stick kept looking at the girl-bartender because she was so fresh and clean looking she could be in an orange juice or a suntan lotion ad. She had a glow to her, perfect tan, perfect white teeth, a tall girl with nice easy moves, natural. She wore a little nameplate that said her name was Bobbi.

They had come up from Miami to Lauderdale in Rainy's new van to meet this guy Chucky and run the errand for him.

The place they were in was called Wolfgang's, a marina bar on the Intracoastal at Sunrise. Outside, every half hour a bell would start dinging and the bridge would go up to let a few cruisers and sail-boats go by. Inside, then, somebody down at the end of the bar would blow what sounded like a foghorn, a baritone moan and everybody, all the late afternoon fun-seekers, would break up. There was a terrace outside with an awning where you could sit and drink and watch the boats go by. Otherwise, it was like a lot of bars with rose-tinted mirrors and high-gloss wood-grained plastic. A Happy Hour bar.

Everybody was sure working at it.

Didn't these people have any problems?

Even Rainy Moya seemed happy, feeling the beat and giving the oval edge of the bar funky little finger slaps like it was a fifty-foot bongo. Stick thought it was disco, the music coming out of turned-up speakers somewhere. He mentioned the word disco and the guy on the bar stool to his right—maybe the only guy in the place older than Stick, a hairy bald-headed guy wearing mirror sunglasses and a nautical blue-with-white-piping beach outfit—said disco was out, nobody discoed no more. Stick didn't like the guy looking at him, hanging on everything he said to Rainy. He asked what people did now if they didn't disco and Rainy said they fucked. Rainy said man, you been away too long, you got to get caught up with the scene. The music still sounded like disco. Latin disco. Rainy said no, man, it's fusion, it's rock, it's a lot of beats. Where you been?

Stick thought he had kept up. Eleven Block, for honor inmates in maximum security, had its own lounge area on the floor of the cellblock with a color TV. But maybe he had missed a few important events and passings. Nobody had told him when Warren Oates died last spring. He had heard about Belushi but not Warren Oates. He subscribed to magazines . . . He did a hundred push-ups and sit-ups a day the first year and toward the end of the seventh year . . .

Rainy and the tourist in the beach outfit were talking past Stick, vouching for each other, the guy saying everything was different now and Rainy saying that's right. The guy saying especially the broads. Rainy saying that's right, nudging Stick and saying listen to him. The guy saying he was married twice but not now, all the stuff around, a guy would have to be out of his mind to get married. Stick glancing at the guy—thinking no way, never, not this guy—and seeing two of himself, his face distorted, sickly, in the guy's mirror sunglasses; he looked a little better in the tinted glass behind the bar, but the girl-bartender, Bobbi, giving all the loudmouths a nice natural smile, meaning it, not putting it on, made him feel old. Why was she happy, working in this place, watching people get smashed? . . . Rainy was saying that's right, man, you don't have to waste no time buying drinks you don't want to; you see a chick you ask her she want to do it, man; she don't, okay, no problem, man, you go ask the next one.

Stick left his bourbon and went to the men's room. He was tired of hearing guys talk, guys wanting you to believe they were street, guys saying *man* all the time. He shouldn't have called Rainy. Well, maybe call him and have a drink, but he shouldn't have promised him anything. Stick washed his hands with the fragrant pink soap that came out of the dispenser, washed them good and stared into the clear mirror at his features. Pale, solemn. Who was that? Like looking at someone else. Back in another life before Jackson he could narrow his eyes at his reflection—hard-boned but not bad looking—and say, "That's it, huh? That's all you got?" Then grin and catch a gleam in there and know that if common sense, intelligence, caution, all the straightarrow stuff ever failed him there was always bullshit to fall back on, live by your wits and a tight sphincter. But there was no gleam today. White skin, white shirt, he looked like he just got off the bus with a cardboard suitcase. He came back from the men's room and nothing had changed.

Sliding up on the bar stool, he said to Rainy, "Is he coming or not?"

Rainy looked at the clock face in a miniature ship's wheel behind the bar. Five-forty. Rainy said, "He don't get here by six, man, we go to his place. It's right there, across the bridge." He nodded toward the sunlight out on the terrace—across the waterway that was like a wide canal—to the dock and sloping lawn of a condominium.

The tourist turned to look as Stick did, giving

Stick the back of his mangy head, bare on top, sun-
burnt, oily strands of hair hanging over his terrycloth collar. Stick heard Rainy say, "Bobbi? . . .
Hey, Bobbi . . ." and now Stick caught a glimpse of
his two faces in the mirror sunglasses as the tourist
turned this way again, the tourist keeping his nose
right in there. The tourist saw Rainy trying to get
the good-looking girl-bartender's attention and
called louder than Rainy did, "Hey, Bobbi!" She
looked up, capping a strainer over a martini shaker,
pouring, raising the shaker up and down, twisting
off that last drop. "Get your ass down here," the
tourist said. "We need you." He said to Stick, "I
wouldn't mind some of that. How about you?"

Stick looked at the guy hunched over the bar,
hairy arms, big hand wrapped around a gin and
tonic. Stick said, "You got short eyes? That your
problem?"

The guy's forehead creased. "What?"

Stick turned away. The girl was coming over to
Rainy now. She looked like Cybill Shepherd, tall,
that type, but younger. She was about the healthi-
est-looking girl Stick had ever seen. Outdoor-
looking in a pink knit shirt with a little alligator on
it, one of those polo or golf shirts—but not like the
other girl-bartender who wore hers tight with her
breasts sticking straight out, encased—no, Bobbi
wore hers loose with a natural sexiness in the way it
hung and the way it strained against her when she

made certain moves. She seemed almost too young to be working in here.

Stick's daughter was fourteen. He hadn't seen her yet. He'd called, spoken briefly to his ex-wife . . .

Rainy was saying to the girl, "Chucky been in?"

She shook her head. "Haven't seen him." She said, "No, so far it's been a perfect day."

"I wasn't sure he stuck his head in and we might have missed him," Rainy said.

She said, "Are you serious? How could you miss Chucky?"

Stick liked her tone, the easy confidence. He'd bet she was aware and didn't miss much. She said, "You guys want another one?" looking from Rainy this way, directly at him now. Stick shook his head. Her eyes lingered a moment and he felt a lift and wanted to say something to her.

The tourist said, "You can do me. Fact I'd let you do just about anything you want to me."

She said, "Big deal."

The tourist said, "Honey, it might be the biggest deal you ever saw. If you get my meaning." He reached over to pat her hand, resting on the bar.

She raised her eyebrows and began to say something as Stick said to the tourist, "Keep your hands off her."

The tourist looked over. "What?"

Bobbi said, "The way it goes, don't touch what you can't afford."

Rainy was off his stool. He came around with his hand moving across Stick's back. He said, close to him, "Hey, come on, man, let's take it easy."

Stick said, "Short eyes . . . Look at him."

The guy said, "The hell's he talking about?"

Rainy, still close to Stick, said, "For who, man? We're in a bar."

"Look at him," Stick said.

"All right, it's all right, man, we got to leave anyway. It's time to go." Rainy kept his hands on Stick's shoulders, turning him away from the tourist, getting him down from the stool.

The tourist took off his sunglasses, squinting, sitting up straight. "What'd he just say?"

"It's okay, we got to go," Rainy said and looked at Bobbi, who hadn't moved. "Lemme have the check. No, we'll be back. I'll take care of it later. Okay?"

Stick heard the guy say, "Jesus Christ, some kind of weirdo . . ." but didn't look at him or at the girl. He was strung up and had to get out of here.

They left the van in the parking lot and walked across the bridge with the traffic moving toward the ocean, tires humming on the metal grid. Stick breathed in and out. He could feel the sun on his back and could feel the Atlantic Ocean two blocks away, beyond the mile-long public beach with its blue cabanas stacked up for the day. He began to come down.

"Man, I see your face," Rainy said, "I know I got to get you out of there."

Stick said, "You hear him, what he said?"

"What did he say? He's jiving her a little. He has some drinks and goes back to the Holiday Inn. Has to sit there and look at his old lady."

"He told you he wasn't married. Didn't you hear him?"

"Hey, listen to you. What difference does it make? He's got an old lady or he don't, nobody cares." Rainy reached up, laid his hand on Stick's shoulder. "Man, you were the one taught me how to be cool, you remember? Showed me how to make it, not take everything personal, you remember that? Serious things, yeah, you go all the way, but not bullshit things. It's the same out here, man. You got to tell the difference, right? You didn't have to prove nothing. What was that in there—little bullshit play with the girl Bobbi? She don't care. She gets that shit all the time."

Stick didn't say anything.

"You're out with the civilians now," Rainy said, "you dig? It's a free country out here, man." He poked Stick's shoulder and let his hand drop. "Buy some new clothes and get laid a few times you feel better."

They moved into the shade of the fifteen-story

condominium and started up the drive. A Cadillac stood by the entrance; two guys in suits, sportshirt collars sticking out, were talking to the doorman, looking this way now.

"They work for him," Rainy said.

The two guys were watching them come up the blacktop grade, both with hands in their pants pockets, giving them dull stares. Stick could see them standing in a cell-block yard in work clothes, down jackets. You could wear anything you wanted at Jackson—if you could keep it and not have to give it to some colored guy with a knit cap down on his eyes. Walk in cherry they would try to take your clothes first, if your clothes had any style, then get around to trying for your body. Most of the cons there were black. Still, you saw the tough white guys with the solid bodies and dark hair. That type, they all had the thick dark hair and stood like they were daring you to move them out of the way. The difference here, Stick realized now, these dark-haired guys were probably Cuban. They were serious mean looking, but not as big as the dark-haired guys he was used to.

"You know them?"

"Maybe," Rainy said. "I'm not sure. He's got plenty of people hang around him."

"What's he scared of?"

"Are you kidding me?" Rainy said.

2

IF HE HAD TO MAKE a decision over the phone as opposed to just shooting the shit, Chucky liked to
take the call in his den where he had a conference
speaker system on his eight-foot desk and, over by
the door to the living room, a hat-tree loaded with
different kinds of hats and caps. He'd put one of
them on—the salty yachting cap or the big straw
cowboy hat, the hardhat if somebody was trying to
give him a hard time, the long-peak fisherman's cap
if he was being philosophical—and move around
while he carried on the phone conversation.

When he was moving, Chucky believed, it was
like he felt his mind and body on "high" and fully
alert, his neurons flashing, making the right connections. It went back to when he was hyperkinetic
as a little kid: ten, eleven years old, Christ, he went
through something like four dogs, ran the ass off
them; they'd come dragging into the house, their
tongues hanging out, gasping. He said when he got

to running full out even hounds'd throw it in, fuck it, look up at him with those sad eyes.

Chucky said he mellowed out quite a bit since he'd grown up, found a plateau he could live on in peace. The steps: flunked out of Wake Forest prelaw. Reached an incredible screaming high in Nam, seven months in-country to a time, two hundred days compressed to a time he couldn't move to save his mind, had no way to release the panic short of killing himself and tried to, tried like hell . . . and was brought down with Thorazine at the VA hospital in Memphis. The final step, Miami, where Charles Lindsay Gorman III passed through his Chucky Buck phase, hustled, got rich and found happiness on a maintenance dosage of Valium and 'ludes: before meals or whenever his motor got stuck on high idle.

The effect of his medication was like swimming under water, only without any water. Floating in lights. He still moved, felt the urge, but he wasn't moving kinetically now, he was floating. He'd load up and let the mood move him along. Cock the straw boater on the side of his head and do a soft shoe on the parquet floor of the den, shuffle stiff-legged to this draggy Kool-and-the-Gang beat he'd turn on softly in his head. Just float, experiencing hundreds of thousands of colored lights popping inside his head like trip flares, only without a sound. See, Chucky said, your hearing gets so acute you have to soundproof your head, turn the decibels way down.

For some reason he had found himself explaining this phenom to the young guy working for the Cubans, Eddie Moke—the person he was talking to right now on the phone—and Moke had said, "That's what you do, uh, float? I think you got brain damage, man. I think you ought to check it out." With that frozen sound Moke had, barely moving his mouth. The boy was a study, trying hard to effect the grungy look of a heavy-metal rock star, the headband, the illustrated disco shirt open all the way . . .

He should never have told Moke about floating and doing the soft shoe. The only reason he had was because of the way Moke sat on his spine, giving himself curvature, practically lying in whatever chair he was in, and Chucky had asked him how he could stay like that without ever moving, like he mainlined cement. You would say things to Moke and he wouldn't respond unless he had to and then would barely move his mouth. And Chucky would take another swing at it, yes, just like trying to bust cement. The Latins dressed up and posed and gave you snappy TV lines—"What's happening, man?"—but this Moke, he'd lock his jaw like a stoned rocker and give you dreamy slit eyes. Hardest thing in the world, trying to talk to him on the phone . . .

Chucky said to his conference system, "You still there?"

Moke's voice, a nasal twang partly hidden in there, said, "Yeah, I'm here."

"Well, what do you think?"

"I think you better pay the man."

Chucky, circling his desk, ran stiff-curled fingers through his hair—the wiry blondish waves kinking back on his head—made a glide over to the tree and put on his orange hardhat, set it low over his eyes.

"I'm *going* to pay him. That's not the question I asked you, boy. Have I ever said I didn't intend to pay?"

The speaker system remained silent.

An idea edged its way into Chucky's brain. What if the boy kept his mouth shut because he felt alone, like some redneck manure-spreader among all the Latin dandies? What if the boy was simply self-conscious? It had occurred to Chucky there was another image that would fit him better. A bronc-stomper was what Moke should be playing, not some candy-ass rocker.

But that analysis would have to wait.

Chucky continued circling the desk. "To answer the question, no. I told Nestor that. I told *you, you* told *him*." Keep the record straight. "He gets delivery tonight. Two-hundred thousand paid in full. In hundreds—Lionel says he got all used hundreds and a Samsonite bag tested by a four-hundred-pound gorilla, so we know it won't come open, right? Blow away. But giving him a *person* along with it . . . that's pretty weird shit we're talking about there, you know it? I think it slips Nestor's mind he's living in Miami, Florida, now. You know what I mean? Mention to him if you would, we're part-civilized here. Our gods don't think much of human sacrifice."

"They don't?" Moke's voice said.

The boy could be dry if you fed him lines. Chucky moved from his desk toward the balcony, then remembered something and changed his direction. At the door to the living room he removed his hardhat and pressed in close to the door panel to look through a peephole.

The girl sat at the near end of the sofa, giving Chucky her left profile from about fifteen feet. More than pleasant looking though not sensational. She sat paging through his latest copy of *Shotgun News* with some degree of interest. Sandals, slim legs crossed, she'd go about a hundred and five. It looked like a beige sundress under the white cotton blazer, the sleeves pushed up a little on her arms. Nice tan. No jewelry except for the Cartier-style watch with the leather band. Blond-streaked hair to her shoulders, cut off he would say abruptly, a manageable style, simple—rather than all swirly curly the way Chucky liked a girl's hair. She didn't look anything like he'd been picturing her since talking to his friend Barry and arranging the date. No, she looked like somebody's sister, like she'd smile a lot with healthy uncapped teeth, hands folded in her lap and say, "Gee, Mr. Gorman . . ." She also looked, from here, about eighteen years old. He'd see in a minute if she was any good.

Chucky swapped the hardhat for the snappy yachting cap he tilted low over his eyes. Moving back to the desk he said, "Tell Nestor . . . tell him before he starts free-basing this evening, gets to trembling and becomes devilish . . . I expect a call."

The phone speaker remained silent.

"Tell him we have customs, too," Chucky said. "Gringo customs. We kill a chicken, we eat it, we don't shake beads and sprinkle its blood around. He wants a life for a life, he has to ask for it himself. It has to come from on high, not told to me by some messenger boy."

Silence. Though Chucky knew this one wouldn't last.

Moke's voice said, "I expect you realize how much you need him, you want a good source."

"Like I need a three-foot yang-yang," Chucky said. "The man comes through, why not, all the dough he's making. But I'll tell you, the association is far from comfortable. Nestor, all he has to do is see *The Godfather* on TV, he goes freaky for a week. The point here is, he *knows* I wasn't playing that tune. I *didn't* set him up. I made an honest mistake . . ."

"You made a dumb mistake."

"Which I'm paying for. But you tell him, hear? I'm sitting on the cashbox till he calls me."

Silence.

"You got it? Grunt once for yes, two for no."

"You threaten him you know what he'll do."

"Tell me," Chucky said. "Keep talking while your mouth's still open."

"He'll cut off your product or your *cojones*, one."

Chucky said, "Do you know how many times in the past ten years I've been cut off, sold out, fucked over, picked up, jerked around one way or another and yet, look-it here, who's still king of the shit pile?" Pink warning lights began popping before his eyes and he paused to let them settle, melt down, wanting to use only a portion of his energy. He said, "It's dumb to get mad at the help for what the master's doing. I got a young lady waiting out'n the living room wants to proposition me . . ."

Moke's voice said, "You calling that little piss squirt my master? Jeez-us Christ."

It stopped Chucky cold. He cocked his head, looking at the telephone machine on his desk.

"There may be hope for you yet," he said, beginning slowly. "I've seen white boys, fine young men, take on that greaseball strut, that curl to the lip, and land in a federal correction facility for showing off. Isn't anything the DEA despises worse'n a white boy turned spic or hippie on 'em. You worked for me I'd dress you up, Mr. Moke."

"Thank the Lord Jesus I don't," Moke's voice said, still not hiding that unruly twang.

Push him some more. "You believe," Chucky said, "I can't change your life or even bring it to a close?"

"I would like to see you step up and try," Moke's voice said, with enough pure bottomland in it to make Chucky break into a grin as he stepped over to the tree and exchanged the yachting cap for the big straw cowboy hat.

He reached back in his mind and across the river then—take Crump Boulevard from the VA hospital—all the way over to West Memphis to get more of a shitkicker edge to his tone and said, "Tell me something, I'm curious. Where you from? I'm going to say . . . you ready? I'm going to say inside of fifty miles of some snake bend in the Red River. Am I right or wrong?"

There was a long hesitation before Moke's voice said, "How'd you pick that out?"

"I'm right, huh? Where you from?"

"Texarkana."

"You don't mean to tell me. Come on," Chucky said, "I was going to *say* Texarkana and I chickened out. I just had a strange feeling."

"You did?"

"Listen, tell me something else. What's a cowboy like you doing working for a pack of breeds?"

"Making wages," Moke's voice said.

Chucky waited a moment, holding himself still. "I bet you've never been turned loose, kicked outta the chute, so to speak. You know what I'm saying? Allowed to show what you can do."

"I bet I haven't neither."

"You don't take part in that weird *santería* shit, do you?"

"They start painting chickens I go on over to Neon Leon's have a cold beer."

Chucky waited again. It was hard.

"Hey. I just had a thought. What would you say to coming by here for a few cold ones, tell some lies? Say tomorrow? I got a hunch about something."

"What's that?"

"I don't want to talk about it over the phone. Let's wait till tomorrow."

"I suppose I could stop by," Moke's natural voice said.

"Fine," Chucky said. "Yeah, hey. Tell that weird

Cuban I need a word with him. You suppose you could do that for me?"

"I'll see what he says," Moke's voice said.

"Shake her easy," Chucky said.

He sighed, worn out, switched off the system. Like trying to get a little girl back in olden times to take off her panties. It was hard labor, what you had to do to cover your ass and stay ahead. Work work work:

Moke did strongarm chores for the Cuban. Moke would be a dandy choice—dumb, eager and right there—to take the Cuban out should the need arise.

3

SHOTGUN NEWS, **KYLE MCLAREN LEARNED**, offered a lot more than shotguns. It was a tabloid-size catalogue of military weapons and gear: rifles, handguns, nasty-looking submachine guns, knives, machetes, steel whips . . . steel *whips*? . . . Dutch army helmets, mustard gas in a handy ten-ounce aerosol container . . .

It occurred to her she might have to do a double check on Mr. Gorman, ask around, learn a little more about his lifestyle. *Shotgun News* did not go with the brocade draperies, the formal, traditional furniture, the huge Hudson Valley landscapes in the heavy gilt frames. Or did it? Maybe his mother had decorated the place. Maybe Chucky Gorman was hardline NRA, ready to defend his property against Communists, Cubans, Haitians or citizens of Miami in general; living thirty miles north might not be to him a safe enough distance.

There was a phone with extension buttons—one

of them lit—on the marble coffee table, no ashtray, no other magazines. *Shotgun News* was it.

How about a nice MIA-E2 semiautomatic rifle with matching handguard, sling and bipod? Set it up on the table and get them coming over the rail of the fifteen-story balcony.

It occurred to her, also, to move from the sofa. The sliding glass doors to the balcony were directly across the room, the draperies pulled back all the way, so that she faced sun-reflected sky flat on the glass, a west exposure. If Mr. Gorman sat across from her she wouldn't be able to read his expression. But as Kyle waited and the sky paled, lost its fire, her mind changed with it.

Why bother to move? To begin with, she was almost certain she was wasting her time, that she would not be able to relate to a grown man who went by the name "Chucky." She could recall only one person in her whole life named Chucky and he was a little kid back in New York, a spoiled little pain in the ass, in fact; so there you were. The profile she had on this Chucky described a man:

Thirty-two who looked at least forty. Originally from Georgia, a well-to-do family that milled cotton for generations, carried Chucky on a remittance for a time—he'd had some kind of mental problem—then cut him off, disowned him. It didn't matter though, because Chucky did all right on his own: invested, bought real estate, belonged to a good club . . . But what did he do exactly?

Her friend Barry Stam, who was also a client and had indirectly arranged this meeting, said, "Ask him. See what he says." Barry, with his put-on innocence, eyebrows raised. "I'll be interested to hear your impression, what you think of him."

"Does he have money? I mean a lot."

"Wait and see," Barry said, deadpan. "He's an unusual type. Colorful, you might say."

She waited, all right . . .

Almost a half hour before a door finally opened and there he was.

As for Kyle's instant impression—as Chucky came in with his shirt hanging out, wearing untied sneakers, baggy pants and a straw cowboy hat, grinning—she had to believe this Chucky wasn't much older or much different than the other Chucky she had once known on East Thirty-first Street in New York. This one was a great deal larger and in his heart, beneath all that bulk, he could be a *Shotgun News* freak, a hardline conservative, an eccentric with Old South connections, but he sure wasn't anyone's image of a serious businessman.

Look at that sweet young thing.

Chucky believed he loved girls who were sweet

and wholesome, without guile or wile, because he didn't know any. But here was one right in his own living room. He felt alive.

Then felt the cowboy hat perched on his thick crown and raised his eyes to make sure that's what it was. He said to the sweet girl, "Whoops, you caught me playing." He pulled off the hat as he walked back to the den, sailed it inside and slammed the door closed.

"Now then . . . So you're Kyle McLaren." Sounding like he couldn't believe it. Which was true, though he gave the words more amazement than he actually felt. "I enjoyed the newsletters you sent. You write all that stuff in there?"

She said, "Yes, it's part of the service." But seemed just a bit vague. Now getting her neat mind in order.

"And you come all the way down from Palm Beach to see me? I appreciate it."

She said, "Well, I get around—"

"Hey, I bet you do."

"I travel quite a lot," Kyle said. "So I don't consider the drive from Palm Beach a major effort."

That sounded pretty neat and orderly. Chucky slipped over next to the coffee table to look down at her, get a closer view. Delicate girl features—a touch of blush, lip gloss maybe, just a speck—but with a backpacking outdoor look about her. Her right hand rested on a straw handbag next to her.

"You don't have a little mini tape recorder in there, do you?"

He heard her say, "No, I don't. Why, do they inhibit you?" as he turned and walked a few steps toward the balcony. Stopped and turned back to her with his grin in place.

"I know people these days'd have you patted down before they'd say a word. Which doesn't sound like too bad an idea." He paused, catching her solemn expression, and said, "I hope you know when I'm kidding."

Kyle said, "Why don't you give me a call sometime when you're not"—picking up her handbag—"and I happen to be down this way."

Chucky said, "Hey, come on, I'm serious now. Look-it how serious I am."

But she glanced toward the door and so did Chucky at the sound of three light raps. Chucky said, "Yeah? Who goes?" and one of the double doors opened.

Lionel Oliva, in a pale-blue double-breasted suit and silky gray sportshirt, stepped in from the hall. He said to Chucky, "Rainy is here. What should I do with him?"

"Jesus, Rainy," Chucky said, "that's right. Put him in the den."

"There somebody with him. Rainy say is a friend of his."

Chucky squinted. "You got one of my shirts on."

"You gave it to me," Lionel said.

"Yeah, I guess it's all right," Chucky said. "Rainy's insecure." He started to turn away and stopped. "Lionel? You ever see the guy before?"

"No, it's somebody he met, you know, where he was up there."

"Yeah, I guess it's okay," Chucky said. The door closed as he turned back to Miss Kyle McLaren . . .

All eyes. Look at her looking at him, the little broad from Palm Beach in her pure and spotless sundress, clean undies and a light cotton blazer, perfect for business or casual wear, for that cocktail at the Everglades Club with an important client or maybe even Mr. Right . . . He could see a shot of her and this clean-cut bozo in *Town & Country*.

"What can I get you?"

"Nothing, thanks."

"You don't drink?"

She said, "I don't care for anything." Sitting on the edge of the sofa. "Why don't we try to do this another time?"

"No, look, you're here," Chucky said. "Let me ask you one question, we can play it from there. Okay?"

She nodded. "All right."

"What do you think of gold?"

"Right now? I like Swiss franc futures better."

"Come on, how do you see it as an investment? What I want to know is, you going to give me a straight answer or a lot of words?"

"Well, first of all"—she sounded vague again—"you don't invest in gold, you speculate. The British fleet moved on the Falklands last spring and the price rose twenty-three points the first two days . . ."

"There. That's what I mean by words," Chucky said, moving in on the coffee table again. "Now you're going to tell me about uncertainties in the world market, devaluation of the pound, all those Wall Street words. Right?"

"And as the fleet sailed," Kyle said, settling back into the sofa but not taking her eyes from his, "*Evita* was still playing in the West End. If you find that interesting maybe you'd like to back a Broadway play. It offers about the same risk as grain futures, but it's way more fun. Or, if you like movies, I can show you a film offering that doesn't look too bad."

Chucky's grin this time was honest, sincere. "Very clever. Movies, I never thought of movies. You know what the last one I saw was?"

"*Gone with the Wind*," Kyle said. "Do you do much trading?"

"In what?"

"I mean are you active in the market."

"Well, you know, now and then. But hey, listen.

If I invested in a movie, would I get to meet any starlets?"

The girl just stared at him.

"I'm serious," Chucky said. "Something like that, that sounds interesting. But let me tell you where I'm at, okay? The particular problem I run into . . . No, first you tell me a few things. See if you're the type of expert I need."

She said, "What do you want to know, my background, business experience?"

"Yeah, where you been, how old you are . . ."

"I'm thirty-one," Kyle said. "I started out as an analyst at Merrill Lynch, moved to Hutton to handle accounts . . . came down here and opened my own office two and a half years ago . . ."

"You married?"

"No."

"You fool around?"

"Mr. Gorman, I have to tell you something."

"Please, Chucky. Everybody calls me Chucky, even the help."

She said, "Chucky," carefully, as though she was trying it out. "All right . . . Chucky." She bent her head down and up, brushed short bangs across her forehead. "I'm getting a kink in my neck, looking up at you."

"Hey, I'm sorry." He took several steps back. "How's this?"

"Why don't you sit down?"

It was as though the idea hadn't occurred to him. He said, "Yeah, I could do that, I guess." And came around the coffee table to sit sideways on the sofa, arm extended, his hand resting against the high rounded back.

She said, "Can I ask you something?"

Her eyes surprised him. A soft blue. Calm. No gee-whiz expression lurking in there. Ah, but the hands were folded in her lap.

"Ask anything you want."

She said, "What are you doing?"

Chucky stared, see if she'd look away. But those calm eyes didn't move. There was a slight bump in her nose. That and the shoulder-length hair cut off abruptly and without any swirls gave her the outdoor look. Her mouth, very yummy, lips slightly parted . . .

He said, "I think I'm falling in love. No, what was the question? You want to know what I'm doing. You mean right now as of this point in time? I'm interviewing you."

She said, "Oh," and nodded with a thoughtful expression.

"Aren't I?"

She said, "Do you know what I do?"

"Yeah, you're like an investment counselor. Right? Tell people what to do with their money."

She nodded again. "That's right. But I specialize, you have to understand, in private placements, growth opportunities, usually going into new companies that need equity capital."

Chucky said, "Yeah, but why do I have to understand it as long as you do?"

"I want to make a point," Kyle said, "so that we understand one another."

Quiet voice to go with the quiet eyes. No girlish tricks. Yes, a first. Chucky was sure of it.

"I spend most of my time," she said now, "finding the opportunities. I'll look into as many as fifty companies to find one or two with what I consider above-average potential."

"How do you find 'em?"

"Leads from people I know. Bankers, lawyers, stockbrokers . . . So you can understand that if I were to show you a limited partnership opportunity that looks promising, or a start-up company that's about to go public, I've already put a lot of time into it. And time is money, isn't it?"

"I've heard that."

"So when you say, at this particular point in time, you're interviewing me, you have to understand something else."

"I do? What?"

"That the chances of my turning you down as a client are far greater than your not accepting me as your financial advisor."

"Jesus," Chucky said, "and you look like such a nice sweet girl."

"I am a nice girl," Kyle said. "Sweet? I don't know. If you mean passive, submissive—"

"No, I understand," Chucky said. "What you're saying is you don't take any shit from anybody, or at least your clients."

"There you are," Kyle said, and gave him a nice-girl smile. "Should we try to be serious, or would you rather not?"

"What do you do," Chucky said, "you scare the shit outta your clients? I have to say, I heard a lot of good things about you."

"From whom?"

"Well, Barry Stam, one. Some others at Leuca-dendra. I get down there to play golf once in a while." He paused and said, "I don't know if I should be telling you that?"

"Why, because Barry's a client of mine?"

"Let me put it this way," Chucky said, "if you're going to ask Barry about me, then I might have to open my soul, tell some secrets so as to give you the straight dope"—he grinned, turning it on and off—"so to speak. Yeah, we're friends, play golf, fool around. But Barry, whether you know it or not, is very impressionable. He likes to—well, he has a certain image of himself and likes to associate with people you don't ordinarily, you know, find in country club circles. You know what I mean?"

"Tell me," Kyle said.

"He likes to think he's on the inside, knows

where the action is. That's why he hangs around the Mutiny, Wolfgang's, places like that. You follow me?" She seemed to nod. "Anyway, I heard a lot of good things about you; though I don't know if you can help me out any. See, I've talked to advisors, financial planners. These guys, they come in here in their dark-blue three-piece suits, the alligator cases, graphs, all kinds of statistics, and you know what they do? They blow smoke at me. That's bad enough, trying to understand what they're talking about. Then, when I go to tell them about my particular situation, explain my plight, so to speak—"

The phone on the coffee table rang, a light showing.

Chucky got up. "I have to take that."

She seemed surprised he didn't pick up this phone.

"Would you like me to leave?"

"No, stay put," Chucky said, walking away. "I won't be but a minute."

Kyle watched him slide open the glass door, step out on the balcony. There was another phone on the metal patio table. He picked it up and turned to the railing as he began to speak, hunching over now in the privacy of the fifteen-story drop, his shape clearly defined now against the sky. A very strange-looking guy. Big all over, high waisted, narrow through the shoulders, the broad hips of a woman . . . and a sagging crotch. Chucky was a picture.

She could imagine this Christmas sitting around the table with her dad and her two older brothers—"I've got to tell you about Chucky. You won't believe it"—her mom and her brothers' wives in the living room while Kyle and the boys talked about stock gambits, swindles, high rollers, placed bets on the Super Bowl, raked over Reagan, David Stockman, the Federal Reserve Board, made fun of dogmas and people in high places and would laugh until her mom stuck her head in the door with her look of quiet amazement. Her dad had been on Wall Street since she was a baby and remained, he said, because he didn't know how to do anything else. She would never tell him she made more money than he did, with her snobby Gucci-Cartier approach to investment counseling; though it was her dad who'd told her rich people loved to be pushed around—as long as they believed they were being pushed exclusively. Her dad was dry, the cynic who'd never cheered, screamed or cried until her brother Jim moved up to the Red Sox from Pawtucket, had a 12-2 record by the All Star break his first year, pitched three scoreless innings and finished the season 18-8. Jim was a stockbroker, now, still in Boston. Her brother Mike had made it through Columbia Law and was now an agent in the New York office of the FBI.

She pictured telling Chucky about "my brother the Fed" and had to smile. He could be tiresome, but at least he was different. She might go with Chucky.

4

STICK TRIED THE LEATHER CHAIR behind the giant desk, swiveling slowly from side to side as he stared at the phone system, at the dull orange glow in one of the extension buttons.

He said, "I bet what's his name, Chucky's talking to somebody. You want to listen in?"

It brought Rainy away from the glass doors, coming over with his shoulders hunched like he was tiptoeing, not wanting to make any noise.

"Come on, man, don't fool around."

"I haven't touched it."

"He's got phones all over this place," Rainy said. "You know how many phones he's got?"

"Four," Stick said. "Five?"

"Five, shit. He's got . . . I think he's got one, two, three, four . . . five, six, seven"—Rainy seemed to be picturing them as he counted, punching the air with one finger, giving it short jabs—"eight, nine, he's got like twelve phones up here."

"That's a lot of phones," Stick said. "He must like phones, huh?"

"He has to have them," Rainy said. "Chucky owns the whole top floor up here, the apartments like connected together. Cost him, I hear, a million dollars. Shit, that's nothing to him. Some of his guys stay here. That one, Lionel Oliva, he's like his bodyguard. Chucky has an apartment he keeps a broad in when he's got a broad here, you know, staying. I don't know if he's got one staying here now or not. Chucky goes through broads, man. They don't stay too long. He gets rid of them or they get nervous being with him and have to leave. Some guys—did I tell you that? They say he's a switch-hitter, but I never seen him with anything but a broad."

Stick said, "No chicks, huh?"

Rainy said, "What?"

"Nothing," Stick said. He'd think about it, see if there was a distinction between a chick and a broad. Or ask Rainy about it sometime. He got up from the desk where he was making Rainy nervous and looked around the paneled den. The wood walls and floor made the room seem bare.

Stick went over to a row of framed color photographs of groups of men in sporty attire. A group with golf clubs. A group standing by a row of sailfish hanging by their tails. A group having drinks on the fantail of a yacht. The name, lettered in gold on the stern, was *Seaweed*. This one interested Stick because there were two girls in string bikinis standing among the soft-looking guys in their Easter-egg outfits, the girls acting coy, trying to appear surprised, their mouths saying *Ohhh* to whatever the guys were doing or saying to them. Stick looked a little closer. One of the girls wore a gold slave chain around her bare middle—yeah, and the comedian next to her with the wide-eyed who-me? look had his hand behind the girl and was pulling the chain tight so that it dug into her nice flat belly.

"The one in the pink shirt on the boat?" Rainy came over and pointed. "That one. That's Chucky."

Stick didn't say anything right away. His first impression, Chucky was one of those poor miserable slobs everybody picked on when they were kids, washed his face with snow, and he'd slink off rubbing his tears and snot, to go eat some candy.

"Is that Chucky's boat?"

"I don't think so. If it's his he never ask me to go for a ride."

"Nice-looking broads."

He said it to see if Rainy would correct him, tell him no, they were chicks. But Rainy didn't say anything and Stick turned away from the photographs.

There was a dartboard hanging on the wall, the paneling around it gorged with tiny holes.

There was a TV set. At first Stick thought there were two standing side by side but then saw the smaller one was a home computer. Seven years ago he remembered computers as big metal boxes. Now little kids were playing with them. He had not played any of those games yet himself; they looked complicated.

He picked up from the floor a straw cowboy hat with a big scoop brim and looked inside it. The "Crested Beaut" model, with the initials CLG engraved in the sweatband. Stick placed it on the hat-tree that was piled with hats and caps of all kinds. Different-colored golf caps, a yachting cap, an orange hardhat, a straw boater, a red military beret, a long-billed fisherman hat, a New York Yankee baseball cap, a tennis hat. The guy seemed to like hats and telephones.

Stick walked over to the glass doors, slid one open and Rainy said, "Lionel told us to wait here, man."

"I won't go too far," Stick said.

It was warmer outside than in and felt good. He'd have to get used to air conditioning again. The sun was going fast now, laying off beyond where the Everglades would be, just the top part of it showing now, fiery red, but you could look right at it. You could almost see it going down.

Directly below, on the waterway, it seemed hours later, already getting dark down there, the boats

showing their running lights, and there was a string
of dull amber bulbs along the awning of Wolfgang's
outside terrace. Stick was looking almost straight
down at it and could hear the music, a faint pulsing
beat he would swear was disco. They'd have to remember to go back after and pay the tab. He could
picture Bobbi, the friendly bartender, the easy way
she had with the young guys coming in high-fiving
each other, making loud remarks. Rainy was right,
he had to lay back and get with the rhythm of it
again. Loud remarks that could get you stabbed in
Jackson didn't mean a thing outside. Just guys
showing off, trying to act like studs. That Bobbi
was sure nice looking . . .

Stick straightened from the metal railing, looking down the length of the balcony, and saw a
heavyset guy with his shirt hanging out, maybe
thirty feet away, and it took him by surprise. At
first he thought the guy was throwing up, the way
he was leaning over the rail; but now he straightened and did a little pivot and Stick saw he was
talking on the phone. It had to be Chucky. Even
without the pink shirt he had on in the boat picture, yeah, that would be Chucky. He didn't look
like the type of guy who owned the whole top
floor of a condominium. He looked to Stick like a
guy, if he was ever in Jackson, would be somebody's live-in old lady before he ever got out of
R and G.

* * *

Chucky was saying into the phone, "I'm not holding out on you, don't say that. You and I been doing business . . . Come on, you know goddamn well I would never . . . What? . . . *No*. Why would I want to cut off my source, for Christ sake? Look, we been all over that. I goofed, okay? I got taken in same as you. Listen, I even had his plates run on the computer, they didn't show . . . What? . . . Okay, yeah, you're right . . . Nestor? . . . Hey, Nestor, come on, it's done, it's over with . . . Yeah, I'm sorry. I told you that, Christ, how many times? All I want to know—and I appreciate your calling—I was wondering now you've had a chance to think it over, you know, calm down some, how about I pay you the two hundred and we call it square?" Chucky leaned over the rail again, concentrating as he listened to the heavily accented voice. Finally he said, "Hey, if it's that big a deal with you . . . No, but I got to tell you it's weird." Chucky straightened again, looking out at the very top curve of the sun, all that was left. "Am I arguing with you? I'm saying it's weird, that's all, but how you see it, amigo, that's up to you . . . What? No, as far as I'm concerned it's out of my hands once I send the man with the cash. Like any other drop . . . No, I don't want to hear any more about it. How you tip the boy is up to you . . ."

* * *

Kyle watched him replace the phone and straighten very slowly to pause and look out at the sky. Different now—he'd been animated during the phone conversation, shoulders hunching, arm extending, gesturing, his big rear end swaying as he leaned over the rail. For several moments he stood noticeably still.

Now he was moving again, wound up, coming back in with a painted-on smile, shaking his head.

"How about stock in a bulletproof vest company? Jesus, the way things are getting around here . . ."

He seemed to want a response to that, waiting, the grin turning to a little-boy sly look.

Kyle said, "There's a U.S. affiliate of an Israeli company that makes bulletproof ski jackets, jumpsuits, mostly casual wear. They come in nylon or corduroy with removable panels of a DuPont protective fiber. I think Kevlar Twenty-nine." And waited to see if that impressed him.

Chucky stared back at her. "Guy I was just talking to, he's looking for U.S. investments, loaded, wants me to find him something. But you know what I get from stockbrokers, the investment experts?"

"Tell me," Kyle said.

"They say things like—you ask 'em about the

market, they say, 'Well, it's due to take a fairly dynamic upturn if prevailing uncertainties related to
interest rates and the price of bullshit futures can be
resolved during the coming quarter. . . . ' I don't
like uncertainty," Chucky said, moving again. "It
upsets my tummy-tum and when I eat I get consti-
pated, I get cramps. But you know where I'm coming from, don't you? I don't have to spell it out."

"No, I would just as soon you didn't," Kyle said.
"An interest in bulletproof vests and—how did you
put it?—'the way things are getting around here,'
and by that I take it you mean down in action-
packed Miami."

"See?" Chucky said. "You know."

Kyle hunched forward, leaning on her knees.
No, it wasn't going to work with Chucky standing
up. She sat back again, brushing at her bangs with
the tips of her fingers.

"You see, Chucky, when a client comes to me
with nervous disorders, popping Gelusils and so
forth, I tell him first of all I'm not a doctor. And second, if the deals I suggest are keeping him awake
nights, then he should be in treasury bills or money-
market funds. Beyond that . . ." Kyle shrugged.

"No, my problem . . ." Chucky said and hesitated.

Kyle came forward again, slowly. ". . . Is getting
someone to sympathize with your problem. Isn't
it?"

"There," Chucky said, "you know exactly where I'm at. They come in here in their dark-blue three-piece outfits, the black wingtips, guys they look like they shower and shave about four times a day. I tell them I got a very special problem . . ."

Behind Chucky, on the balcony, a man in a white shirt looked in as he walked past the open sliding door. Kyle saw him briefly, there and then gone.

"No, that's not true," Chucky said. "I don't say anything about a problem. It *becomes* a problem when they start fooling with their glasses and these tight little knots they've got in their prep ties like they never heard of dealing in cash before. It's like, I go in Holy Cross over there for a few days, see if I got ulcers, gastritis, whatever. Have the upper and lower GIs, the barium enema . . . You know you get to look at your insides on TV now? The doctor goes, 'Go ahead, take a look.' I tell him, 'You outta your mind? I want to see my bowels, for Christ sake?' . . . I go to pay, the cashier, she doesn't see any hospitalization written down on my papers, she goes, 'Don't you have Blue Cross?' No, I tell her I'm paying cash. Her mouth drops open down to here. 'But you owe four thousand three-hundred and eighty-two,' something like that, '*dollars* and fifty-three cents.' I go, 'Yeah? What's the problem?' She doesn't know how to handle it if you pay in cash. Same with these guys in the dark blue suits . . ." Chucky was moving, turning.

Just as the man in the white shirt, on the balcony, was passing the doorway again, glancing in as he went back the other way.

"Hey!"

Chucky stopped him as Kyle watched, surprised. "You mind telling me what you're doing here?"

"I'm with Rainy," Stick said.

"You don't look like you're with Rainy to me," Chucky said. "You look like you're walking around my home taking in the sights. What're you, an appraiser?"

Stick turned to walk away.

"Wait a minute," Chucky said. "Wait just a god-damn minute there. I asked you a question. You're walking around my place like somebody invited you in—you see anything you like?"

Kyle watched the man stand awkwardly for a moment, as though he didn't know what to do with his hands or didn't know how to answer. Though his expression, staring at Chucky, seemed at ease. It caught her by surprise when he stepped into the doorway. He looked around the living room, taking his time. He looked directly at her.

Then looked at Chucky again. He said, "No, I guess I don't," and walked away.

Chucky turned to Kyle. "You believe it? Jesus Christ." He started for the balcony but turned again, doing his pivot step, and said, "The hell with it. I'll get it straightened out."

Kyle said, "You don't know him?"

"I never saw him before in my life." Moving again. "We're having a time here getting down to business." He turned to her, rubbing her hands together. "You don't want a drink, huh?"

Kyle shook her head. "No, but go ahead."

"You see why I get ulcers, people walking in. I don't mean as a habit, but I tell you, I get involved now and again with some weird folks," Chucky said. "Did Barry—you mentioned he's a client of yours—did he tell you much about me?"

"He said, 'Wait till you meet him,'" Kyle said, "and gave me that sidelong look over his glasses with his eyebrows raised."

"I can see him," Chucky said. "Well, the gist of it is, I got funds looking to go to work and I don't know where to put 'em. Not only because I don't read *The Wall Street Journal*, but like I mentioned not having Blue Cross–Blue Shield, people don't know how to act you say you deal in cash. You get away from condos, which I'm sick to death of, getting jacked around by the developers, having to discount my dough—I don't even like condominiums, I don't know what I'm doing living in one." He paused. "But it's safe up here, you know it? It's pretty safe, usually."

Kyle said, "You don't have to bare your soul. In fact, I would just as soon you didn't."

"Anyway, what's my goal, the American dream,"

Chucky said. "What else? Put money in some gim-
mick everybody *has* to have, get rich and retire. No
more worries, no more looking over your shoulder.
So the boys in the dark-blue three-piece suits come
up here, the wingtips, I start talking, they start
pulling at their little ties. I think I ever showed them
the actual funds, emptied out the suitcases and the
ice coolers, piled it all on the table, they'd strangle
to death."

Kyle was nodding, trying to be objective about it
and discovering that she was accepting Chucky's
problem without too much trouble. It surprised her
that she felt no aversion. But then money was simply money. It had no intrinsic moral value. It passed
from hand to hand . . . and a one-hundred-dollar
bill in Miami today could be in Minneapolis tomorrow, one of a thousand others just like it buying a Bridgeport milling machine.

She touched her throat. "Well, I'm not wearing a
necktie."

Chucky looked at her with a gleam. "No, you're
not, are you?"

"I'll tell you right now though," Kyle said, "I
don't do laundry."

Chucky grinned. "That's cute. But how does it
help me?"

"Well, I don't see why I couldn't advise you,"
Kyle said. "Get you into an equity situation that
looks promising. I've got several. Barry bought into

a beautiful little company in Dayton last month. They make instrumentation to measure analog and digital signals."

"I see high-tech in my future," Chucky said. "Computers. That's where I understand it's at." He saw Kyle staring at him, waiting. "*I* read. You think I'm not up on all this shit?"

"By the time you read in *Time* magazine about a trend," Kyle said, "it's over. That's when you sell short if you're going to do any trading at all. Don't worry, I'll find you something. If they want your investment bad enough you can deliver it in one-dollar bills in a wheelbarrow. So don't worry about that either . . . As long as you pay my fees by check. Can we agree to that?"

"No problem," Chucky said. "Boy, you're fun, you know it? You're so girlish and yet . . ." His expression began to change, the gleam becoming smug. "It's not going to bother your, let's say, your propriety any, doing business with me?"

"You have a lawyer, don't you?"

"You kidding? I got a law *firm*."

"And they charge you fees."

"Up front, a retainer . . . Yeah, I see what you mean." Chucky grinned, still with that smugness. "So I won't worry any about your personal ethics." He winked. "Just kidding."

Kyle said, "Good, and I won't worry about your

drug habit." She gave him her nice-girl smile. "And I'm not kidding."

Lionel came in with the suitcase and laid it on the desk. It seemed to Stick like a ceremony: all of them standing around waiting, Rainy taking the suitcase now, bringing it down to his side and hefting it. "Tested by a four-hundred-pound gorilla," Chucky said, "so we know she won't come apart on you."

Rainy was grinning. "You always say that."

Stick waited, nothing to do. Lionel was looking at him with a sleepy expression, heavy features slack. Rainy had said Lionel's name was Oliva, a Cuban; all the guys, he said, that worked for Chucky were Cuban. He had five or six of them hanging around this place, some others when he needed them. Stick tried staring back at Lionel, not giving it much, and Lionel held on for about five seconds before looking away. Chucky had hardly looked at him at all since coming in from the living room, alone. The girl must have left. She had seemed out of place here. She looked like a social worker with money, if there was such a thing as that. Or a tennis pro. She had looked at him: she had those eyes that knew things but didn't tell you what she was feeling.

Rainy was saying, "I was thinking we should have a gun. One of us."

It took Stick by surprise. He wanted to get Rainy's eye and shake his head at him. But maybe he didn't have to. Chucky was saying, "You tell me you're bringing Bozo here with you 'cause there's nothing to it, he's going for the ride. So what do you need a gun for?"

Rainy said, "You always give me one before. Like Brinks, man, for just in case. Why is it different this one?"

Chucky said, "You want the job? You want the job, get outta here . . . Lionel?"

Lionel went over to the door and stood waiting to see them out as Rainy said, "How about the pay? Five grand you said."

"We'll take care of that tomorrow," Chucky said. "I'll be here, you know I'm going to be here . . . Now go on, get out . . ."

Chucky punched out a number on his phone system, walked over to the hat-tree and set the "Crested Beaut" model over his eyes. When Moke's voice came on, Chucky said:

"Delivery's on its way."

Silence.

"You hear me?"

"I ain't deaf, am I?"

Just dumb, Chucky thought. He said, "For the other part of the deal, instead of Rainy, how about you take the bozo that's with him? You think you could do that?"

"It don't matter none to me," Moke's voice said.

Chucky said, "Hey, partner? See you tomorrow."

Moke was starting to work for him already and didn't even know it.

5

RAINY, BEHIND THE WHEEL OF the Chevy van, would glance at Stick as he spoke and from Stick back to the four lanes of freeway and the red taillights moving in the dark.

"The way I understand it, Chucky owes the money because it was his fault Nestor Soto had to put up a bond, the two-hundred thousand, to get one of his guys out. Then when the guy left and went to Colombia it was okay with Nestor because he say Chucky has to pay him. See, Chucky knew a guy from New York or some place he thought was a good guy. He see him in the Mutiny, different places, he knows the guy is buying product, right? Now this guy tells Chucky he wants to make a big buy—I don't know how many kilos, man—I'm talking about coke. So Chucky is thinking okay, no problem. He'll broker the deal, put the guy in touch with Nestor Soto and make about five-ten percent from the guy, everybody's happy, right? Except what do you know, this guy from New York, man, he turns out he's a deep narc, man, from the BNDD. Sure, he put it together, they raid this place Nestor has down in Homestead on the canal, kill one of his guys, bust the other one—that's the two-hundred-thousand bond—take all his shit, man, and Nestor believe Chucky put the stuff on him. What else is he going to think? Nestor is crazy anyway. Sometime they call him El Chaco, from some wild place where he was born. El Chaco. He believe in *santería*, man, like voodoo. He start free-basing, he kill these animals as a sacrifice, with a knife. It can scare the shit out of you, you see something like that. Chucky explain it to him, no, man, he was surprised as Nestor the guy was a narc. He say, ask anybody at the Mutiny, they tell you. Nestor, he finally say okay, but Chucky has to pay him for the bond, you know, that Nestor lost."

"Forfeited," Stick said.

"Yeah, forfeit. The court don't give it back. So that's it, man, in the suitcase. He always say that, Chucky? About the gorilla." Rainy grinned. "Oh, man . . ."

"Why'd he pick you?"

"What, to take it? He ask me."

"He's got all those guys—why didn't he send one of them with it?"

"I tell him I need a job, some money. So . . ."

Stick thought about it, trying to accept Chucky doing Rainy a favor. "What's he on?"

Rainy glanced over. "Who, Chucky? 'Ludes, man. You can tell, uh? How he moves?"

"Like he's walking in mud," Stick said.

Following 95 through Miami, Stick couldn't believe all the cement that had been poured since he was last here, when he was married and living here . . . He had begun thinking about his former wife, Mary Lou, when Rainy had to brake hard in traffic not watching his lane, and Stick felt his bucket seat slide forward and had to plant his feet. His wife's Camaro had had a seat like that. He would adjust it, there, but it would break loose within a few days and give them something to discuss when his wife wasn't complaining about the hot weather, about not seeing her friends, about her mother driving her crazy . . . till they moved back to Detroit and she began complaining about the cold, busing, about the colored taking over the shopping malls. Now she was back here again, Stick believed, because she missed bitching about her mother. They were a great pair, with their mouths turned down and set that way for all time. He hoped it wouldn't hurt his little girl, always hearing the negative side of things. His little girl's name was Katy. She had sent him handmade birthday and Father's Day cards, her school pictures some years, and twenty letters during the time he was in prison; more than half of them written when she was twelve. He'd call tomorrow . . . get a present for her . . .

They left the freeway and after that Stick didn't know where they were, somewhere in South Miami; all the streets, up-down and across were numbers. Finally Rainy turned a corner at Southwest Seventy-Third Street and pulled up in front of a place with a sign that said Neon Leon's. They had to meet a guy here, Rainy said, who would tell them where to go. A guy name Moke.

Stick said, "Why don't you give him the bag? Get it over with."

"I have to give it to Nestor Soto or his father-in-law, a guy name Avilanosa, nobody else," Rainy said. "Nestor don't advertise, I have to find out where he is . . . Lock your door."

Stick watched Rainy go into the place—a lounge or a restaurant, it looked new, whatever it was, flashy. *Neon Leon's.* Hot shit. Places like this and Wolfgang's made Stick tired thinking about them. He was getting old. Getting on and nothing to show for it. He'd earned five dollars a week in Jackson as a clerk-porter in the Guidance Center office, filing, mopping floors, cleaning toilets, and managed to come out with 680 dollars. A hundred and a half to get to Florida; a week paid in advance at the Hotel Bon-Aire on South Beach . . . he had about three hundred left. He'd go as high as a grand from Rainy for sitting here in the dark guarding Chucky's suitcase with almost a quarter of a million in it. Christ . . .

Moke came out, let go of the door and Rainy had to catch it. Stick watched him approach this side of the van as Rainy came around and got back in.

"He's going with us."

When Stick opened the door Moke said to him, gesturing with his head, hair to his shoulders, "Get in the back." He seemed stoned, half asleep, holding his left arm, the elbow, pressed in. He had on an old worn-out leather jacket zipped partway up, nothing under it but bare skin. Stick would bet he had a couple of tattoos on him somewhere, crude, threatening artwork.

"I got to get out," Stick said, "before you get in, don't I?" Wanting him to move back.

Moke said, "I guess if you're stupid."

Rainy was patting the inner side of his seat. "Through here, man. Just come through here."

Stick edged around between the seats to the rear compartment, hearing Moke say, "Where'd you find him at?" in that lazy, know-it-all tone so familiar, a twang of pure ignorance.

Moke climbed in and slammed the door. Then looked around at Stick. "Let me have the suitcase. Make sure you assholes aren't pulling any shit here."

The compartment bare, Stick was about to sit on

the case. He got it up in front of him, kneeling on the carpet, and thought about shoving it hard into Moke's face. He could feel his heart beating.

Moke took the suitcase, laid it on his lap and fooled with the clasps until he got the top half raised. Rainy glanced out the side windows, then switched on the interior light. Stick raised up on his knees. He saw neat rows of banded one-hundred-dollar bills filling the suitcase. Moke picked up one of the packets and riffled through it, picked up another one, raising it to his ear and did it again. "Yep, it's all there." Rainy started to laugh. Moke half-turned to put dull eyes on Stick.

"The fuck you looking at?"

Rainy said, "Hey, where we suppose to go, man? Let's get the show on the road."

Stick got a good look at those sleepy eyes before Moke straightened around again, told Rainy to go on over to 87th Avenue and head south.

He could still feel his heart beating.

What he had to do was tell himself, keep telling himself, he had nothing to do with this, he was along for the ride. Take a moment to think, realize where he was now and not just react to things.

That guy he had read about last winter, the one who wrote the book inside and they got him a parole, that guy hadn't stopped to think. Maybe the other guy, the guy working in the luncheonette who told him there was no place for customers to go to the bathroom there, the health department or something didn't allow it, maybe he had said the wrong thing and the guy just out had felt his heart beating. That was understandable. But out here you didn't use a knife on somebody who said you couldn't take a leak. Inside you would have pissed on the *guy*. But outside—he shouldn't have even had the knife on him. He shouldn't have been *out* to begin with after they knew he had killed inside and didn't think anything of human life and after he had spent all that time in the hole. They could've read the guy's book and known they shouldn't ever let a guy like that out. It was so different out . . . All the lights, for one thing, all the headlights and streetlights, the neon lights, all other people's lights that had nothing to do with you. But inside you all lived together in the same fluorescent light or lights in metal cages without shades. You were in the same kind of light together all the time. If a guy like Moke ever gave you that look or tried to lean on you various ways, everybody was watching and you better back him off or else sew up your asshole because if you gave the guy the first inch he'd take the rest any time he wanted.

You were lucky in there, Stick began to think. Jesus, you were lucky. You know it?

He had backed some of them off, the hot-shit guys in the wool-knit caps, but he wouldn't have backed them off the whole seven years if he hadn't been lucky and found a six-four, 240-pound soul-buddy by the name of DeJohn Holmes. One moment thinking he was going to die against that cement wall. The next moment DeJohn's face grinning, showing him glints of gold and a pink tongue, DeJohn saying, "Man, you my frien'. Don't you know that?" Stick shaking his head, still thinking he was going to die, and DeJohn saying, "Man, I hear you the one did the motherfucker put me in here. Tell me your pleasure, you want weed, you want shit, tell me what you want . . ."

Moke had been saying, "Turn here, hang a left the next corner," saying, "I got a Two-eighty Z'd put this fucker on the trailer in reverse." Saying, "About a Hunnert and fifteenth. It's before you get down to Montgomery . . ."

Now he said, "Past the school."

"I don't know where in the hell I'm at," Rainy said.

"Go on around the other side . . . Yeah, see the drive? In there."

Rainy said, "We going to school? I think it's closed."

They moved along the side of the old building, a playground or athletic field extending off to their left.

"Park along here," Moke said, "facing out. Turn your engine off."

"I can't see nothing," Rainy said.

They sat in silence.

"You got any weed?" Rainy said.

Moke didn't answer him.

"How about some music?" Rainy said. Then said, "Here comes somebody. Man, I hope it ain't cops."

Stick kneeled up. He saw headlights coming across the field toward them, creeping, coming out of darkness. In the beams now he saw a baseball diamond.

Moke said, "Pop your lights on and off . . . I said *off*, asshole!"

Stick remained quiet, watching as the headlights came to a stop maybe fifty or sixty feet away, along the third base line. The headlights went off. Then came on again glaring, switched to high beam.

Moke said, "Okay, get out," and watched as Rainy opened his door and stepped down. Moke shoved the suitcase at him. "Wait now. I want this boy to take it over," glancing around at Stick.

Rainy said, "Man, I got it, I'll take it. What's a difference?"

Moke said, "This boy here's suppose to take it's what I'm saying to you."

Rainy said, "No, man, I'm the one," backing away from the van with the suitcase.

Stick was looking at Moke's face, eyelids heavy in the light beams. He said, "Why would I do it? I come along for the ride."

He heard Rainy, outside, saying, "I'm going, okay? I want to say hi to Nestor. I haven't seen him."

Moke was shaking his head. "Jeez-us Christ—hey, come back here, will you!"

Stick saw interior lights go on as a door opened behind the headlights, giving shape to a full-size American car. A figure appeared at the right front fender. Rainy was in the beams now, out in front of the van. He called out, "Nestor? . . . Who is that?" Raised the suitcase in one hand and gave it a pat with the other. "I got it, man!"

Moke said, "Well, shit, I don't care."

All that was happening was there in front of Stick, watching from a second-row seat. He saw Moke's right hand dig inside the worn-out jacket.

Moke saying, "We'll make 'er a two-for-one special, today only."

Stick yelled out, "Rainy!"

Through the windshield he saw Rainy look back. Saw the figure by the headlights raise something in his hands and saw the muzzle flash as he heard the burst of gunfire, a hammering sound out in the open. Saw Rainy, outside, stumble and saw nickel-plate gleaming inside, the big revolver coming up in Moke's hand.

Stick lunged hard with his hands and shoulder into the back of Moke's seat and felt it rush on its tracks and stop dead and heard Moke's grunt as his head slammed against the windshield. Stick didn't wait, stop to look. The headlight beams lit up the compartment, showed him the rear-door latch. He banged through the doors and left the van running, digging hard, that hammering sound chasing him until he was around the corner of the school building.

With no idea of direction he walked residential streets of tile-roofed bungalows concealed in shrubbery, aroused a few relentless dogs, came out to commercial lights again, finding South Dixie Highway without knowing where it was. He waved down a taxi, let the driver look him over, told the driver South Beach and didn't say another word after that. They had to leave city streets and traffic, break free onto MacArthur Causeway before he opened the window to feel the breeze coming off the bay and to stare at distant solitary lights out in the Atlantic Ocean, listening in his mind to Moke saying, *This boy here's suppose to take it . . .*

Suppose to die.

* * *

They sold nickel bags inside for seven bucks, they sold regular cigarettes, shampoo, all that kind of stuff; they sold shine made from potatoes, spud juice at ten bucks a gallon, or let fruit juice stand till it turned and drank that. Stick's former partner, Frank Ryan, died of the potatoes in the prison hospital.

DeJohn Holmes said he could have anything he wanted. A sateen jacket? Blue and gold with his name on the back? *Stick*. Look nice, be a man of fashion.

Here was the strange part. It wasn't any of the colored guys in the wool-knit caps he had to watch.

No, out of five thousand eight hundred and something losers shuffling around, hanging out in the yard, getting high, chasing sissies, it was a white guy named Luther doing two to five who stared at him a few weeks, circled in and finally told Stick he was going to kill him. Why?

(Just like, why would he have thought he had to watch Moke? He wasn't mixed up in that business.)

It didn't make sense: sitting there in the Big Top, the dining hall, one morning with his cold scrambled eggs and having this stone-eyed asshole biker chewing with his mouth open telling him he was going to put a shank in him when he least expected. The colored guys—Christ, he got along fine with the colored guys and they knew all about him, from DeJohn Holmes.

DeJohn was one of the "mayors" at Jackson and ran a section of the yard, taking cuts on the card games and numbers and renting out weight-lifting equipment by the quarter hour when he wasn't using it. "Stay by me when you need to," DeJohn told Stick. "I'll show you how to jail, not lose any good time mixing up with crazies."

But why did Luther want to kill him?

" 'Cause he see you talking to me when you should be hanging out with the white boys. Start with that," DeJohn said. "Man like him, he don't even know how to brush his teeth. You watch him 'cause you don't know when the bug is going to go out on him and he turn hisself loose. Maybe he thinks in his stone mind you somebody else or you remind him of somebody stepped on him one time. Or he like to be like you and he can't. He say he going to shank you and you say watching the motherfucker eat is enough to turn you sick to death anyway. But see, he so slow in the head he has to think, man, to blink. So I get him assigned the meat shop and let him see he fuck with my frien' Stickley what can befall him."

Pure luck. Getting next to DeJohn, being discovered by him. DeJohn's story:

"A man point at me in Recorder's Court, City of

Detroit, say yeah, that's him, that's him. Say I'm the one come in his place with a gun and cleaned out both his cash registers. Yeah, that's him. I draw thirty to life for the third and final time around. Now that man that pointed—not because I took his cash receipts but took his woman, *one* time, *one* night only and she love it—that man was Sportree, who died of gunshot at the hand of my frien' Ernest Stickley, Jr.," DeJohn said. "They some details missing, but it was some funny business following when you and Frank robbed the J. L. Hudson Company in downtown Detroit and got ate up."

Stick was careful. He said he was doing his time for a grocery store in Oakland County, not any homicide or robbery in downtown Detroit.

DeJohn said, "I know that. It's cool." He said, "Believe me, my man. You my man and it's cool. But it don't change you did Sportree and the dude was with him."

Stick said, to DeJohn only, okay, but it was unavoidable.

DeJohn said, "They all unavoidable when you have to do it. Like the two brothers in the shopping mall, in the parking lot, I believe was Northland."

Stick said yeah, that had been unavoidable too, the two brothers wanting to *mug* him, for Christ sake, take his groceries.

DeJohn showed his gold and his pink tongue.

"Groceries, yeah, shit"—enjoying it—"and the cash underneath the Wheaties from the store where you and Frank did your shopping." DeJohn said, "What they say, you could have got a hundred years just for the cars you used on those jobs. You take the fall on the grocery store, but they got Frank on the big one, didn't they? The Hudson's store."

Stick wondered how he knew all that.

DeJohn said, "You famous, baby."

When Luther made the move it was at a time when Stick was playing basketball in the yard. He left the game wheezing, out of shape, put on his work jacket and sat bent over on a bench trying to get his breath. He felt the wet on his back and thought at first it was sweat. He began to smell something . . . Christ, gasoline, and heard it when Luther dropped the match on him and *wouf* the back of his jacket went up in flames and he dove head-first over to land on his back on the cement and roll from side to side grinding in that hot sting . . . seeing the guy standing there with the Windex squirt bottle of clear liquid watching him.

DeJohn said it was the man's style and they should've known. "But the man lied to you, didn't he? Say he was going to shank you."

Three days later there was an accident in the butcher shop. Three witnesses in wool caps and white aprons swore Luther was splitting pork ribs with a cleaver, missed and cut off his left hand.

DeJohn said, "Man was lucky, wasn't he? He could have been seriously hurt and bled to death." He said, "I told him that, too."

There was all kinds of luck.

Stick sat on the cement porch of the Hotel Bon-Aire, listening to elderly people with New York Jewish accents complain about high prices, about Medicare and how Reagan had betrayed them. The hotel was light-green stucco, four stories, and seemed more like a retirement home than a hotel. Stick could feel the old people staring at him; one asked if he was with the government, looking things over.

August, no tourists, but still a lot of people on South Beach.

He crossed the street always lined with cars and went out on the sand past the clumps of sea grape and the Cuban families cooking over charcoal, eating at the picnic tables, and lay in the sun listening to bits of voice sounds coming to him in Spanish. They sounded like they were arguing but looked like they were having fun. Try and figure out Cubans. He would lie in the sun not moving and think about going up to Stuart or Daytona, or maybe over on the west coast around Naples, work construction. He could always drive a transit-mix, he'd done enough of that before.

With the hot glare pressing on his glasses and his eyes closed tight he would try to look into the future to a place where a man forty-two, starting over, could find something interesting and make up for lost time. If he was going to work he'd have to stay in Florida and get back in construction. Not around Miami, though. Or Detroit. People up there with seniority were drawing unemployment. He didn't look so far ahead that he pictured himself an old man on the street, he pictured himself *now*; but he couldn't, no matter how hard he thought, see himself *doing* anything.

He still hadn't spoken to his ex-wife or his daughter. Now, the way things were, he wasn't ready.

He was going to buy some clothes and get lucky there. The manager of the hotel, an old bent-over guy, showed him laundry packages of stuff a guy had left in his room Stick could have for thirty bucks. Different-colored shirts with little polo players on them, nice pants just a little tight, a couple light jackets, everything clean and neatly folded, fairly new stuff but without that brand-new look, which Stick liked even better. The manager said this young fella that left the clothes was here in May, went off to Key West for the weekend and never came back. The manager settled for twenty. Stick went out and bought a pair of sneakers with blue stripes on the sides.

They were the most comfortable shoes he'd ever owned. In the early evening he'd walk up Collins Avenue from Seventh Street as far as Forty-first sometimes, up around the big hotels, and on the way back find a nice quiet bar, have a few bourbons over crushed ice, suck on that good stuff and feel himself, after a few evenings of it, beginning to settle down and get his confidence back. He burned the first day in the sun. But by the fourth day he looked like he was working construction again, getting tan faster than he ever had before. His hair even looked different, lighter; he let it fall in its natural bent instead of combing it back behind his ears. Four days and he looked like a regular Florida native. Next he would be going to discos, doing those slinky numbers with the ladies. There were enough of them around, he had a waitress or two hitting on him every night; but he wasn't anxious to move in that direction yet. He had to make up his mind about something, take one thing at a time.

He bought a postcard to send to DeJohn that showed a bunch of alligators, one with its mouth wide open, next to a kidney-shaped cement pool. He would sit with his bourbon and stare at the empty white message side of the card, thinking:

*Dear DeJohn, My luck almost ran out on me
the other night . . .*

*Dear DeJohn, man, could I use you right
now . . .*

*Dear DeJohn, Rainy asked me to go with him
on a deal that was supposed to be a Sunday
drive . . .*

But if he was going to go into all that, he'd have
to put it in a letter. Tell what happened. Tell what
he was going to do about it.

Well, the way it looked when he first started
thinking about it, nothing.

Because there was nothing he *could* do. And because it was none of his business, it was Rainy's.
Rainy knew there was always a risk, that kind of
business, but it was how he made his living. It
didn't matter what the deal was and it didn't do any
good to think about it, because he didn't know all
the facts.

Chucky owes a Cuban money. Chucky makes
the payment. The Cuban takes the money—you as-
sume that—and has Chucky's bagman killed. Why?
Because as Rainy said, the Cuban was crazy, that's
all. You were dealing with people, they weren't just
weird, they had machine guns.

What he tried to do during the day, lying on the

beach, taking walks along the surf, was think only about his future. Look at it in bright sunlight. Here it was, the world. What did it have to offer? All he had ever seen was one shady part of it. He found his thinking would come to: pick up a car and take off— And then his thinking would start jumping all over the place.

But in the evening, settled down, feeling himself again, he was able to narrow his view, look at pieces of what had happened and come to a conclusion that had a hole in it but still made enough sense. He believed, first:

They didn't kill Rainy because he was Rainy. They didn't seem to care who they killed. Either one, he or Rainy would do. Moke said, "Shit, I don't care." Or both of them. Moke said, "Make it a two-for-one special."

But Rainy wasn't the first choice.

Stick could see Moke looking at him and saying, "*This boy here's suppose to take it.*"

He had to squint hard trying to understand this part.

Maybe he'd heard it wrong. Or Moke had decided on his own to send him out there with the suitcase; so in Moke's mind he was *suppose to take it* and it was that simple.

Because if he'd heard it *right*, the way it sounded, then somebody had given Moke instructions. Send out the guy with Rainy. And who even knew there was going to be a guy with Rainy? Except Chucky.

So the second thing Stick came to believe:

Chucky was giving the Cuban somebody to kill. Part of doing business. Rainy said Chucky owned the Cuban money. Rainy didn't know he owed the Cuban a lot more than that, he owed the Cuban a life, too. Maybe Rainy didn't serve enough time to learn how those things worked. Stick knew.

He could sip his bourbon and know exactly why Chucky had picked him. Because he had crossed the line, walked where he shouldn't have walked. Because he had given Chucky a look. Because he had inspected Chucky's home, a room in it, and said he wasn't impressed.

"You see anything you like?"

Asking for it. What was he supposed to say, yeah, I love it? Ask him who his decorator was?

Once Stick reached this conclusion he could look back at what had happened, including Rainy's murder, and accept it. He wished he could have helped Rainy. But Rainy and all these people were in the same life. It was how they dealt with one another. To them, inside or outside eighteen-foot walls with gun towers, the life was the same. So if in time Stick could put Jackson out of his mind he'd be able to forget about this business too. Begin by walking away from it.

Except that he began thinking about Chucky

now and the one hole—a question mark, really—in his conclusion.

Chucky might have set them up, but a fact still remained. The suitcase tested by the four-hundred-pound gorilla had been delivered. Didn't Chucky owe somebody five thousand dollars?

On the postcard with the alligators on it he sent to DeJohn, the message read:

Dear DeJ:

So far you aren't missing a thing not being here—as you can tell from that bunch of girls hanging around the swimming pool (over). Listen, I'd even take your old lady, Antoine, before I'd pick one of them. UGGGG!!! Tell the brothers disco is out and Soul is in. God bless you and take care of yourself. I'm going now to seek my fortune. Wish me luck.

Stick

He put on the lime green polo shirt, a pair of khakis faded almost white that didn't need a belt and matched the poplin jacket; he put on his new sneakers with the blue stripes and stuffed the rest of his new wardrobe into a white canvas bag with blue handles. Well, look at sporty, he said to the dresser mirror, liking his color especially, his tan face smiling at him.

For seven years he had worn state clothes. He told DeJohn, turning down offers of sateen athletic jackets and sportshirts, he was reminding himself he was a con and would not pretend to be something else until he was out of there.

Now what was he?

He'd find out pretty soon.

6

HE WONDERED WHY YOU COULD walk into a bar and smell it when it was empty or there were only a few people but you couldn't smell it when the place was crowded.

He wondered why there were more cars in the parking lot than people inside the place.

Coming in from sunlight with his canvas bag Stick opened and closed his eyes in the dimness, saw only a few tables occupied, a couple of guys in hardhats sitting at the bar. It was so quiet he thought at first it was the wrong place. As he stood there the bell rang outside for the bridge to go up but nobody blew the foghorn. Maybe this was the time to come. He wasn't feeling old, he was still feeling pretty good; a little tired maybe. It had taken three and a half hours and seven rides to thumb his way up US 1 from Miami to Lauderdale and to walk to the beach from federal highway.

No, it was the right place. The girl-bartender, Bobbi, was serving the two hardhats.

Stick went down to the other end of the bar where it was still afternoon, sunlight filling the wide opening to the terrace. A good spot. He could swivel a quarter turn on the stool, look across the Intracoastal and see the front of Chucky's building, the blacktop drive curving up to the entrance.

When Bobbi came down the bar in her loose pink-knit shirt and said, "Well, hi, how're you doing?" giving him a cocktail napkin, Stick was sure she recognized him. He said just fine and ordered a Michelob draft. But when she brought the beer and he placed a ten and a five on the bar she said, "What's that for?"

"The other day, remember, I was in here with Rainy?"

She said, "You were?"

"You held the tab 'cause we were coming back later."

It took her a moment. "That was last *week*." She seemed to study him, cocking her head. "You were with Rainy?"

"Remember the hairy guy? Made a pass at you?"

"That was you?"

"No—guy in a beach outfit, long hair. He grabbed your hand."

Her mouth opened. She said after a moment, "The one, you called him . . . short eyes?"

"Yeah, I might've."

She was nodding, thoughtful. "Yeah, I remember." Then frowned. "What's it mean? Short eyes."

"Well, usually, I guess it refers to a child molester."

She didn't speak right away, putting something together in her mind. Then seemed to have the answer, sure of it.

"You were with Rainy, weren't you? Up in Michigan."

"Jackson," Stick said. The beer tasted good; it was one of the things he had missed the most.

"I used to write to him," Bobbi said. "Well, I wrote a couple times. Yeah, I remember now when you said that I thought, it sounds like something you'd hear, you know, where you and Rainy were."

"In prison," Stick said. "It's all right to say it. We were in prison together."

"But why'd you call him that?"

"That's what he looked like to me. At that time. I know—it wasn't any of my business."

"I'm used to it. You should see some of the old farts come in here, try and make out. Bunch a dirty old men."

"I can believe it," Stick said. He didn't feel old at all this time. He felt in shape, the way she was looking at him, confiding. He saw her with him in brief flashes, a balcony on the ocean, her eyes smiling in amber candlelight, wine glasses, soft bossa nova, a dreamy look as she stretched, reached behind her and slowly pulled off the pink shirt. She said:

"Where's Rainy? I haven't seen him."

Stick shook his head. "I haven't either."

"I don't think he's been in since the last time, when you were here." She smiled then. "Yeah, I remember you now. Boy, have you changed." She seemed at ease with him, like they were old friends.

"It's nice to be remembered," Stick said. "Sometimes, anyway." He pushed the glass toward her. "Why don't you give me another one of those."

She drew several more for him while he watched the boats go by and saw, finally, the dark-haired Cuban-looking guys in their tight suits and sportshirts across the way . . . and began to think of another time in another bar, in Detroit, sitting with Frank Ryan while Frank told him his rules for success and happiness in armed robbery. And Stick, fresh out of the Wayne County jail, feeling as lucky and confident as he did right now, had listened. He could have walked away from Frank and saved himself seven years.

He could walk away from this place . . .

A heavyset dark-haired guy in a pale blue suit and blue print shirt came in from the terrace, passed behind Stick and stood at the empty bar a few stools away. He rapped on the rounded edge of the bar with a car key and said, "Hey, Bobbi!"

Stick turned to look at his profile. It was Lionel

Oliva. Lionel ordered a rum and tonic. As he waited, lightly tapping his key on the bar, he called out to Bobbi, "Turn a music on. This place is dead."

Stick said to him, "How's it going?"

Lionel looked at him, stared a moment with no expression of interest and shrugged. He turned back to wait for Bobbi.

Stick felt himself relax more as he sipped his beer.

He could walk away clean. Go out to the parking lot. He'd noticed when he came in a Mercedes, a couple of Cadillacs, a brand-new Corvette he could get five grand for easy, even without a delivery order . . . and not have to go up to the top floor of that condominium, try and talk Chucky out of it and worry about getting thrown off a fifteen-story balcony.

The prize out in the parking lot was a Rolls Silver Shadow, light gray, that was about fifteen years old and in show condition. Though the 'Vette would be easier to move. Get some plates off another car, drive up to Atlanta and unload it. Fly back tomorrow night, see his little girl . . . Except a 'Vette, the new ones, they say you had to punch a hole through the steering column and it was easy to butcher. The old-model Rolls would be a lot easier to get into and take off.

Lionel walked past him with his drink, going out

to the terrace. He didn't look back. And they had stared at each other in Chucky's place.

Bobbi came over. He thought she was going to mention Lionel, but she said, "That tab you were asking about? I remember, it's taken care of."

"Who paid it?"

"You were suppose to meet Chucky that time?" Stick nodded. "Well, when you didn't come back I put it on his charge. Is that all right?"

"That's fine. You can put these on it too, you want."

"Chucky always forgets to sign, so we have a pen that writes just like his."

"I'll have to thank him," Stick said.

"That was his bodyguard was just here. So Chucky'll probably be in."

"Yeah? What's he need a bodyguard for?"

Bobbi said, "I make drinks, but I'm not dumb. You know as well as I do if you're a friend of Rainy's, and that's all I'm gonna say."

"I don't blame you," Stick said.

He watched her walk away and began thinking of his partner again, Frank Ryan: sitting in the bar telling Frank he was going to Florida to see his little girl—Christ, almost seven and a half years later he still hadn't seen her . . . No, he'd listened to Frank tell him that in the area of taking money that didn't belong to you—as opposed to lifting goods you had to fence—the method that paid the most for "percentagewise" the least amount of risk was armed robbery. He'd said, big deal. After all that buildup. And Frank had said, "Say it backwards, robbery comma armed. It can be a *very* big deal," and had even quoted actual statistics, saying they could follow his rules for success and happiness in armed robbery and make three to five grand a week, easy. That was when he should have walked out, right at that moment, when he didn't have a dime, but was calm inside. Confident, reasonably happy. And most of all, free.

He caught Bobbi's eye. Coming over she said, "Same way?"

Stick shook his head. He said, "No, I think it's time to check out." He hesitated and said, "I'm going to see my little girl."

Bobbi said, "Oh?" and sounded surprised. "How old is she?"

"She's fourteen now," Stick said. "You remind me of her. You sort of look alike."

He walked out feeling absolved, almost proud of himself. Though he couldn't help catching another glimpse of her taking off that pink shirt in amber candlelight, the waves breaking outside in the dark . . .

Barry came off the *Seaweed* with its port side still three feet from the dock, engines rumbling low, inching the fifty-eight-foot Hatteras gently into berth.

Chucky and a girl named Pam and Barry's friend Aurora stood by the deck chairs in the stern watching Barry, wanting to stop him. Not wringing their hands exactly, but caught in a tableau of surprise: Chucky in a striped red-white-and-blue T-shirt down over his hips, the two girls in skimpy little nothing bikinis.

Chucky said, "You coming back, what?"

Aurora, dark hair shining, voice whining, said, "Bar-*ry*! Will you wait, *please*!"

Barry was pointing to the stern line his deckhand had thrown onto the dock, Barry gesturing, saying something to Lionel, who stood there in his light blue suit and didn't seem to know what to do. Barry's captain sat up on the flying bridge of the *Seaweed* observing, unconcerned behind his sunglasses, as the deckhand ran forward and jumped dockside with the bowline.

Barry looked up, squinting. He said to the boat, "Rorie? Chucky's going to run you home, babe. Okay? I gotta run."

Chucky said, "I am?"

Aurora, pouting, said, "You promised we're going to have dinner."

"I got a call," Barry said. "Didn't I get a call? I was on the goddamn phone—how long? You saw me."

Aurora said, "You're always on the goddamn phone."

Barry said, "Call you later, babe."

Aurora tried once more to stop him. "Bar-*ry*!"

But he was gone.

Bobbi's face brightened, broke into a big smile as she saw him coming. Then tried to turn it off but couldn't and a small grin lingered as Barry came over to the bar, his expression blank. Not grim, not serious; blank.

He made a gun of his right hand, index finger extended, and cocked it at Bobbi's face.

"What's the last thing that goes through a bug's mind as it hits the windshield?"

Bobbi said, "I don't know, what?"

"Its asshole . . . Where're the keys?"

"What keys?"

"The car keys. Cecil was here, right? Tell me he was here."

"He was here."

"And he gave you the keys to the Rolls."

"Uh-unh. He tried to give me a hard time though."

Barry put the palm of his hand to his forehead, said, "Oh, Christ," and did a half turn before looking at Bobbi again. "He was drinking?"

"I don't know why you ever hired him in the first place," Bobbi said, serious, with innocent eyes.

Barry said, "Hey." He paused for emphasis. "I'll take care of Cecil. Okay? You say he was drinking?"

"He had a few."

Barry shook his head, then leaned on the bar, weary. "He leave the Rolls? I don't know what good it'd do me, but tell me at least he left the car."

"I wouldn't know," Bobbi said. "He came in, sat down right there. Didn't have his uniform on . . ."

"It's his day off."

"Had four Chivas with a couple of beers and left, pissed."

"Pissed off."

"That's what I said."

"There's a difference," Barry said. He slapped the bar and said, *"Shit."* Then glanced toward the terrace at the sound of Chucky's voice—Chucky coming in with the two girls. They were wearing short beach covers to their hips, looking nude underneath. Barry said to Bobbi, "They sit around drinking, it's Chucky's party, not mine. Don't give Aurora any martinis; she'll lay every guy that comes in." He looked toward the terrace again as he moved down the bar. "Rorie, I'll see you later, babe. Call you as soon as I can."

He heard her say, "Bar-*ry!*" but kept moving down the length of the bar, out.

* * *

Stick watched the guy in cutoff jeans and plain white sneakers—he had very hairy legs—come tearing out of the place and run over to the Rolls-Royce. He tried the door. Locked. He bent over to peer into the car, shielding his eyes with his hands. Then started yanking on the door, trying to tear the handle off. Then straightened up and banged his fist on the roof of the car, swearing, saying Jesus Christ and goddamn it. Really mad. Having a little tantrum. Stick wondered—assuming the guy had locked his key in the car—what there was to get so excited about.

Stick was sitting on Wolfgang's front steps under the awning, at a point where he'd decided this was not the place to pick up a car, not in daylight—he'd have to go to a shopping mall or a movie theater parking lot—when this little guy in the cutoffs came flying out. Dark hair down over his ears. At first Stick thought the guy was Cuban, all the Cubans around. But then decided no, no Cuban who could afford a Rolls was going to run around in cutoffs and a yellow alligator shirt hanging out. No, the guy was probably Jewish, a rich young Jewish guy in his early thirties. He reminded Stick of Frankie Avalon, the hair, or a young Tony Curtis.

Stick said to him, "You need a coat hanger?"

Barry looked over at Stick for the first time. With

hope, or surprise. Then seemed to lose it and put his hands on his hips, shoulders rounding, though he seemed to be standing up straight.

"No keys. It wouldn't do me any good even if I got in."

"You lose 'em?"

"My asshole driver's suppose to drop the car off, leave the keys at the bar. Sounds easy, right? Take the keys out, hand 'em to the girl? Totally wrong."

"Can you give him a call?"

"Where? It's his day off. Wherever he is he's smashed by now. That's it for Cecil. No more of this bullshit, I'm telling you . . ."

Stick got up. He brushed at the seat of his new faded khaki pants. Smoothed the front of his lime green shirt with the little polo player on it. He was going to pick up his canvas bag, then decided not to, not yet. Look interested, but casual about it.

He said, "Maybe I can help you."

Barry said, "What, get in the car? All I had to do was get in the car I'd break the goddamn window. I got to get *in* and I got to be in Bal Harbour"—he looked at his Rolex—"shit, in less'n forty minutes. And I need stuff that's *in* the car and I gotta make about five phone calls on the way."

"You got a phone in the car?"

"I got two phones. Channel Grabber in the car, another one in a briefcase in the trunk."

"What year's the Rolls?"

Barry paused. "Sixty-seven. Silver Shadow, man. They stopped making 'em not too long after."

Stick nodded. He said, "I bet you I can get in and have it started in . . . fifty seconds."

Barry paused again. "You kidding me?"

"Bet you a hundred bucks," Stick said.

Barry said, "You're *not* kidding, are you? Jesus Christ, you're serious."

He watched Stick hunch down over his canvas bag, zip it open and feel around inside. Watched him take out a coat hanger. Watched him feel around again and take out a length of lamp cord, several feet of it with metal clips at each end.

Barry's mouth opened. He said, "What're you, a car thief? I don't believe it. Jesus, you want a car thief—you think there's ever a car thief around when you need one? Honest to God, I don't believe it—right before my eyes." He paused a moment. "What were you going to do, swing with my car?"

"Hundred bucks," Stick said, bending out the coat hanger without looking at it.

Barry stared, his expression grave. "The Polack runs in this place, he says, 'Gimme a coat hanger quick. My wife and kids're locked in the car.'" He raised his arm to look at his Rolex, paused and said, "Go!"

Stick wasn't going to appear hurried. He walked over to the Rolls and had the coat hanger ready by the time he reached the car door, worked it in over the top of the window and lowered the hooked end to the door handle without fishing, got an angle on it and tugged, twice, three times. Pulled the coat hanger out and opened the door. He said to Barry, "Now pop the hood."

"The bonnet," Barry said. "With the Rolls Silver Shadow, man, you get a bonnet."

Stick got in under the hood, Barry watching him with interest, seeing how he clipped one end of the lamp cord to the battery and the other end to the ignition coil. Stick bent the coat hanger into a U-shape then touched the solenoid activator terminal with one end, the battery terminal with the other. The starter whirred, the engine came to life in a roar and idled down. Stick turned his head to Barry. "How long?"

Barry looked at his watch. "You just made a hundred bucks. About . . . four seconds to spare. Not bad."

Stick lowered the hood, the bonnet, and brushed his hands together. "One problem, though. You're going to burn out the ignition you run it this way. You have to get a ballast resistor put on."

Barry said, "What do I have to worry about my ignition I got you, the phantom jumper. Get in the car, you can tell me all about yourself . . . your record, how many convictions, anything you want. *You* drive."

Stick was still at the front end. "I wasn't planning on going to Bal Harbour."

"What're you talking about?" Barry said. He was by the door on the passenger side now. "The engine dies I'm fucked, right? You have to jump it again. Come on, you got me into this, you got to make sure I get home."

Stick said, "Bal Harbour? That where you live?"

"You'll love it," Barry said. "Get in the car."

7

AT FIRST STICK THOUGHT HE was talking about cars to whoever it was on the phone, saying, "No, long term I'm only looking at convertibles now," like he was going to buy a fleet of them. "Short term, yeah, I'll listen." But then, Stick realized, he was talking about stocks and bonds and probably had a stockbroker on the other end of the line. The guy asking about "capital-gain potential" and "default risk."

Here they were cruising south on 95, traffic beginning to tighten up, following the same route he and Rainy had taken last week.

The guy, Barry Stam, had the phone wedged between his cheek and shoulder as he wrote words and figures on a yellow legal pad, scrawled them on a slant with a gold pen. The guy sitting there in his cutoffs and sneakers, *The Wall Street Journal* and dark-brown alligator case on his hairy legs. It was a picture, something Stick had never seen before. Driving away from Wolfgang's, the guy said, "Barry Stam," offering his hand. Stick took it, saying "Ernest Stickley." And the guy said, "But they call you Stick, right? What else."

He was saying into the phone now, "Gimme it again. Parkview? . . . Yeah, million and a half at, what was that, eight and a half? . . . Eight point seven . . . Yeah, I got it. Due when? . . . What? . . . I know it isn't, for Christ sake, it's a municipal. Listen, I may help you out, Arthur. Gimme a minute to ponder, I'll get back to you."

Stick kept his gaze straight ahead in the traffic, down the length of that pearl-gray hood, squinting a little against the afternoon glare. It was cool and quiet inside, nice feel to the leather seat.

"You got to keep it working," Barry said, punching a number on the phone system. "We sleep, you and I, right? But money never sleeps, man. Play golf on the weekend, the money's still working its ass off. Work work work . . ."

Stick said, "You talking about it earning interest?"

But Barry was on the phone again. "Hi, babe. Me again . . . No, the boat's in Lauderdale, I'm on my way home." Relaxed now, comfortable, a warmth to his tone that wasn't there with the broker. "I just talked to Art. I mean Arthur please, what's the matter with me. He's got a tax anticipation note, million and a half at eight point seven due in July . . . Parkview public schools." A police car screamed past them, lights flashing. "What?

The fuzz're after some poor asshole . . . *No*, not me, for Christ sake. You know I'm an *ex*-cellent driver."

Stick looked over and Barry was waiting, gave him a wink. With his thick dark young-movie-star hair down over his ears and forehead the guy looked like he was acting into the phone.

"Yeah, due in July, the fifteenth." He paused, listening. "Why June?" Writing something on the legal pad now. "Yeah, okay, I'll see what he says. Hey, Kyle? . . . Love you, babe." He listened for a moment, a grin forming. "Hey, come on. Don't say it less you mean it." He listened again. "Wait. When do you get back? . . . Then why don't you come into Miami? Save some time. I'll pick you up . . . Sure, no problem . . . Okay, babe, have a nice trip. I'll see you."

He rang off and punched another phone number. "Lemme have Arthur." Waited and said, "Arthur? Gimme a June fifteen come-due on the Parkview note I'll do you a special favor, take the whole load." He waited, but not long. "End of June I'm into"—he searched over the yellow pad with his pen—"housing or some goddamn thing. Or is it soybean futures? I don't know, I can't find the . . . What?" He listened and then said patiently, " 'Cause the funds're promised, Arthur, earmarked. Out of this into that. It never sleeps, man. It doesn't even stop to fucking catch its breath. Don't you know your business, for Christ sake?" Glancing at Stick, but getting no reaction. "Yeah, all right. Lemme know." Near the end now, trailing off. "No, call me at home . . . Hey, Arthur? No more government securities. Keep that shit to yourself for a while . . . Yeah, all right."

Stick let him make a few notes and put the yellow pad in the case before he glanced over.

"You do a lot of investing, uh?"

"You want a simple yes or no or an in-depth answer?" Barry said, reaching around to drop the case and the newspaper on the backseat. He crossed his legs then, got comfortable. "What you should ask is what I do when I'm not investing, trading or speculating in this and that. And the answer is, nothing. 'Cause whatever I'm doing, I'm also at the same time investing, trading or speculating. It's like it's my life force. You understand what I mean? Like you're breathing while you're doing other things, but if you weren't breathing, man, you wouldn't be doing *anything*." He seemed mildly pleased with himself. "That answer your question?"

Stick wondered why he'd asked it. He gave Barry a nod. Barry was looking at him, staring.

"What do you do? When you're not hot-wiring cars."

"Same as you," Stick said. "Nothing. Only when I'm doing it I'm not investing, trading or speculating. When I do nothing, I believe in doing nothing."

"How many cars you steal in your career?"

"Somewhere between three and four hundred."

"There any money in it?"

"I don't know, I don't do it anymore," Stick said. "That was a long time ago."

"You just happen to have the jump-wire in your bag."

Stick didn't say anything to that. Why bother.

"Lemme try an easy one," Barry said. "You live here? In Florida?"

"I used to."

"You do any time?"

Stick kept his eyes on the road. "Some."

"Raiford?"

"No. Up north. You ever hear of Jackson?"

"No shit," Barry said, impressed. "That's heavy duty."

Stick glanced over at him.

"For car theft?"

"Robbery."

"What kind? From a building? Little B and E?"

"Armed."

"No shit. Don't tell me a bank . . ."

"No banks," Stick said, beginning to warm up, not caring what he told the guy, or maybe wanting to impress him. "Banks are for thrill-seekers."

"How many convictions?"

"I did a bit in Milan before. Wasn't much, ten months."

"What's Milan?"

"Federal. It's up near Detroit."

"UDAA?"

"No, but I got probation on one of those. The next one I went to Milan on. You go, normally, from joy-riding to unlawfully driving away; then you go big-time, transporting across a state line and you get the feds after you. Familiar?"

"Why do you say that?"

"Well, before you started not doing anything while you're playing the stock market," Stick said, "I think you were a lawyer."

"That's very perceptive of you," Barry said. "I practiced a couple years, picked up on contracts, all that corporate bullshit, how to avoid paying taxes . . . So you had two raps up in Michigan, you come down to where the action is . . . You going for three?"

"I came here to visit my little girl."

"Really? I love it—an early Robert Mitchum. Nice guy gets fucked over . . . 'It's a bum rap, I didn't do it, I swear.'"

"I did it," Stick said.

"And now you're sorry for all your past sins?"

"Most of 'em."

"Most of 'em," Barry said, "the ones you got nailed for. I love it. How'd you make out in the joint?"

Stick looked over. "How'd I make out?"

"You have to take a lot of shit?"

"There isn't anything else they offer."

"But you made it okay? Got rehabilitated?"

"Yes sir, I've learned my lesson."

Barry said, "You want a job?"

Stick glanced at him. "Doing what?"

"What you're doing. Driving."

"You mean be a chauffeur? I've never done it."

"Well, if you've driven three, four-hundred different cars, right, that's what you said? You must have a pretty good feel for it."

Stick was watching the green freeway signs. "Bal Harbour, where do we get off?"

"Hundred and twenty-fifth. It's the next one. Goes over to Broad Causeway."

"What happens when we get there?"

"What do you want to happen?"

"I mean if I don't take your offer? You going to give me bus fare or what?"

"Jesus, you're already into me for a hundred bucks."

"You owe me a hundred, but I haven't seen it yet," Stick said. He looked at the rearview mirror and began edging over, into the lane to his right.

Barry said, "Don't worry about it, you'll get it."

Stick got over to the far-right lane, followed the exit ramp off, descending, turned left on 125th Street and moved along slowly—in more traffic than he could ever remember, it seemed everywhere you went down here—until he was able to swing in next to the curb at an Amoco station and set the hand brake.

He turned to face Barry now. "When?"

"When what?"

"When do I get the hundred?"

"Jesus Christ," Barry said. "You don't trust me?"

"I don't know you," Stick said. "You could've come in first in the bullshit finals and I didn't hear about it. Last week I was in a deal with a friend of mine, we didn't ask for our pay up front and we missed out. My friend, I can't tell you how *he* missed out. Now, I don't know. It wasn't the kind of deal you can take the guy to court, you know, and sue him."

Barry seemed amazed and Stick wasn't sure if he'd been listening.

"You don't trust me . . ." Barry said.

"If I did I'd have to trust everybody I meet, wouldn't I?"

"You're the one did time, for Christ sake, not me!"

"That's right," Stick said, "and I'll tell you how it works in a place like that. You owe somebody you better fucking pay up as quick as you can. You make people wait in there or they get the wrong idea about you, your mom gets a letter, you passed away in surgery. The way it works here, I get out of the car, take my jumper and go home."

"Hey," Barry said.

"What?"

"It's cool." Giving him the level-eye look now. One of the boys. "You want me to pay you right this fucking instant? All right, I'll pay you. I thought, I guess it was my presumption, you understood." Very serious now. Rolling to one side as he spoke, digging into his back pocket to bring out a fold of currency in a silver clip.

"Where I'm coming from. Understood what?"

"That my word—when I give my fucking *word*, when I tell a guy on the phone I'm putting up a million and a half for a tax anticipation note it means I'm going to come across with a million and a half and he *knows* it. I don't have to sign anything, he *knows* it. You follow me?"

"I should've upped the bet," Stick said.

"I say I owe you a hundred, here . . ." Barry snapped off a clean new bill and extended it. "Here's the hundred. Are we all right? We square?"

Stick took the bill. He said, "Thank you very much." Put the Rolls in gear and they continued west on 125th Street, followed the causeway across the upper neck of Biscayne Bay, passed through Bay Harbour Islands and came to the Atlantic Ocean at Collins Avenue, a much different Collins Avenue from the one down in South Beach—a fifteen-minute ride from the Amoco station on 125th and neither of them opened his mouth, made a sound, until they were looking at the ocean and Barry said, "Left."

Now they were in Florida postcardland, surf and sunny sky, lush tropical greenery. Stick took it all in, watched it get better and better. They turned left again, off Collins, and came to a gatehouse. A guard in a white shirt with epaulets and a blue pith-helmet—the guy was *armed*— waved the Rolls through, not even ducking down to look in, and now it got even better than before, though with a manicured look: a maintained tropical park of white walls and high trimmed hedges, palm trees against the sky, all kinds of flowering plants, occasionally a black-topped drive and a glimpse of wonderland . . . worlds away from a bleached house in Norman on an oil lease or a flat on the west side of Detroit, playing ball in sight of railroad switchyards and the stacks at Ford Rouge.

"Next one on the right," Barry said, "we're home."

Stick turned into the drive, 100 Bali Way, fol-lowed the blacktop through a patch of jungle and came in view of the house, white with a whiter roof; it reminded Stick of a mausoleum, neat and simple. Barry said, "Around back." They came to a turnaround area of cobblestones, four garage doors, a covered walk leading to the house and Stick couldn't believe the size and sprawl of the place. Like an assortment of low modules stuck together, open sides and walls of glass set at angles, the grounds dropping away from the house in gradual tiers, with wide steps that might front a museum leading down to the terraced patio and on to the swimming pool. A sweep of manicured lawn extended to a boat dock and a southwest view of Biscayne Bay, downtown Miami standing in rows of highrises beyond. On the far side of the swimming pool, past shrubbery and palm trees, Stick saw a red tennis court with a red striped awning along one side and beyond that a second house that was like a wing of the main house, a module broken off and moved two hundred feet away. Stick's gaze came back to the row of garage doors.

"How many cars you have?"

"Four," Barry said, "at the moment." He got out, then stuck his head back in and reached for his attaché case. "It's all right to be impressed. I am and I own the joint."

Stick sat behind the wheel taking it in. He saw a woman in a green robe standing on the terrace, looking this way, brown hair with gleams of red in the sunlight.

Barry yelled at her, "Babe, how you doing!" Then ducked into the car again and glanced at Stick as he got his *Journal*. "The lady of the house. You'll have to drive her around too, but usually just over to the club. Leucadendra. It's in Coral Gables, if you don't know where it is. I doubt if she knows how to get there. But I'm the one you have to impress. You're not an alcoholic, are you?"

"I never thought about it," Stick said.

"That's a good answer. Cecil'd say he was going to an AA meeting and come back smashed. Well, you get a guy out of a rehab center you take your chances."

Stick said, "Why do you want to hire me?"

Barry stood slightly bent over, looking in. "What do you mean, why do I want to hire you? I'm offering you a job. You're sitting in the car already, I don't have to go to the service."

"What's the job pay?"

"Jesus Christ," Barry said. He straightened and bent over again. "Two bills a week, room and board. All you can eat—got a great cook. But no fucking the maids, they're nice girls. The broad that comes in does the laundry, that's up to you. What else you want to know? . . . Clothes, I buy the uniforms."

"I have to wear a uniform?"

"Jesus Christ," Barry said, "what is this? Yeah, you wear a uniform. A three-button, single-breasted suit. You wear a black one, a dark gray or a light tan, depending. That sound okay to you?"

"Where do I live? I have my own room?"

"I don't believe this," Barry said. He half-turned, nodding toward the garage wing. "There's a two-bedroom apartment in there you share with the houseman but, yes, you have your own room. Now, you want the job or not? Jesus . . ."

"Let me explain something so you understand," Stick said. "See, I did seven years straight up day to day in a room six and a half feet wide by ten feet deep. I know I have to overcome stumbling blocks, bad luck of all kinds and a tendency now and then to take shortcuts, you might say, or I could go back there or a place like it. But while I'm out, and as long as I stay out, I can choose where I live. So why don't I look at the room and then I'll let you know. How'll that be?"

Barry said, after a moment, "Sure." He didn't seem to know what else to say.

8

CHUCKY WAITED OUTSIDE. Because when he mentioned Wolfgang's on the phone Kyle said she didn't do business in bars. Not snippy about it, fairly low key, in her natural style. Stating a fact. She said she was going to be down this way and wanted to drop something off. Or, if he liked the looks of the stock offering he could sign a letter of intent.

He told her lay it on him, he'd sign on the dotted line. Told her he had a pressing engagement and *had* to be at Wolfgang's and if she'd make an exception this time he'd never let it happen again.

What he wanted was for Kyle McLaren to meet Eddie Moke, and say something nice to him. A small favor to ask. Also he wanted to impress the boy. He wanted Eddie Moke in his pocket as an Anti-Cuban Protection Guarantee. A white-boy buffer between Chucky and the crazies. Somebody who thought American but worked for the chickenkillers. Chucky did not intend to make any more quarter-million-dollar offerings for honest mistakes.

He stood there in his size 44 red-white-and-blue striped-T-shirt, boat freak or patriot, talking to the parking attendant who'd come on for Happy Hour, talking about cars. The young-kid attendant, seeing the gray Porsche roll in, said, "Now there's my idea of wheels. Shit, a Nine-twenty-one."

And Chucky *knew* it was going to be Kyle. Dove gray Porsche with a stylish faint orange pinstripe. She was her own girl, wasn't she? Palm Beach, stock portfolios and high-performance iron. Mom and dad'd trip over each other getting to her. He got his smile ready and there she was:

In pale yellow, plain dark sunglasses, a zip-up case in one hand, brushing at her bangs with the other. He liked her hair better this time, it was blonder in outside light, yes, had a nice outdoor look that was *her*. A good-looking broad with brains. He wondered if Pam and Aurora had finished their drinks yet . . .

Aware of everything at once moving around in his head, floating in and out of his mind's vision, pictures and now live action in the pale yellow dress. Ready?

"Kyle!"

She flipped up the sunglasses coming over, then removed them. She said, "Chucky," almost matching the intensity of his greeting. But immediately her expression relaxed, again composed. She said, "Well, are you ready to become a corporate shareholder?"

Chucky said, "If I don't have to read any small print. Hey, come on inside, I want you to meet some people." Going up the steps, his hands lightly touching her back, he said, "Would you do something for me?"

She looked at him but didn't seem surprised.

"What?"

"Tell this boy I'm going to introduce you to that you like his hat."

Chucky brought a chair over to the table, waving at people, asking how they were doing. Both of the girls, Pam and Aurora, made room; but the young guy drinking beer out of the bottle, introduced simply as Moke, didn't move.

Very serious, with that official American-cowboy funneled brim curving down on his eyes. Grim. While his body tried to appear casual—the indifferent stud.

Kyle said, "I like your hat. It has a lot of character."

Moke stirred. He looked at her, looked past her, came back to her, then stretched to look out at the room, showing her his pointy Adam's apple, vulnerable white throat. He might not have heard what she said, with the rock beat, a bell dinging outside, a foghorn blaring inside among cheers and forced laughter—poor timing.

She leaned close to the table. "I said I like your hat."

And got a reaction this time. Moke touched the brim, moved it up and then down on his eyes again. The strands of dark hair to his shoulders didn't move.

"It's an original Crested Beaut," Chucky said.

"I like your shirt, too," Kyle made herself say, though she wasn't sure why. The shirt was light blue with dark-red roses across the yoke, pearl buttons open almost all the way down the front, bony chest showing. "Are you a cowboy?"

"Moke's from Texas, the real article," Chucky said. "Hey, Moke?"

Moke shrugged, like it wasn't anything.

"I believe it," Kyle said. And that was enough of that. She wondered what Chucky was doing. If he was putting on a show. If he felt the need to have people around him.

The girl named Pam, Kyle assumed, was Chucky's. She had more hair than Kyle had ever seen before on a human head. Ash blond. More than all of Charlie's Angels put together, making her face seem tiny, hiding in there. Her hand, bearing a diamond solitaire, rested on Chucky's arm. She yawned but seemed content.

The other girl, Aurora, was dark-haired, cat-faced, with bedroom eyes, languid moves; she wore rings on seven of her fingers, a diamond, an opal, intricate designs in gold. She didn't yawn, she wound the straw from her collins around her thumb, pulled it off and wound it again.

Chucky said, "We were out with Barry earlier today, cruised up from Dinner Key. Little boat party."

"I know," Kyle said. "He called me as I was leaving home."

Pam said, "Every time we go out'n the boat"—she spoke slowly, dragging her words—"and then come in here after and go, you know, to the ladies' room? I wash my hands and all, comb my hair. And then, whenever I look at myself in the mirror after we've been out on the boat? My zits look bigger."

"They are," Aurora said.

Chucky said to Kyle, "You work out of your house, uh?"

"I have an office there."

"These two work out of their house, too," Chucky said.

Pam slapped his arm. "What's that suppose to mean?"

Aurora said to him, "I thought you were going to take me home." The whine in her voice surprised Kyle; she had expected a purr. She heard Chucky say, "You want to leave, call a cab." And the whine again: "You big shit, Barry said you're suppose to take me." They weren't bedroom eyes, they were joyless, at best sleepy.

Chucky said, "Hey, when'd I start working for Barry? You want to go home, go home. You want to wait'll we're through here, I'll take you. Now you be a good girl."

Aurora said, "Well, why can't Lionel take me?"

" 'Cause Lionel's busy."

Moke said, "Doing what, eating? I ain't seen that sucker do nothing else." Moke grinned, his eyes slipped over to Kyle to get her reaction.

She smiled, an act of courtesy, and regretted it.

Encouraged, Moke said, "Yeah, Lionel, he gets his snout in the trough he'll feed all day you let him. Won't he?"

Chucky said, "Well, he is a size, all right."

Moke said, "He was mine I'd keep him out'n a feed lot."

"Why don't I leave this with you," Kyle said, setting her case upright on her lap. She zipped it open and brought out a printed binder and a few loose papers. "You can take your time, read over the prospectus and give me a call . . . not this week, though. I'm going to be in New York."

"I can't wait," Chucky said. "Let's get 'er done now."

"He can't read, is what his trouble is," Moke said. "Can you?"

Kyle kept her eyes on Chucky. "You want to do it *here*?"

"It'll be a first," Chucky said. "The only legit deal ever made in this place."

Kyle said, "Well..." and placed the bound prospectus in front of him. "It's a software company, been in business two years."

"Software," Moke drawled, "they make that toilet paper don't hurt none when you wipe yourself?"

Pam said, "God, you're sickening."

Kyle didn't look up. "They've developed a series of programs for personal computers." She glanced at Chucky. "You wanted to get into high-tech."

"Love it," Chucky said. "I got a computer myself. I show it to you?"

Kyle shook her head, surprised. "No, you didn't."

"I don't know how to operate it," Chucky said. "I got a fourteen-year-old kid comes in when I need him, name of Gary. Gary can key into Dade and Broward County, both their systems. I ask him to run a license number? Gary can tell me in about ten seconds if it's on a county or government vehicle or belongs to a pal. All the time popping his bubble gum."

Moke said, "You shitting me?"

"Ask it the birth date of your favorite trooper," Chucky said, "case you want to send him a card with a little something in it."

Kyle said, "Well, you only plug into Dow-Jones with this one. They're specializing in programs for mailing lists, forecasts, cost analyses, budgets, word processing. They've somehow organized an eighty-eight-thousand-word dictionary inside ninety-three K bytes of disk space, if that excites you . . ."

"Dig it," Chucky said. "What else?"

"Well, the market," Kyle said, "is definitely there. It's been increasing by a third each year, while this particular company has tripled its revenue over the past two years and they're now reasonably sure of a three-hundred-percent annual growth rate through at least 'Eighty-five."

Aurora said, "How do you know all that?"

Kyle looked up to see the dark-haired girl frowning at her. "I'm sorry. What?"

"How do you know about all that kind of stuff?"

"I read," Kyle said. She placed a typewritten letter before Chucky that was addressed to an investment banking company in New York, then went into her case again for a pen. "That's the subscription form. Sign where you see your name at the bottom and you'll be a one-and-a-half percent shareholder in Stor-Tech, Inc."

Aurora said, "I mean but how did you *learn* all that?"

"She's smart, what she is," Moke said. If anybody wanted the answer.

"I've got an idea," Kyle said to poor puzzled Aurora frowning at her. "I'll give you a lift home and tell you all about it on the way. How's that?"

Chucky said, "Hey, come on, you're not leaving us, are you?"

"Have to," Kyle said. "Isn't that the way it is, just when you're having fun . . ."

Bobbi raised her arm straight up, called to Chucky going out to the terrace and waved the check at him. She watched him come back through the customers standing around by the opening, Moke right behind him in that stupid cowboy hat.

"You want to sign or pay for it?"

"I'm a signer," Chucky said. "Gimme your pen."

Bobbi had to go over to the cash register to get it. Lying there on the back counter was the drink check her boss wanted verified, so she brought that with her and held it out to Chucky with the ballpoint.

"Gabe says I have to show you this one I signed your name to. From last week."

Chucky took the check, looked at it. "You write just like I do."

"I try to save you the bother, but Gabe can tell the difference."

"Just come straight out from the loop and put a little tail on it. This one here you can almost read," Chucky said. "You didn't give yourself a tip."

" 'Course not. You think I'm trying to rip you off?"

"Not my sweet girl," Chucky said, still looking at the check. "Who was I with? I don't remember."

"Well, actually," Bobbi said—she was afraid he was going to ask that—"you weren't here but Rainy said put it on your tab"—Chucky looking up at her now—" 'cause he and this guy he was with were supposed to meet you, but you didn't show up."

"Last Thursday?" Chucky said, his big pupils staring right at her now.

Moke was in close to him, leaning on the bar and looking at the check past Chucky's shoulder. Bobbi raised her hand to smooth her hair in back, fooling with it for something to do and saw Moke, the creep, staring at her armpit. Moke was weird. He'd sit at the bar sometimes and just stare, hold his beer bottle by the neck in his fist, never taking it away from his mouth, and giving it a little flip with his wrist when he wanted a sip. When he was being funny he'd ask for a straw with the beer and wait for her to laugh. He was going to wait a long time, the stupid shit. What a 'tard.

"He say I was coming in?" Chucky asked.

"Who, Rainy? Yeah, you were supposed to meet 'em here," Bobbi said. "Rainy and this friend of his. He was here about an hour ago, I just saw him."

"Rainy was?" Chucky seemed confused.

"No, not Rainy. His friend."

"While I've been here?"

"I don't know. Maybe. I didn't notice."

Chucky had straightened. "Not while I been here." He turned to Moke. "You see him?"

"See who?" Moke said.

"The guy, the one that was with Rainy last week. You know, went with him . . ."

Now Moke straightened up from the bar. "He was in here? When?"

"She says just a while ago."

"I don't know," Bobbi said, instinct telling her to back off, "maybe it was a couple of hours ago." She didn't like the look on Moke's face. Or Chucky's, for that matter.

"Musta just missed him," Chucky said. "What'd you say his name was?"

"I don't know his name. Only he's a friend of Rainy's."

"Slim fella, with brownish hair," Chucky said.

She had never seen Chucky so intent, serious. A moment ago she was going to say something about how much Rainy's friend had changed, his appear-

ance, like he'd been sick and now was all better, but
changed her mind and said, "Just ordinary looking,
I guess."

"Where's he staying?" Chucky asked her.

"I don't know." With irritation now, to show she
was getting tired of this. "Ask Rainy."

Neither of them said anything.

Moke seemed about to, then raised his eyebrows
and grinned. Then rubbed his hand over his mouth
and looked away, like TV actors did, acting innocent. Immature or stupid—Bobbi believed you
could go either way with Moke and be right. Even
stoned he was a simple study.

Chucky said, "Well, it doesn't matter." He bent
over to sign the check.

And Moke said something that would stay with
Bobbi for a long while after. He said, "It was dark
time I seen him, but I'd know that sucker again, I
betcha anything." With an eager sound to his
drawl.

She was glad she didn't tell them how much
Rainy's friend had changed. She wondered if he'd
come in again. She wondered what she'd say to
him, if he did.

They were on the walkway of the bridge, crossing
toward Chucky's condo, Lionel trailing behind.
Moke said, "Girl says ask Rainy. That'd be some

deal. Get one of them air tanks you put on your back for diving, pair of flippers . . ."

"I don't want to know anything about that," Chucky said.

"Well, you better see about this fella. I tell Nestor he's gonna say find him and take him off the street."

Chucky wiped at his face with the palm of his hand. He wanted to run. Run home, run up fifteen flights of stairs, that elevator was so slow, and pop some caps; when he was wired he had to move right *now*. He said, "She must've made a mistake. The guy wouldn't be hanging around here, so don't worry about it."

Moke took hold of Chucky's arm, bringing him to a stop in the middle of the bridge walkway, people giving them looks as they had to step off the curb to go around. Lionel came up but Moke didn't pay any attention to him or the people, saying to Chucky, "You're the one sent the fella with Rainy. *I* saw him run off. Avilanosa's standing there with his Mac-ten smoking, man, *he* saw him run off. Avilanosa goes, who was that? I tell him, beats a shit outta me. Some guy Chucky wanted taken out."

Chucky, trying to keep his jaw tight, said, "The guy was with Rainy. I didn't even know him. Listen, I gotta go."

"Yeah, you said to me on the phone, take the bozo with Rainy. You recall that?"

"I might've at the time," Chucky said, moving, twisting his shoulders, wanting to snap his fingers. "It doesn't matter if I said it or not, right? I'll take care of the matter. The guy's around I'll find him."

Moke said, "You fuck Nestor again, man, he'll send Avilanosa. And there won't be nothing in the world I can do about that or want to try—no matter how many goddamn hats you give me, partner . . . Hey, you hear me!"

Chucky was running with the appearance of jogging, just in time moving to hold back the panic beginning to seep through his nervous system. If Moke touched him now, if Moke tried to stop him . . .

He felt exactly the way he had felt when he was twelve years old and had killed the dog with his hands.

9

THE HOUSEMAN, CORNELL LEWIS, SAID, "Does it please you?" Making it a point, maybe, to show Stick he had manners, but not putting him on.

Stick didn't expect a double bed with a view of palm trees out the window. He said, "I think I'll take it."

"I bet you will," Cornell said. "So, we got the bathroom between us, tub and shower. . . ." He moved off and Stick paused to take a look at the bathroom: the clean tile, the seat on the toilet. "We got us our rec room I like to call it, with the color TV . . . refrigerator and stove over there . . . if we don't want to eat in the kitchen with the help."

"You cook?"

Cornell looked at him. "Yeah, I cook. Don't you?"

Stick said, "I cook probably better'n I fix cars—he's going to find out."

"Nothing to fix on his," Cornell said. "They

break down he trade it in, get a new one . . . Come on, I'm suppose to show you the rest. The master want you to be acquainted where everything's at. He yell to you, 'Hey, Stickley, bring me a phone out the morning room.' You know which one's the morning room no matter what time of day it is. You dig?"

"Yeah, but I don't work inside."

"He like his driver to be versa-tile, do things around the house, help out when they have company. 'Cept Cecil. Cecil broke things, generally fucked up and didn't give a shit. Beautiful human being. So Mr. Stam kept him out of the house. Shoulda put him on a chain."

"I haven't heard anything good about Cecil," Stick said. "You get along with him?"

"Get along with Cecil you need a whip and a chair, or one of those cattle prods? First place, he don't like black folks and in the second place he hates 'em. He should be back any time, pick up his mess."

Stick said, "He doesn't even know he's fired, does he?"

Cornell made a face, an expression of pain. "Not yet."

It seemed more like a museum than a place where people lived: all marble and glass or wide open, full of hanging plants and flower arrangements, potted palm trees. Looking across some of the rooms or down a hall it was hard to tell what was outside and what was in.

The living room was like an art gallery: two steps down to a gray marble floor and a sectional piece in the middle, pure white, where about a dozen people could sit among the pillows and look at the paintings and pieces of sculpture that didn't make any sense at all. The room was pale gray and pink and white except for a black marble cocktail table. There were white flowers on it—no ashtrays—and several copies of a magazine, fanned out, called *Savvy*.

Stick went down into the living room, stood before a canvas about ten feet by five, gray shapes that could be parts of the human body, organs, bones, scattered over a plain white background.

"What is it?"

Cornell said, "Whatever your imagination allows."

He stood on the marble steps taller than Stick: a light-skinned black man of no apparent age but with the body of a distance runner: as neat as the decor in pressed gray trousers, black suspenders over a white dress shirt open at the neck, polished black loafers with tassels: the houseman nearly ready for evening duty.

"You have to do any of the cleaning?"

"The maids," Cornell said.

"Well, they do a job," Stick said.

"No trash, no dust," Cornell said, "or cold drafts coming in broken windows." He paused. Stick was looking at him now. Cornell said, "You from the block, aren't you?"

Stick came back toward him, still looking around, pausing at a polished stone that could have been an owl if it had eyes. He said, "I think you're guessing."

"I might have been," Cornell said, "but you answered the question, didn't you?"

"Well, as they say . . ." Stick said.

"What do they say where you were?" Cornell seemed even more at ease, ready to smile. "I come out of Raiford, then some trusty time at Lake Butler four years ago and found my new career."

"Jackson," Stick said.

"Mmmm, that musta impressed him. Yeah, Jacktown, have riots and everything up there."

"I think he liked it," Stick said.

"What the man likes is to rub against danger without getting any on him," Cornell said. "Make him feel like the macho man. You know what I'm saying?"

"He goes," Stick said, " 'How'd you make it in the joint?' Like he's been there. He sounds like a probation officer."

"I know it . . . Come on." Cornell turned and

they moved off. "I know what you saying. He ask how you make it like he knows what it is you have to make. I try and tell him, start with the doors clangin' shut. Every place you go the door slide open, the door clang shut. Go in the cell, *clang*, you in there, man. He act like he knows . . . That man ever took a flop there people would pass him around, everybody have a piece."

"Dress him up in doll clothes," Stick said, "and play house. But he wants you to think he knows all that."

"Wants you to think he's *baaad*, what he wants you to think. You understand what I'm saying to you? Yeah, like he's the one knows and he's testing to see if *you* know, 'cept he don't know shit less you tell him." Cornell was looser now, coming at Stick with that quick clipped black way of street talking. "You see by some of the rough trade he associates with what I mean. People he has in his *house*, man, you see their picture in the paper, some state attorney investigation, that kind of thing. It's why he hired you—why he hired me. See, he sits there at the club with his rich friends? Say, 'Oh yeah, I go right in the cage with 'em. They wouldn't hurt me none. No, I know how to handle 'em, how to treat 'em.' He tells *every*body. You understand? So there happen to be a fugitive warrant out on you someplace—you know what I'm saying? You best fly your ass out of here."

"I did it straight up," Stick said. "I'm done. For good."

"You hope to Jesus."

Stick said, "He get you out of a halfway house or coming through the window?"

"Shit," Cornell said. "You know how he found me? Man didn't know nothing about me, I was doorman at a place down the beach, this big private condominium. He comes driving up—place is full of cars on account of this reception somebody's having. See, I didn't park cars, I have to stay there by the door. But Mr. Stam, he slide his window down, his hand riding on it, he got this ten sticking out from between his fingers. He say to me, 'You got room for one more, haven't you?' and shove the bill at me, like go on, take it. So I do, I tuck it in my shirt. I say to him, 'No, sir, we full up,' and walk away. He gets out of the car and comes over to me, stands right here." Cornell held the palm of his hand straight up in front of his face. Then lowered it to his chin. "No, more like here. Like he's the little manager and I'm the umpire. You know what I'm saying? Right here. He say, 'What are you, some kind of smartass?' I go, 'You offer me the money, shove it at me to take it. Wouldn't I be a fool not to?' He turn and come back and he's got his lip like pressed against his teeth? He say, 'You got nerve, kid. I like a kid with nerve.' Takes a c-note out of his pocket from a roll, hands it to me and says in his natural voice again but real loud, 'Now park the fucking car!' I go, I scratch my head, I go, 'Oh, tha's what you wanted.' We doing this skit, see? He go in the party, come out a little later, I'm still there. He say, 'What do you do, man, when you not impersonating a doorman?' See, I know the man's crazy, likes to fool, so I tell him the truth figure he'll think I'm giving him some shit. I go, 'Well, I hustle, you know, I deal, I steal, sell TV sets and silverware out the back door.' Man love it. He say, 'You polish the silverware 'fore you fence it? You know how to do that?' Coming on to me now. 'You the cool cat with the hot goods?' All that kind of shit. Now it's part of his routine. They have company, I come in with a tray of canapés to serve the guests? He'll say to one of the ladies, 'Watch your purse, Sharon, here comes Cornell.' Then what I do, I grin and chuckle."

"Doesn't bother you?" Stick said.

"Bother me how? Put on the clown suit, man. Grin and chuckle. 'Yessuh, Mr. Stam.' Say to the lady, big blond lady name of Sharon, 'Oh, that Mr. Stam, he *ter*rible what he say.' Put on the clown suit and they don't see you. Then you can watch 'em. Learn something . . ."

He seemed thoughtful. Stick said, "Learn what?"

"I don't know. *Something*," Cornell said. "There must be *some*thing you hear listening to all these rich people can do some good."

"Something they don't know they're telling you," Stick said.

"Yeah," Cornell said, dragging the word. "You got it."

"Only you don't know what you're listening for."

"Not till I hear it," Cornell said. "But when I hear it—you understand me?—then I'll know it."

"You been listening for four years?"

"What's the hurry?" Cornell said.

Right, and if he never heard magic words of opportunity what was he out? Cornell was playing his grin-and-chuckle game with himself, Stick decided. Which was all right: he'd probably admit it if you held him down. On the other hand listening and being ready, not sitting back on your heels, there could be something to it.

He wondered where the man was.

"Phoning," Cornell said. "When you don't see him he's phoning. When you *do* see him he's phoning."

"People with money like phones," Stick said.

"Love 'em," Cornell said. "It's a truth you can write down, memorize."

"I met a guy has twelve phones," Stick said.

"Twelve's nothing," Cornell said. "Mr. Stam's got seven in the garage part counting the ones in the cars. Must be fifteen in this house and the guest house and four, five outside." He said, "Here, look in as we go by the den."

Sure enough, there he was on the phone, sitting at a black desk in a room painted black, sitting in a cone of light from the ceiling, holding a red phone. Stick caught glimpses of gold and red. What stopped him was the blown-up black and white photo of Barry, about six feet of him from cutoffs to yachting cap, eyebrows raised in innocence, his expression saying *who, me?* The black and white Barry behind and above the real Barry on the phone.

Why was it familiar? The expression.

Cornell said, "Hey," in a whisper and they moved on. Now Cornell was saying the man liked black 'cause it was restful, kept him calm swinging the big deals. Loved a red phone with the black.

Stick, listening, kept seeing that *who, me?* expression in his mind. The man had not looked familiar in the car, not someone he'd seen before . . . until he thought of another photo in a group of photos on the paneled wall of a den . . . all the guys in their Easter-egg colors and the two girls on the aft end of the yacht . . . the exact same *who, me?* expression on the guy next to the girl with the gold chain digging into her tan belly, *yes*, the guy next to her. Who, me? I'm not doing anything.

Jesus. Barry and Chucky . . .

He could be wrong. The same expression, but two different guys that looked somewhat alike, the same type.

"Now the man's wife, Miz Diane Stam," Cornell was saying, "she something else. You see her here, you see her there. What the man says she does, she putzes. Putzes around the house trying to think up things to be done. Then she give you a list. Man loves phones, the woman gets off on lists. List say put all the books in the library in alphabet order by the author's names. List say put red licorice Jelly Bellies in the black den, put mango and marzipan Jelly Bellies in the morning room . . . There she is. Grape ones in the living room."

They were coming through a pantry into the kitchen.

The woman still had on the green robe, a thin, silky material. She was talking to the cook. Cornell waited. Stick would bet, judging from the way the robe hung, she had those round white breasts that looked full of milk and showed little blue veins. She was about thirty, a good age. When she turned to them Cornell said, "Miz Stam, I like you to meet your new driver. Stickley."

She was looking at him but could have been

thinking of something else. Vague brown eyes, pale complexion, thick brown hair pulled back and tied with a piece of yarn.

"Stickley?"

"Yes, ma'am."

The kind he thought of as a soft, comfortable woman, slow moving, passive—they always had that pale white skin.

"Stickley . . . is that English?"

The kind if he saw her alone in a bar he'd feel his crotch come alive and then he'd be anxious, nervous, going through the opening remarks and was sure he sounded dumb.

"Yes, ma'am, it's English," Stick said. Though he had never considered himself or his people from anywhere but the Midwest.

"That's nice," Mrs. Stam said. "Well then . . ." Stick waited, but that was it. She walked out of the kitchen.

He met the cook, Mrs. Hoffer, a bowlegged old lady in a white uniform: strong-looking woman, she swiped at Cornell with her neck towel when he patted her behind, but Stick could see she liked it. He told her he was glad to meet her and she said, "You too, kiddo."

Cornell put an arm around her shoulders. "This lady makes super blintzes, don't you, mama? Makes knedlachs, piroshkis, what else, kugel, all that good stuff. I'm showing her some gourmet tricks, like how to save her bacon grease and pour it in with the collards."

The kitchen was a pretty friendly place. Stick met Luisa Rosa and Mariana, the maids that Cornell called the Marielita Twins from Cooba. They smiled and stayed fairly close to one another, both in yellow uniforms with white aprons. Cornell said he was teaching them to speak American, how to say, "I'm feeling depressed because of my anxieties," and "Have a nice day."

No—Stick decided—Cornell wasn't listening for magic words. He was home.

After supper, coming back along the breezeway to the garage, he began thinking of that big blown-up *who, me?* photo again—wondering if he could stick his head in the den, take another look—and a strange thing happened. He saw a yacht tied up at the dock now. Big sleek-looking cruiser that had to be fifty feet long. He went down to the dock, began pacing it off from the bow, counted twenty strides and looked at the stern.

Seaweed. And beneath it, *Bal Harbour, Fla*.

He walked back to the apartment in the garage, now relating Barry's *who, me?* expression to the cruiser in the photo in Chucky's den, but still not sure of something.

Cornell was wearing a pearl gray tie now with his gray trousers, slipping on a lightweight black blazer.

"You going out?"

"Man, you think I wear this to go *out*? Look like the undertaker."

"There's a boat tied up at the dock."

"*Boat*? That's a halfa million dollars worth of cabin cruiser, the *Seaweed*. The man makes some of his great escapes on it."

"I thought maybe somebody stopped by."

"We got company coming, but not by sea." Cornell buttoned his blazer, turned sideways to the dresser mirror to look at himself. "You a lean, handsome motherfucker, ain't you?"

"He has parties on the boat, uh?"

Cornell turned from the dresser. "What you trying to find out I might help you with?"

"Our boss, I wondered if he's got a friend by the name of Chucky."

Cornell's face broke into a smile. "Chucky? You know Chucky? You do, there some things you haven't told me."

"They pretty good friends?"

"They play together sometime. How you know Chucky?"

"There was a fella name Rainy Moya at Jackson, used to work for him."

Cornell shook his head. "Don't know any Rainy

Moyas. But Chucky, shit, Chucky's the head clown, our man's star attraction, his *in* with the bad guys, the wise guys, all those guys . . . What you looking at?"

Stick waited.

Cornell said, "Yeah," taking his time, "there some things you have not told me."

"I got to talk to somebody," Stick said.

"Don't get me into nothing, man, I'm clean, I'm staying clean."

"I need to find out something . . ."

"I got to go to work."

"Wait a minute, okay? I want to ask you a question, that's all. I think," Stick said, and hesitated. "I practically *know*, Chucky set up a guy, the one I mentioned. Rainy. Sent him to drop a bag knowing he was going to get whacked. Guy steps out of the car with a gun big enough to kill Jesus. But you tell me Chucky's the head clown, lot of laughs." Stick waited.

Cornell said, "Yeah? What's the question?"

"Is he or isn't he?"

"I got to go to work," Cornell said.

Stick fell asleep. He wasn't sure for how long. He was watching a James Bond movie on television, sitting up in a comfortable chair, but when something touched him he jumped and the news was on.

Cornell said, "Didn't mean to scare you . . . Mr. Stam would like you to come out to the patio."

Stick had to look up at him. "That all you going to tell me? How should I dress?"

"You fine like you are."

"What's the problem?"

"Cecil," Cornell said. "Cecil come home mean and ugly. Don't like the idea he's fired."

"I been waiting for him to come and get this stuff out of there," Stick said, "so I can go to bed."

"Well, he's here now. Mr. Stam want you to have a talk with him."

"I didn't fire him, *he* did."

"Then come tell Mr. Stam that."

"What's the guy think, I took his job?"

"Ain't any way to know what Cecil thinks."

"Yeah? What's he like?"

"Cecil? He's an ugly redneck mother*fucker* is what he is. And he don't *like* nothing."

"Wait a minute," Stick said. "I get into this—then he's got to come here and pick up his *clothes*? After?"

Cornell said, "Man, what can I tell you?"

It was an informal get-together. Friends over for a few drinks, some cold shrimp and crablegs: Barry's lawyer, his internist and his yacht broker and their wives in casual dress, light sweaters over shoulders, their faces immobile, softly illuminated by patio lights buried among rows of plants, candles on the buffet table and a circle of torches burning on black metal poles.

Barry and Diane wore white caftans, Diane among the guests while Barry stood in his robe, in the ritual glow cast by the torches, to face Cecil, who hung against the portable bar.

Cecil would shift his weight and the cart would move, the bottles chiming against each other. He would reach behind him, take a bottle by the neck and swing it backhand to arc over the heads of the guests—no one moved—and splash in the swimming pool. Several bottles floated almost submerged in the clean glow of underwater lights.

Barry held his elbows in, palms of his hands extended flat, facing up. He would gesture as he spoke, then return to this palms-up pose of resignation.

"Cece? . . . What can I tell you?"

"You already tole me, asshole. If I heard you right." Cecil was drunk enough to stumble. He would cling to the cart as he raised a bottle of Jack Daniel's to his mouth.

"That's what I mean. What more can I say?"

"You can say it ain't so, pussyface. We'll talk her over."

Barry was solemn. "Cece, you're not giving me much reason to even listen to you." He glanced off into the dark. It looked like someone was coming. Finally. "I don't want to call the cops, Cece, but I don't know. I press charges you've got a parole violation. Right?" Barry looked at his guests, picked out his lawyer. "David? Wouldn't you say he's on dangerous ground?"

The lawyer stirred, sat up straighter. He said, "Well, I suppose it's possible . . ."

The figure, coming from the general direction of the garage, was cutting across the slope of lawn now. Carrying something at his side. A bucket? Something round, with a handle. A second figure, Cornell, trailed behind.

Barry said, somewhat louder, "Well, Cece, it's up to you. I'm going to ask you once more to leave quietly."

"And I'm own ask you to bite this," Cecil said, palming his crotch. "Little pussymouth Jew-boy, you might be pretty good."

"That's it, all she wrote," Barry said. "You're paid up and your replacement's right here, so get the fuck out. *Now.*" He stepped back toward his guests, looking at Stick coming into the torchlit patio . . . The hell was he doing? Carrying an old two-gallon gasoline can . . .

Stick walked past Cecil without looking at him, not wanting to. He'd seen enough of Cecil already: that hard-bone back-country type, cords in his neck and pale arms, big nostrils—Christ, hearing the guy blowing air through his nose to clear it. You did not talk to the Cecils of the world drunk; you threw a net over them if you had one. Cops and prison guards beat their brains in and they kept coming back. Stick walked over to the buffet table. He placed a glass on the edge, unscrewed the cap on the gooseneck spout of the gasoline can and raised it carefully to pour.

Cecil said, "The fuck you drinking?"

Stick placed the can on the ground. He picked up the glass, filled to the brim, turned carefully and came over to Cecil with it. Cecil stared at him, weaving a little, pressing back against the cart as Stick raised the glass.

"You doing? I don't drink gasoline, for Christ sake. Is it reg'ler or ethyl?"

Stick paused, almost smiled. Then emptied the glass with an up-and-down toss of his hand, wetting down the front of Cecil's shirt and the fly of his trousers.

There was a sound from the guests, an intake of breath, but no one moved. They stared in silence. They watched Cecil push against the bar, his elbow sweeping off bottles, watched him raise the fifth of Jack Daniel's over his head, the sour mash flooding down his arm, over the front of his shirt already soaked. He seemed about to club down with the bottle . . .

Stick raised his left hand, flicked on a lighter and held it inches from Cecil's chest.

"Your bag's packed," Stick said, looking at him over the flame. "You want to leave or you want to argue?"

He was making his bed, changing the sheets, when Cornell came in, leaned against the door frame to watch him.

Cornell said, "I don't know what you worried about Chucky for . . . Mr. Stickley."

Stick looked over at him. "I don't know if I am or not. You never answered the question."

"Hospital corners," Cornell said. "Know how to do all kinds of things, don't you? You about scared the shit out of the guests. They all had a double Chivas and went home to bed." Cornell came into the room, looking around at nothing; the walls, painted a light green, were bare. "You ask me is Chucky a clown or what. Could he have had your friend killed? Ask Mr. Stam, no. Chucky's the funky white Anglo-Saxon cocaine dealer, weird, but wouldn't hurt a soul. Ask on the street, that's another something else. They speak of Chucky, say bad things about him. Set up his own man, set up his mama, wouldn't make no difference. Works with de Coobans and stays zonked on the 'ludes. Way you want to never never be."

"He come here to visit?"

"Time to time," Cornell said. "But as I say, man know how to play with fire shouldn't have to worry none."

Stick brought up the green plaid bedspread over the pillows, then pulled it back down again and folded it across the foot.

"You want to know what was in the can?" He looked up at Cornell. "Water."

Cornell said, "Sure, 'nough?" His grin widening. "Shit . . . you telling me the truth?"

"Where was I going to get gasoline?" Stick said. "Drive all the way over the Amoco station?"

10

WHEN WAS THE LAST TIME he had a choice and picked out his own clothes?

He wore state clothes. He wore sporty clothes left by the guy who went to Key West and didn't come back. Now he had a black suit, a gray one and a tan one a tailor in the Eden Roc Hotel had chalked, altered and delivered in three and a half days as a special favor to Mr. Stam. Two seventy-five a copy.

The last time would have been in '76, but he couldn't remember the clothes, outside of a Hawaiian shirt that had sailboats and palm trees on it.

He was to wear a white or light blue shirt, black regular tie. He was to wear the black suit with the black Cadillac, the gray suit with the Rolls, the tan suit with the beige Continental. He could wear anything he wanted when he drove Mrs. Stam; usually she took the green Mercedes.

Stick said, "In the morning when I get up, do I sit

around in my underwear, wait till I find out what car we're taking?"

"That's very funny," Barry said. "No, you don't sit around in your underwear, I tell you the night before." His eyes serious, questioning. Like he might be having a few doubts. "You keep the cars washed, gassed, ready to go, either for a time I tell you or within ten minutes of my call. You think you can handle that?"

Saying it to a man who had never been in the armed forces but had recently taken seven years of penal shit and was full up. Stick waited a moment, as though he was getting it straight in his mind but concerned about something. He let himself ease back and said, "Yes, sir. But if we have to synchronize our watches we're in trouble. I don't have a watch."

He would remember Barry's solemn eyes staring at him. Where were the one-liners?

He asked Cornell about it later on: the guy seemed different from one day to the next.

Cornell said, "What's wrong with you? I explained, didn't I? The man's top bill. *We* don't say the line, the man says the line. What we do, we grin and chuckle. Shit, I told you that."

Stick said, "Yeah, but he gave me a watch to use."

"Sure he did," Cornell said. "The same time he wants you to respect him he remembers you coming with that gasoline can . . . Man wants you to be stupid but happy."

They took the Cadillac limousine to Leucadendra. Barry sat in back and made phone calls. He talked to his broker, Arthur, told him he'd get back to him. He dialed three numbers asking for someone named Kyle, was unable to find her and was short with Arthur when he spoke to him again; he'd get back. Then spoke to a girl who was "Rorie" at first—Barry laying down a field of soft snow about how much he missed her—then "Aurora" as he explained almost deal by deal how busy he was, why he hadn't been able to see her. Stick, all dressed up in his black suit, would glance at the rearview mirror and see Barry in his tennis whites acting into the phone, telling the girl he was on his way at this very moment to a meeting with his lawyers, but hey, how about meeting on the boat later, around six or so.

He said to Stick, "You know the difference between a wife and a mistress? . . . Night and day, man."

Stick looked at the rearview mirror. "That's right, isn't it?" With a note of appreciation, but not giving it too much.

"Sometimes you ask yourself," Barry said, "is it worth it?" He waited for Stick to look at the mirror again. "Bet your ass it is."

Stick looked at the mirror again and nodded. Why not?

They drove into the grounds of Leucadendra past fairways to the tennis courts that were off beyond the stucco Spanish clubhouse with its red tile roof. Getting out, Barry pointed to a side entrance that went into the men's grill and told Stick to "park over there somewhere and hang out, I'll be an hour or so."

Barry walked off carrying three tennis racquets in an athletic bag, a sweater tied around his shoulders. Stick watched him from the air-conditioned car. It was about ninety degrees out there, the sky almost cloudless. He put the Cadillac in "drive" and swung it around.

Park and wait. All right.

But wait a minute . . .

It startled him, something he had failed to consider: that on a job like this he could spend more than half the time doing nothing, waiting. Twenty minutes from Bal Harbour to Coral Gables, now he'd be "an hour or so." Did that mean more than one hour but less than two? If Barry played tennis and then had drinks and maybe lunch in the men's grill . . . Stick realized he could be hanging around here for two hours at least. Or even three hours . . . Driving, he was doing something, he could shut himself off from the man in the backseat. But waiting, he was waiting for the man to come and set him in motion again. Wind him up. He could wait all day and have no right to complain—"Hey, you said you were going to be an hour or so"—because waiting was part of the job. Chauffeurs waited. There were some right here, standing by their cars lined up in the circular drive. Three uniformed chauffeurs. Older guys, all of them in their late fifties or early sixties.

Watching him from the shade. They'd know the Cadillac from the vanity plate, BS-2. The Rolls was BS-1, the Continental BS-3. Mrs. Stam's Mercedes bore a conventional number. Stick got out and walked up the drive. Yeah, they were at least in their sixties. All three wore dark uniforms, white shirts, glasses.

The one wearing a chauffeur's cap, cocked a little to one side, said to him, "Looks like Cecil finally got let go." Stick nodded, coming up to join them—a younger look-alike in his uniform, the new guy—and the one in the chauffeur's cap glanced at the other two. "I told you. Didn't I tell you?" Then to Stick again, "He got looped once too often, didn't he?"

"I guess so," Stick said.

They shook their heads talking about Cecil and it surprised Stick that they seemed disappointed. They told their names: Harvey with the cap, Edgar and John, who didn't say much, and told who they worked for as though Stick would recognize the names. They smoked cigarettes with one hand in their pants pocket and referred to other club member names that Stick realized he was supposed to know. He saw that you acquired a casualness in this job: Yes, you knew all those people and nothing anyone said surprised you. Though Stick let what they said surprise him when they got around to Cecil again, talking about his memory, how ignorant he was but had this knack for remembering things. While Owen, who was Mr. Stam's driver before Cecil, Owen would jot things down he couldn't remember. The three talking among themselves about Cecil and Owen, Stick listening.

Until Harvey turned to him and asked, "How's Mr. Stam doing on that deal he's got in California, that seed company?"

"I don't know anything about it," Stick told him but paid closer attention now. These old guys were taking their time but gradually moving in on him, the new man.

Harvey said, "You play the market?"

Stick said no and the three of them acted mildly surprised. "Gee, that's a shame," Harvey said, "sitting where you are, right there in the catbird seat."

Stick knew he was supposed to ask Harvey what he meant, so he did.

"Working for Barry Stam," Harvey said, sounding surprised.

"We ask him, what looks good, Mr. Stam?"

Edgar said, "and he tells us. Gives us some pretty good tips."

The one named John smirked, said, "Not bad a'tall."

Harvey said, "You know, over-the-counter stuff mostly, companies nobody knows anything about."

Edgar said, "Or some hasn't reached the counter yet. Some of those brand-new stock deals he gets into."

Stick said, "Well, I hear him talking on the phone. It's about all he does."

Harvey said, "That's right. Now Cecil, he'd recall the names and numbers for you from mem'ry. Owen, he'd have to jot 'em down. But Cecil, he was like a jukebox. You put a coin in him and he played you a tune. Look off at number two fairway there, get a squint on his face and go right down a list of stocks, tell you the bid and the ask."

Edgar said, "He did pretty well, too."

John said, "*Well*? He cleaned up."

Harvey said, "I betcha he was making a hundred a week, easy."

Stick said, "Cecil played the stock market?"

"No, from tips," Edgar said.

"Don't confuse the man," Harvey said. "Cecil'd give us a stock tip and get the regular kind of tip back. But I'm not talking about a buck or a five. A good one, like a new company Mr. Stam was going into? That could be worth fifty bucks."

Stick said, "You guys must do all right, you can afford a fifty-buck tip."

Harvey looked at Edgar and back to Stick. "I work for a lady who don't know shit but what her broker tells her and her broker don't know shit either outside of what's on the Big Board. You follow me? Ten years ago Barry Stam was a little smarty kid'd get mad and hit his tennis racquet down on the pavement, bust about two a week. Today little Barry could buy this whole club they ever wanted to sell it. He started out with a rich daddy like everybody else around here, but he passed his daddy by—I mean he could buy his *daddy*, he wanted to. Started in real estate but makes all his money from stock investments now, mostly the last few years. He's the man with the touch a gold. So if I give old Mrs. Wilson a tip sounds good to her, she gives *me* a tip and then I turn around and split it with Cecil. You see how it works? And not just with me or Edgar or John. You can work it with pretty near any one of the fellas you see here."

"Waiting around," Stick said.

"Yeah, right here."

Stick said, "Doesn't it bore the shit out of you?"

Chucky was looking at a ton and a half of next to top-grade Colombian marijuana that had a street value of almost two million dollars. Nestor Soto had bought it in Santa Marta for forty dollars a pound, brought it up from Colombia by sea and air and delivered it to Chucky for two hundred dollars a pound. Now Chucky would turn it over to jobbers and dealers in odd lots—eating extra pills for the next two days—and double his investment.

It was pressure time in the old horse barn—off NW 16th Avenue, out past Hialeah—waiting to move the grass. Dishonest people in the business could hear about it and rip him off. Or somebody could cop to the DEA or the FBI or the BNDD or Dade County Public Safety and they'd confiscate the load, smoke it up in the municipal incinerator and he'd still have to pay Nestor six hundred grand. Within forty-eight hours, that was the deal. Nestor could even steal it from him, sell it again to some other dealer.

Chucky had guys with shotguns in the stables, out in a stand of scrub pine and down NW 16th in a car with a PREP radio. Lionel carried a radio hooked to his belt, his suitcoat hanging open. Chucky wore his hardhat and a long white lab coat, his duster, that he left here on a nail or draped over the handle of a pitchfork.

He said to Lionel, "What I should do, I'm thinking seriously, get out of the wholesale end, work strictly as a broker. I didn't have to stockpile I could be a normal human being." Looking up at the bales, seeing daylight through the rickety boards.

He imagined a wind raising dust across the yard, swooping in to blow away the barn, rip the lab coat from his back and he'd be standing here with his stacked bales, exposed. "I brokered I could do it all on the phone. Or having my dinner where people stop in. Way I used to do it. What do you need?—see Chucky Buck, the first booth there."

"Sounds good," Lionel said, "but you don't make no money. Five, ten bucks a pound."

"I'm talking about just the weed. What's this load worth if I brokered it? I wouldn't make the deal for less'n thirty grand, on the telephone, never have to look at it. Okay, take the thirty and buy half a kilo of good Peruvian flake. You see what I mean? Look at this pile of horseshit—look at it."

"I'm looking at it," Lionel said.

"Cost me what, six hundred grand. Same as ten kilos of Peruvian. Only you don't have to lease a fucking barn to stockpile coke. Listen, this stockpiling—I didn't have to sit on it and wonder who in the hell knows about it outside of enough people we could have a dance we all got together, I wouldn't have this pressure. Right here's where I feel it," Chucky said, slipping a hand inside his white lab coat to touch his abdomen. "Locks up the intestines, man. Every night I'm watching the late news I have a vodka and citrate of magnesia . . . You saw they found Rainy. You see it? It was on the news and this morning's *Herald* had it, way in the back."

Lionel shook his head. "I don't think so."

"You don't *think* so," Chucky said. "You mean—here it's about the same guy you handed a suitcase to goes out and gets shot six times and maybe you saw it, maybe you didn't?"

"No, I don't guess I did."

"They pulled him out at the Bay Front yacht basin. Cause of death gunshot. And they identify him 'cause he's got his wallet in his pocket with the driver's license. You believe it?"

"Yeah, well, it's too bad. I like Rainy okay," Lionel said. "I work for a guy three years ago; man, I didn't like to work for him at all. He got shot, too. I was very happy about it . . . ."

Chucky wondered if Lionel was going to make some kind of point, but never found out. Lionel's walkie-talkie squawked and began speaking to them in Spanish. Lionel unhooked it from his belt and spoke back to it in Spanish, Chucky waiting.

"He say it look like Nestor's car coming. The white Cadillac."

Chucky straightened. "How many?"

"He say only three. It look like Moke and Avilanosa with him."

Chucky said, "Shit," and stepped over to the barn opening to see the car already approaching, its dust trail blowing into the pines that bordered the road in from the highway. Coming past the stables the car drew two of Chucky's men from the shade to follow along behind, one of them with a pump-action shotgun.

Moke, getting out, glanced back at them unimpressed. He had on his cowboy hat, the front of the brim bent down on a line with his nose. He said to Chucky, "Brought somebody wants to visit with you, partner." Moke wearing his new shitkicker image for all to see.

Avilanosa, coming from the driver's side, was another type entirely and Chucky felt no vibes from that direction. He saw Avilanosa as primitive man in a plaid sportcoat: the cane cutter, with his big hands, his big gut, his bowed legs, who served as Nestor's bodyguard and current father-in-law. A Cuban redneck. Chucky found it hard even to say hi to him. Though he did, with a grin.

"Well, how you doing?" Saving his concentration for Nestor, hoping to read the wooden-face little dude before he surprised him with some new demand.

Nestor got out of the backseat of the Fleetwood Cadillac to stand gazing about through tinted glasses as though he'd never been here before. It was typical of him—the sandbagger—he'd distract you while he crept up, get you looking the other way. He raised his hand now in a limp gesture of recognition and gold gleamed, a diamond flashed in dusty sunlight. The little king with gigolo hair and mahogany skin. Nestor passed himself off as Spanish Cuban; but there were people who said he was part Lengua Indian from the wild, miserable Chaco country of Paraguay originally—raised on the alkaline flats and fed spider eggs. Which had made him evil and mean. Another primitive passing for a South Miami dude. Chucky felt he should be trading him beads instead of crisp new cash.

He said, "Nestor," grinning, "you're some kind of rare exhibit, you know it? You're a fucking floor show, man, all by yourself, and you don't even have to perform."

Nestor seemed to like that. He smiled and said, "Chucky," coming into the barn shade, his dark-brown suit losing some of its silky sheen. He looked at the bales of grass, nodding. "You got it okay, uh? It's very good grade Santa Marta. You like it?"

"It's all right," Chucky said. "If I'm lucky, I don't get ripped off or busted I'll make a few bucks . . . You hear about Steinberg? You remember him?"

"Yes, of course," Nestor said, "but I don't see him for, I think, five years."

"Right, he was busted in 'Seventy-eight and ran out on his bond. I just heard they picked him up again out in California. But you know how they found him? You remember that big goddamn St. Bernard he had?"

"Yes, of course. Sasha."

"Right. And you recall how many different names Steinberg used? I don't know what he was using out there, California, but he never changed the dog's name, Sasha. How do they find him? Through the vet. Sasha's doctor."

He got a smile from Nestor, that's all. Not enough to loosen him up, if he needed it.

"The moral of the story," Chucky said, "the *punto*, any time you go a.k.a. you better be sure everybody with you does too. You had a goat, didn't you? Different animals?"

"They all die," Nestor said.

"Oh," Chucky said. With the awful feeling he'd said the wrong thing. He wasn't going to mention chickens.

Nestor said, "What is it you wear? You dress like you gonna kill something. This place a *carniceria*?"

Chucky held his arms out, showing off his lab coat. "Just one of my many outfits."

"You look like you gonna kill the *pollo*."

Shit. "Not me, Nestor." And couldn't help saying, "I like chickens." He felt Avilanosa come up on him and turned enough to see the pitchfork— Christ!—and tried to get out of the way, hunching. But Avilanosa only gave him a tap with it, hitting the tines flat on top of his hardhat.

Nestor smiled. "Like that you kill the cow, yes?"

Avilanosa tapped him again, a little harder. Chucky felt the jolt down through his neck.

"Yes, for fat cows," Nestor said.

Avilanosa raised the pitchfork again and there was nothing Chucky could do but grin and hunch his shoulders playing pie-in-the-face straightman to the free-basing Cubans. But this time Avilanosa used two hands and brought the edge of the pitchfork down with force and Chucky was driven to his hands and knees, pole-axed, the hardhat cracked down the middle rolling away from him. He felt Avilanosa's foot jab him in the ribs to push him over, head ringing, an awful pain down the back of his neck. Now he saw Avilanosa and Nestor looking down at him. He saw Moke, his arms folded. Turning his head he could see his bodyguard, Lionel, standing by the barn opening, two more figures behind Lionel against the sunlight. Now a bale was coming down on him and he tried to roll away but a foot held him. Another bale came down, more bales—his head was free, he could see the faces, but he couldn't move his arms or his legs, the bales piling on top of each other, some rolling off. The weight didn't hurt but he couldn't move. He tried. *He couldn't move.* He tried again, straining, looking at Nestor, pleading with his eyes. *He couldn't move!* And now he began to scream . . .

Because it was exactly the same as the time at

Dau Tieng with the 25th Infantry—Easy Company—
no place for a boy inducted drunk and living in-
country stoned but not stoned enough—when they
were overrun and he was in the ditch trying to press
himself into muddy invisibility and the VC came
down on top of him, blown apart by their own
mortars: black pajamas and mud slamming down
on him, lying on his back *and he couldn't move*.
Pinned, wedged beneath all those bodies. The
stump of a leg pushed against his cheek, his head
lower than his body. Looking up at green tracers
and the weedy edge of the ditch, the creviced sides
coming apart, sliding down with the pounding
noise, straining his neck to raise his head against
the mud rising higher around his face *and he
couldn't move*! This was when he began screaming
to kill himself, to burst his lungs, rupture his heart,
screaming so hard he saw lights exploding and
didn't know if they were in the wash of sky or inside his head, screaming himself out of his body . . .
to come back to life in Memphis, Tennessee, the VA
hospital.

Avilanosa speared the pitchfork into the bale
close to Chucky's face, inches from it, stooped
down and said, "Hey!" So that when Chucky
stopped screaming and opened his eyes he was
looking through the tines of the pitchfork, impris-
oned.

Nestor stood over him now, frowning as Chucky's

eyes focused and he came back to them. "What's the matter with you? You can't be quiet for a moment? You always like to move when I tell you something. I want you listen, okay? I want this guy was with Rene. You tell Moke it's no problem for you, but I don't hear nothing that you find him."

Chucky seemed to strain to speak, out of breath. "We just heard it, few days ago."

"Yes, it's what I mean. A few days, you haven't done nothing," Nestor said. "But you busy, you doing business."

"With you!" Chucky began to cough with the weight and the odor of the marijuana.

"Try to be tranquil," Nestor said. "Breathe slowly. The man with connections, you can sell this in a day, but you can't find the guy was with Rene."

"Nobody even heard of him," Chucky said, coughing again. "None of Rainy's friends. Nobody." He breathed in and out, trying to calm himself. "All I know, Rainy asked me could the guy go with him. Some guy he did time with, but I never saw him before in my life."

"You don't know him," Nestor said, "but you want him dead."

Chucky said, "It was him or Rainy, so I picked him, that's all. I know Rainy. I told you, I send somebody with the money and it's out of my hands, you do what you want. So that's all I did. He got away from *you*, not me."

"Listen to you," Nestor said. He pinched the crease in each leg of his brown silk trousers to squat close to Chucky, resting his arms on his knees, balanced, his body erect. "You give me a lot of shit, you know it? You send a federal man to do business with me. You send somebody you don't know who he is for me to kill. You say you gonna find this guy, you don't do it. You say you gonna tell me places to put my money, make it clean, you don't do it. Tell me what good you do."

"I've been busy," Chucky said. "I just got into that myself, finding investments. Let me up, Nestor, come on, we'll talk about it."

"I don't want to talk about investment," Nestor said. "I want to tell you find this guy was with Rene. It's the first thing, it's the only thing you have to do."

"I gotta sell this weed, Nestor, or I can't pay you," Chucky said. "You know that."

"You sell it, I don't think about that. I think about this guy was with Rene, who he is, where he is. I think you better find him . . ."

"I'm trying—I'm doing everything I can!"

"Shhh. Listen to me," Nestor said. "You don't find him we gonna have to do the ceremony, make an offering to Changó and Elegua. I can do it, you see, because I'm *babalawos*, a high priest before I came here. I don't do it they get angry and I have some more bad luck. You understand?"

Chucky said, "Come on, Nestor, Jesus Christ," panic edging into his voice again, seeing El Chaco the medicine man looking at him from another century and another side of the world. "What you believe, man, that's fine. But I'm not into that, I'm an outsider, man, I don't know anything about it—*nothing*."

"We return a gift to the earth in sacrifice," Nestor said to the face beneath the steel bars of the pitchfork. "You understand? You find this guy was with Rene or we gonna bury you alive."

Moke, in the front seat of the Fleetwood Cadillac, looked back through the rear window at Chucky's guys standing by the barn opening, turning away from the dust blowing at them. They weren't going to try anything. He adjusted his Crested Beaut, loosening the sweatband sticking to his forehead and looked at Nestor sitting with his legs crossed, hands folded in his lap. Neat little guy, smart as hell.

"Old Chucky," Moke said, "isn't anything he's scareder of'n not being able to move. I don't know why, but it's true."

"There something wrong with him, in his head," Nestor said. "He's a man to pity. But I tell you something, he know how to move the product."

"He thought he was gonna get offered up right there," Moke said and looked at Avilanosa driving, his huge fists gripping the steering wheel. "Didn't he?"

"He believe it," Avilanosa said, almost smiling.

"Sure, he did," Moke said, being part of this Cuban business, looking at Nestor in the backseat again. "You pull that *santería* on 'em they start pooping apple butter, I swear."

"Yes, it's good to use," Nestor said. "Save you a lot of work. I find out a long time ago, gods can scare the shit out of anyone."

11

HE WAITED THREE AND A HALF HOURS counting lunch at the snack bar, a hot dog, listening to golfers in their Easter bunny outfits describing their lies and how they chipped out of trouble pin-high and blew a five-foot putt, becoming macho and obscenely emotional about it. All these people seemed to have their troubles.

Barry came out in his white shorts and a clean tennis shirt trimmed in blue and yellow. Jumping in back, slamming the door, he said, "Let's get outta here." As they drove through Coral Gables toward South Dixie he said, "They bug you for tips on the market?"

Stick looked at the rearview mirror. "Yeah, as a matter of fact. The other drivers there, they say you've got the touch. You only pick winners."

Voice from the rear of the air-conditioned Cadillac enclosed in tinted glass:

"Is that right? The touch, uh? The people those guys work for, the families, all their dough was handed down, they never had to lift a finger. It's a goddamn good thing, too. If their IQs were any lower they'd be plants, shrubbery . . . The touch, huh? . . . You know how you acquire the touch, Stickley?"

He'd see what it was like to say, "No, sir."

"You work your ass off, that's how."

"Yes, sir."

"They wouldn't know anything about that, getting up and going to work, man. They tell their drivers to hang out, try and learn something. It doesn't bother me, though. They ask you for anything in particular? Certain areas, like oil, high-tech?"

"They wanted to know about, I think one of 'em said over-the-counter stock."

"Yeah, new issues mostly, that's what they like. Tell 'em—I got one for you. Tell 'em to buy Ranco Manufacturing. Which I'm getting ready to unload. But don't tell 'em that. Tell 'em, buy Ranco. Whisper it . . . Shit, tell 'em anything you want, make a few bucks. Gen-uh-rul Mo-tors. You might have to spell it for 'em."

Stick said to the mirror, "How'd you know about the other drivers?"

"I happen to know things, Stickley. Stickley, old boy. My wife thinks you're English. What'd you tell her, you're from Jacksonshire? Oh yes, that's right next to Yorkshire . . . Stay on Ninety-five, we're going to Lauderdale . . . I know things that'd surprise the shit out of you, Stickley. I know, for instance, that fall you took up in Michigan wasn't half of it. I understand you and your partner were in something much bigger. You and your partner. What was his name? . . ."

"Who, Frank Ryan?" Stick said to the mirror.

"That was it, Ryan. You and Ryan had a deal going with some jigaboos that blew up in your face. But before you took your fall—I think while you were out on bond, according to my source, which is A-one reliable—you took out the jigs. True or false?"

Stick did not feel he could tell the story through a small rectangle of glass to a guy sitting behind him, even if he wanted to. He said, "Where'd you hear that?"

"I understand before the big one went down, you and Frank Ryan, there were a couple *other* spades you blew away. You got something against colored people, Stickley? I better tell Cornell to watch his ass."

Stick looked at the mirror, at the young millionaire trying to sound street. "You checking up on me?"

"You mind? Since I'm providing your bed and board?"

"I thought I was working for it."

"Now you seem bothered by semantics. You want me to rephrase it?"

The street tone didn't go with the words. Guy

didn't know how to stay in character. "Who's your source? You don't mind my asking."

"Yeah, I mind. I don't think it's any of your business."

Trying to sound on the muscle now, a hard-nose. The guy should try out for the movies. See if in about a hundred years he could take Warren Oates's place. Christ. Why wouldn't he just relax and enjoy being rich? On the phone again, talking to his Rorie. The little asshole big-dealer sitting in the backseat of his limo in his tennis whites trying to sound like a hardass and coming off like Eddie Fisher doing Marlon Brando. The first thing he should do is get rid of all his phones except one. Maybe two. And drive his own fucking car.

Stick said, "You mind my asking where we're going?"

"I'm on the phone!" Then, sounding tired: "I'll tell you when we get there. Okay?" Indicating to Rorie the kind of shit he had to put up with from the help. Stick was silent, listening now to Barry telling Rorie babe he was sorry about the interruption. Telling her to take a cab and meet him. To be there in fifteen minutes. Voice rising now:

"Because I'm running late and I don't have time to pick you up. You now have exactly fourteen and a half minutes—got it? Be there or that's all she wrote, babe." He hung up.

For a minute or so Stick thought over the situation. He said, "Mr. Stam? When we get to where we're going—"

"Wolfgang's." Barry was dialing again.

"You going to want me to wait?"

Stick looked at the mirror for an answer that, at this moment, could be crucial.

"No, drop me off." He had his hand over the phone.

Stick said, not sure, "I don't have to wait around?"

He heard Barry say, "Go home. Do whatever you want." Heard him say, "Babe?" his tone mellowing. "I'm sorry. I had a bad day . . . Yeah, I know. Listen, you want to come home with me? . . . What?"

Giggling now. Stick watched him in the mirror. The guy was grinning with his shoulders hunched, giggling like a little kid.

"No, I mean on the boat. What'd you think? I'm serious, babe. Don't you know when I'm serious? . . . Fourteen minutes." He hung up.

"I'm not saying she's tough . . ." Barry said.

Stick looked at the mirror.

". . . but she's the only broad I know who kick-starts her vibrator."

Stick kept staring at the mirror until a horn blared next to him and he got back in his lane.

* * *

He was lucky to find an empty seat down at Bobbi's end of the bar. When she came over with the cocktail napkin she blinked her eyes at his suit and said, "Are you trying to confuse me or something?"

"I wouldn't mind talking to you," Stick said, "over a nice dinner somewhere. You ever leave this place?"

She made a face, disappointed. "I come on at five and work straight through. I'd love to some other time . . . You working?"

"No, I'm not a funeral director," Stick said. "You know a guy named Barry Stam? Has a boat here?" She was nodding eagerly as he said it. "I work for him."

"You work for *Barry*? Oh, my God—"

"What do you think of him? You like him?"

"Yeah . . ." though not sounding too sure. "He's cute. He's flaky but he's cute. He always zings me with a—not a joke really—a one-liner, every time he comes in. I see him coming and get ready. Yeah, he's a nice guy, basically, when he doesn't try so hard." She paused, raising her hand. "Ah, now I know what happened to Cecil." She glanced at a customer waving at her. "Be right back. Wait. What do you want?"

She brought him a bourbon, smiling. "And how's your daughter? You have fun with her?"

"Yeah, she's fine," Stick said, tried to think of something to add and was saved. Bobbi left him again. He watched her making drinks—unhurried but very efficient, no wasted motion, pleasant with the customers. He still had to call his ex-wife. He wondered if he was forgetting on purpose, putting it off . . .

Bobbi came back, placed another bourbon in front of him and said, barely moving her mouth, "I'll put it on Chucky's, the dumb shit."

"He isn't here, is he?" Stick glanced over his shoulder at the crowded room. It was packed, noisy, upbeat music and voices filling the place.

Bobbi said, "No, but somebody else is. Don't look around. He's coming back from the men's . . . Sitting down now, about the middle of the bar."

"Who?" Stick looked at the tinted bar mirror.

"Eddie Moke, the creep. He's a friend of Chucky's."

"I don't see him."

"About halfway down. The cowboy hat—God, you can't miss him."

He saw the hat—pale straw with a high crown, scooped brim—and recognized it right away. Or knew of one just like it. Hanging on a hat-tree with about a dozen different kinds of caps and hats.

"Every time he comes in he asks if I've seen you."

Moke stared straight ahead at his reflection in the rose-tinted glass. He raised his fist, holding the neck of a beer bottle, to his mouth. The hat didn't move.

"What do you tell him?"

"Nothing. There's nothing to tell," Bobbi said. "I might've done something dumb though. You know the last time you were here? And I didn't recognize you right away?"

"Yeah . . ."

"I was explaining to Chucky about signing his check—you know, when you were here with Rainy—and I told them you'd been in, like just a little while before. They started asking me your name and if I knew where you lived, I told them to ask Rainy . . . But I shouldn't've, huh?"

"No, that's all right."

"I don't even *know* your name."

"But you might know where I live, now."

He saw her eyes change, her gaze become flat. "Thanks a lot. You think I'd tell those creeps anything?"

"I didn't mean it that way. My name's Ernest Stickley and I live at One Hundred Bali Way. In the garage."

Her eyes became warm again. "Ernest?"

"Stick."

She did a little something with her eyebrows and her shoulders, putting on a dreamy look, and moved off to take care of a customer.

Stick finished his drink, left a five and walked down the bar to where Moke, in a body shirt striped black and yellow, skintight, straddled his stool, hunched over his beer and a paper dish of peanuts: Moke throwing a few peanuts in his mouth, then taking a swig of beer before he'd begin to chew. Stick laid a hand on his shoulder, feeling bone. The hat came around and now he saw dull eyes staring at him from between the curved brim and the bony shoulder.

"You mind my asking," Stick said, standing there in his black suit and tie, "where a cowboy gets a hat like that?"

"Buy 'em at the store," Moke said, sucking bits of peanut from his teeth.

Stick narrowed his eyes at the hat, studying it, giving Moke time to look him over.

"I like that high crown. It stands up there."

"It's a Crested Beaut," Moke said.

"It sure is," Stick said. "You mind taking it off, let me have a look at it?"

Moke straightened, turned to the bar mirror as he lifted the hat carefully, passed it over his shoulder and began brushing at his hair with bony white fingers.

Stick took the hat, held it at various angles, turned it over to look inside. "There's something sticking out of the sweatband."

"Toilet paper," Moke said. "I put some toilet paper in there so'd fit me good and snug."

"Feels like a fine grade of straw," Stick said.

"The best," Moke said.

"Doesn't crease on you, get out of shape?"

"Can't hurt it none," Moke said.

"Let's see," Stick said. He dropped the hat on the floor and stepped on it, crushing the crown flat, grinding it against the polished vinyl tile. He picked the hat up then and placed it on the bar in front of Moke. "Thanks," Stick said.

He walked away. Along the bar, through the foyer and out the front door to the pavement. The parking attendant said, "Yes, sir," coming over, and Stick pointed. "It's right there."

Moke finally appeared. He stood at the top of the three steps, in the shade of the awning over the entrance, holding his crushed hat. He looked at Stick waiting for him. Stick took off his coat. The Cadillac came up next to him and the attendant jumped out. Stick threw the coat in on the seat. He gave the attendant a dollar, said something to him and the attendant walked away. He pulled off his tie and threw it in the car.

Moke came down one step in his cowboy boots, hesitated and stayed there. He said, "I've seen you someplace."

Stick walked toward him now, to the edge of the awning. Moke turned sideways, raised a boot to the top step again. He appeared uncertain, confused by a dude with a Cadillac coming on like a street fighter. He stared hard but was cautious and seemed ready to run back inside if he had to.

"You know me," Stick said, "or not?"

Moke didn't answer. Stick walked back to the car. He paused with his hand on the door to look at Moke again.

"I know you," Stick said.

He got in the car and drove off, west on Sunrise, Moke watching the Cadillac till it was out of sight.

Chucky could recover from anything, including great bodily harm, in a matter of a few minutes once he was home and got his caps working. Oh, my God—the sheer physical relief of coming down, able to move in slow motion again, at this moment bathed and naked beneath a gold lamé robe that brushed the parquet floor as he moved to the mood, gliding past the muted streaks of sunset outside the sliding glass doors. He heard a male French voice singing *Le Mer*, upbeat, big band in the background, drummer pushing, driving Chucky to slip and slide, doing a funky soft-shoe in his sweat socks, his world turned upside down . . .

His natural state like being on speed or semi-blacked-out drunk, remembering things after and asking himself, did I do that? The only one remembered clearly was killing the dog. Twenty years ago, in the beginning. Picking up the little dog nipping at him, running home and choking it and throwing it against the brick wall. Yes. But others . . . Did I do that? Frag the Easy Company CO? The son of a bitch constantly on his back. Rolled the grenade into his hootch and Lieutenant . . . he couldn't even think of his name, was sent home in a bag. Did I do that? Run over the guy who wanted to argue about a parking place? Vaguely remembering the guy coming back toward the car with his short sleeves tight around his biceps, one of those. Took the guy out with a squeal of rubber and ripped off his door . . . Cut some Cuban hustler across the street from Neon Leon's with a steak knife? . . . Well, when he was young and full of the Old Nick maybe, hadn't yet settled down on the right amount of caps. "Brain scan your ass," he'd said to the neurologist, "it's down in my tummy where it starts."

He heard the door open, came around with the beat to see Lionel.

"Moke is here."

And stopped dead in ringing silence.

"Who's with him?"

"Nobody with him, he's alone. He's mad at something."

"You sure? If that cane cutter's with him—I see Avilanosa you're fired."

"What was I suppose to do?" Lionel said. "I couldn' do nothing."

"What good are you"—picking up Lionel's accent—"you couldn' do nothing? Guy's beating me on the head, you stand there."

"I don't know what you want us to do," Lionel said, "you don't say nothing."

"How could I? I'm on the *ground*—you're standing there watching."

"I didn't want to leave you," Lionel said.

Chucky did a slow turn with his arms extended like airplane wings, came all the way around and Lionel was still there, faithful servant who wouldn't leave him. "Send in Moke," Chucky said, holding his pose, ready to fly at the snake, buzz and confuse him. But it was Chucky who was caught by surprise. Moke stepped in and sailed his Crested Beaut hard in Chucky's direction to land on the floor upright, creased and cracked, the crown stove in.

"What'd you do?"

"Son of a bitch stomped on it."

"You let him?"

"Son of a bitch grabbed it, stomped it, run out and took off in his Caddy 'fore I could stop him. License BS-two." Moke looked over at Chucky's home computer. "Ask that thing whose car it belongs to."

Chucky took a moment—all this coming at once. He felt a warm glow rise through him, closed his eyes, pinched the bridge of his nose and said, "Black Cadillac, Florida vanity license plate BS-two. Owner, Barry Stam. Address . . . something Bali Way. The number isn't clear."

Moke was staring, mouth slack. Chucky thought

for a moment of slipping over and kicking him in the balls. It brought a smile and he said, "You mean little Barry Stam took your hat off your head and did a dance number on it? Ah, Cecil was with him . . ."

"Wasn't nobody with him. He grab it and run out."

"Where was this, 'cross the street?"

"Wolfgang's. Nestor said hang out there and wait for the fella if he come back. And what do you know," Moke said, his ugly mouth curling into a grin.

Chucky frowned. "Wait. This guy we're talking about, he's around five-seven with thick dark hair, Jewish?"

When Moke didn't understand something he became mean. "You know what he looks like same as me. Thin fella, 'bout my size. Only now he's all dressed up, got a suit of clothes. I *knew* him. See, I knew him but I didn't. Till he goes, 'You know me?' I still wasn't sure 'cause it was dark in the van that time. Then he goes, 'Well, I know *you*.' And right then I knew who it was."

Chucky was trying to catch up, get the facts straight in his mind. "I thought he stomped your hat and ran. Now you say you talked to him?"

Moke got meaner. He said, "You hear what I'm telling you, fatass? It was the guy was with Rainy we been looking for, for Christ sake!" Quieter then. "Only with a suit on. Driving this black Caddy."

Chucky became a statue, wondering how long he could hold without moving.

Moke said, "Well, goddamnit, say something."

"Son of a gun," Chucky said.

12

WAITING AGAIN. THIS TIME AT Miami International. Down under the terminal near the Eastern baggage claim area. This time in the Lincoln Continental, color coordinated in his tan chauffeur's outfit. While sporty Barry, in a starched workshirt and pressed faded jeans, had gone inside to meet somebody named Kyle McLaren, arriving from New York.

Did he dress like that, Stick wondered, so people would think he worked? Mistake him for a regular guy?

Regular guys didn't have color-coordinated chauffeurs.

Regular guys didn't keep their girlfriends on a yacht tied up in the front yard 150 feet from where their wives walked around outside in flowing see-through robes.

How did they keep their faces straight?

* * *

A little more than an hour and a half ago he had walked from the garage to the pool in his tans, ready to go. Had waited for Barry, swimming his morning lengths, to come up the ladder in his briefs, lean, hairy, very dark, shaking water from limp hands, gold chain glistening. Had looked at his new watch as Barry slipped on a white terrycloth robe and announced it was 11:30. Barry said, "So?"

"You said the flight arrives at one?"

"I said one-oh-five."

"What time you want to leave?"

Barry looked out at the bay, the narrow sea at Miami's high-rise shore, and placed his hands on his hips inside the robe, if not defiant a little pissed off.

"Stickley, anybody gets to an airport more than ten minutes before a flight leaves or a flight arrives doesn't have anything to do."

Stick said, "I didn't know you were busy." Barry looked at him and Stick added, "Very good, sir."

He walked back to the garage to find Cornell standing just inside the door he'd rolled up earlier to bring out the Lincoln. At the edge of shade, holding binoculars to his face, Cornell said, "I knew it." He lowered the glasses after a moment and handed them to Stick. "Look out there at the boat. Tell me what you see."

Stick raised the glasses, adjusted the focus. "A seagull."

"Not that bird, another bird. *In* the boat."

He saw the superstructure dazzling white, the empty flying bridge moving with a slight roll, the yacht close in his vision, riding above the gray-weathered dock pilings.

"Toward the back end," Cornell's voice said.

He saw the figure now, a woman moving about in the cabin, wearing something white, a beach cover hanging open. A young woman with dark hair, long and full around her shoulders.

"See her?"

"Is that Aurora?"

"That's Aurora. The man's number one at the moment. Now look at the man . . . dying."

Stick edged the binoculars left, past trunks of palm trees, brought his vision down to the swimming pool. Barry was at the umbrella table with his morning papers, a silver service of coffee. He faced the bay, holding a section of newspaper folded lengthwise.

"Mr. Cool," Cornell said. "Love it. Love it . . . Uh-oh, here she come."

Stick cut his gaze back to the yacht.

"No, the terrace. Up on the terrace, man. Here come Miz Diane."

Stick made a quarter turn and put the glasses squarely on Mrs. Stam coming through the formal garden to the terrace steps: silky, see-through lavender negligee stirring, sunlight defining her legs as she descended, laying fire in her hair, glinting on sunglasses that concealed her expression.

"Saturday morning soap," Cornell said. "Better than *All My Children* put together. Lady of the house saying to the lady in the boat, 'He might be fucking you, girl, but I got it *all*.' "

Stick lowered the glasses. "She knows?"

"Course she knows. Last night she see him tippy-toeing out the house—she knows. He tell her he has to see Neil, that's his captain, Neil King, he drives the boat like you drive cars. She tell him, 'Neil ain't there, I saw him leave.' He tell him yeah, he has to get these important papers he forgot. Man leaves important papers wherever he wants to go. Now he like to sneak out there again, but Miz Diane's standing over him with the rolling pin."

Stick put the glasses on Mrs. Stam again, seated now on a lounge, lying back, the negligee coming open to show her bathing suit, two strips of lavender, her pale flesh, the inside of her raised thigh.

"She's going to get burned."

"Never tans, never burns," Cornell said. "She don't stay out long enough. Like shady places best."

Stick held the glasses fixed on Mrs. Stam and felt a stirring in his crotch. She didn't have a *Playboy* body, perfect measurements; it wasn't that. What her body did for him, it met requirements fixed in his mind a long time ago, a day of revelation: Back in Norman when he was ten and saw the full-grown woman friend of his mother naked one time, visiting, and had walked in their bathroom and saw that white skin and that thick patch of hair between her legs. Thinking thereafter that was the ticket when it came to a bare-naked woman, pleasure that would turn you inside out just to look at. He was thoughtful bringing the glasses down, squinting in the bright sunlight, wondering if he was a simple soul. But if he was, what was wrong with that?

He said, "What if Diane wants to go for a boat ride?"

"Make her seasick," Cornell said. "The man's crazy but he ain't dumb. This afternoon he'll say, 'Come on, who wants to go out on the boat?' He sometime he even begs her, say, 'You be all right, babe. It's calm out today.' Uh-unh, she won't set foot on it."

Stick looked toward the pool, at the woman's white body resting on the lounge. "What does she get out of this?"

"Anything she wants. Believe it."

"It's a show, isn't it?"

"It's cuckooland, what it is."

"Fun to watch," Stick said, "if you don't happen to be doing anything."

" 'Specially if you listen," Cornell said. "Don't forget to listen."

First Barry was talking, animated, swinging a tote bag up over his shoulder. Now the girl—who would be Kyle McLaren—was giving it back, though with more controlled gestures, raising her hand as a point of attention and using it to brush her hair back from her face. She carried a straw purse and flat leather briefcase in her other hand. A skycap waited behind them with two bags. Stick had not recognized her yet.

He pulled the Continental forward, edging into the third lane from the curb, popped the trunk release and got out. Across the roofs of cars he could see Barry stretching, face raised, looking everywhere but directly in front of him. Stick went back to the trunk, raised the lid. When he looked over again they were coming toward the car, Barry in his starched work clothes, his hand on the girl's arm. She looked familiar . . .

Then recognized her, the girl in Chucky's living room, remembering the streaked blond hair, the girl he'd thought of as athletic, with the calm, knowing eyes. He moved around to the door and held it open.

The girl was saying, "I'm talking about a direct correlation between effort and results. The payoff, and I don't mean money—" She stopped. She was looking directly at him now, close enough to shake hands. "Isn't satisfying enough."

Barry said, "Everybody's got problems, babe. Get in the car."

Away from the terminal Stick's hand went to the rearview mirror—Kyle McLaren was sitting directly behind him—and adjusted the angle to her face. She was relating something about her father, that she'd felt impatient with him for the first time and wasn't sure why. Stick heard her say, "He's always gotten away with being a snob and a cynic because he's funny, with that dry delivery. But this time, I don't know why, it was tiresome and I thought, do I sound like that?"

"I want to call Arthur," Barry said. "Gimme the names, whatever you got for me."

"Today's Saturday."

"And tomorrow's Sunday—Arthur doesn't care. You kidding?"

"I'm trying to tell you something that concerns *me* for a change. Is that all right?"

"Hey, come on, I always listen. I better, I pay you enough."

"I told my dad about Chucky."

Stick looked up at the mirror.

Kyle was looking at the mirror.

Seeing each other's eyes.

Stick's gaze returned to the freeway. They were

on 112 now, going toward the ocean in fairly light traffic. He heard her say, "I practically acted him out, and I do a pretty good Chucky, if I have to say so myself."

"You think I don't listen? You say something like that, it hurts me."

"Just shut up for a minute, okay? First I did Chucky paying his hospital bill with cash. The three thousand and something for his constipation problem. Then, Chucky carrying an ice-cooler full of hundred-dollar bills into First Boston, dumping it on their conference table, the board of directors standing there watching—"

"Where's Arthur's home phone?" Barry had his attaché case open on his lap. "I got it here someplace." He looked over, poked her arm. "Hey. I'm playing with you. Tonight do your Chucky for me. When we have time."

"You're exactly like my dad," Kyle said. "I tell him about Chucky and he says, 'How do you stand the humidity down there?' He's been here once. He took my mother to the Roney Plaza in 'Forty-seven. He could tell then it was a breeding ground for stuntmen and third-raters." Stick heard her say she was tired. She sounded tired, disinterested. He saw her unzip her soft leather case and take out a file folder.

He saw Barry with the phone now, dialing, handing Kyle a sheet of legal paper, saying, "Get

Chucky—you want my advice—get him into commodities and lose his ass, or else he's going to drive you nuts. Here, take it." She was looking out the window and Barry had to wave the legal sheet in front of her. Stick looked away, approaching the 95 interchange, followed the gradual curve down and around to head north. It was a beautiful day, but neither of them had said anything about the weather. He thought of Cornell telling him to listen, maybe learn something.

He met her eyes again, briefly, as she looked up from the yellow legal sheet. She said, "Good, stay with cheap play for the time being. Few more months, anyway. I like Kaneb, I like Fleetwood . . ."

Barry was saying, "Whatta you mean, who is it? Cut the shit, Arthur, and turn on your recorder. I want to go with Kaneb Services"—he looked at Kyle and she held up her hand, fingers spread— "another five thousand . . . Right." He listened, saying "Yeah," then put his hand over the phone. "Arthur says put another ten in Automated Medical. Whatta you think? . . . Hey."

"I'm sorry. What?"

"Automated Medical Labs. I forgot what they do."

"Interferon," Kyle said, "the cancer treatment. They're also working on herpes."

"Jesus, you're kidding . . . Arthur, let's go ahead with Automated Medical . . . No, couple thousand shares . . . You bet." He listened again, nodding. "Let me think about it a minute." He turned to Kyle. "Wake up. Ranco Manufacturing—they were at twelve, they're up to seventeen. Arthur's been telling me all week it's time to get out. Whatta you say?"

It was a name Stick had heard before. Ranco. The one Barry had told him to give to the chauffeurs, but not before he sold his shares.

She was saying, "I'm going to sleep all week."

"Come on, Ranco. It's at seventeen. Sell or not?"

"What's your position?"

"Four thousand shares. It's one you gave me last year."

Stick watched her paging through her folder. He heard her say, after a moment, "Yeah, I remember now. It's a very thin issue."

"Come on, Arthur's waiting."

"The float's only three-hundred-fifty thousand. Ask him what the net earnings are per share. And predicted year-end."

Stick tried to make sense out of it. Barry spoke to Arthur, then put his hand over the phone. "Two and a quarter. Projected to go up another buck a share, but Arthur says we've heard that song before."

Kyle said, "What do they make? Something for the military, isn't it? Water tanks?"

"Right, portable tanks, they pull 'em behind a truck. And some other equipment, all government contract."

Stick saw her face as she looked up. She didn't seem interested. She said, "The P-E ratio for Ranco should be about twenty to one, at least. They're forecasting three and a quarter and the stock's only at seventeen?"

"Come on—do I sell?"

"With that skimpy float it'd be awfully easy to drive the price up. I think Arthur wants to keep it in the house."

"You sure?"

"Tell him you think it's going up," Kyle answered. "See what he says."

Barry: "What're you doing, Arthur, blowing smoke at me? That stock's going to the fucking moon . . . *Yes*, I believe it. You schmuck, what're you trying to pull?" He listened and said to Kyle, hand over the phone, "Arthur says it's volatile, very shaky."

Kyle: "I think Arthur's shaky. Tell him he can have it when it hits fifty, not before. Tell him you want five thousand more shares before it hits twenty or you're going to Hutton."

They turned off the freeway at 125th Street, Stick concentrating, committing to memory Kaneb, Automated Medical Labs, Ranco Manufacturing . . .

And now Kyle was reading from her file folder:

"Titan Valve, two thousand shares at fifteen and a half . . . Delpha Health Services, twelve bucks a share, another two thousand." Biotech Systems . . . KMA Industries . . .

Stick added names to his list.

Barry: "Arthur says the market for IPOs is very mushy. Stay out of it."

Kyle: "That's what Arthur's supposed to say. They have to sell the board up before they try new issues. How many times've I told you that?"

Barry: "Arthur says the fringers aren't gonna make it."

Kyle: "I don't pick fringers."

Barry: "He says the bloom is off the energy rose."

Kyle: "I'm going to be sick in your car."

Barry: "He says high-tech remains first in the hearts of investors."

Kyle: "Tell Arthur good-bye."

It was hard work, driving and listening. Trying to remember that Southwest Bell and British Colonial Hydro were corporate bonds that looked good. That you could make a killing on Firestone if the company was taken over and the possibility kept getting better. By the time they crossed over on the causeway and were approaching Bal Harbour Stick was sure of one thing: Barry would never be the chauffeur's hero without Kyle McLaren.

Barry never let up. As the car swung into the

drive, home, he was talking about somebody named Howard Ruff, who—as near as Stick could figure out—was an investment expert of some kind, an economic forecaster. Barry sounded impressed. "Howard Ruff says buy all the gold you can and silver's even better."

"He'll tell you to buy his record album, too," Kyle said. "If you like the advice of a guy who sings *Climb Every Mountain* and *You Light Up My Life*, I can't help you."

It didn't matter that Stick had never heard of Howard Ruff. He was getting a pretty good idea who Kyle McLaren was.

He got her bags out of the trunk and carried them to the terrace where Kyle was talking to Diane Stam. Barry was heading for the morning room, ducking under the awning that shaded the arched openings in the wall. Stick hung back, watching the two ladies in polite conversation: one with slender brown legs, smiling easily, touching Diane's arm; the other a different type, soft and white beneath a striped robe. They were edging away from each other now but with pleasant expressions; they seemed to get along. Kyle glanced toward him, waiting with her bags. Diane turned away and he followed Kyle along the paved walk that led from the terrace to the tennis court. He had not been to his side of the property before, but Kyle seemed to know where she was going. She carried a tote slung over one shoulder and the briefcase under her other arm. They passed the line of palm trees and under the red-and-white-striped awning—there were deck chairs here and a small bar, empty now—crossed the red clay court and approached the guest house just on the other side, partly hidden in shrubbery. There was a door here; but Kyle walked past it, following the path around front to the bayside of the house.

Turning the corner she glanced back at Stick and said, "We'll let the producer have the sun in the morning. I'll take the room with the view."

He didn't know what she was talking about and was going to ask, what producer? But now they were at another entrance. One of the maids appeared in the doorway as they approached and Kyle said, "Luisa Rosa!" like she was glad to see her, the maid smiling. "How're the anxieties doing?"

"My depression is much better," the maid said, still smiling. "I'm very glad to see you again."

Stick took the bags inside as they stood talking. He looked around the living room, which seemed to be all yellow and white with rattan furniture, fresh-cut flowers everywhere, a bottle of champagne in a silver bucket on the cocktail table with three glasses. He wasn't sure what to do with the bags. The entire front wall was glass, facing the bay, Barry's cruiser tied up off to the right. He won-

dered if the girl was still aboard. He heard Luisa
Rosa laugh. He heard her voice, with its pleasant
accent, say, "Have a nice day."

"You can put those in the bedroom," Kyle said,
"if you will, please."

There were twin beds pushed together with yellow spreads, screens that opened onto a patio and a
somewhat different view of Biscayne Bay. The guest
house was bigger than any house he had ever lived
in. As he came out she was unslinging the tote,
dropping it with her briefcase onto the sofa.

He paused, not sure of the procedure, wondering if she was going to offer him a tip. He hoped
not.

She said, "I've been curious about something for
the past—I guess it's been about two weeks. Do you
remember my being at Mr. Gorman's, in Lauderdale? We were in the living room and you
walked by on the balcony."

"You know I remember it," Stick said. She did,
too. He could feel it between them. "You want to
know what I was doing there?"

She said, "If I'm not being nosy. I'm curious, because Chucky didn't seem to have any idea who
you were, in his own apartment."

"I was with a friend of mine. He was waiting to
see him."

"Do you recall what you said?"

"He asked me—what, if I was an appraiser?" He

smiled as he saw her smile, familiar with each other, and knew what she was going to say.

"Yeah, but the best part"—her eyes smiling now—"he asked if you saw anything you liked, and you looked around, not the least bit hurried, and you said, 'No, I guess not,' and walked away."

"You remember that."

"Your timing was great."

"Thank you. Can I ask you one?"

"What was I doing there?"

"No, I figured that out. You tell people like Barry and Chucky what to do with their money. Barry comes off as the boy wonder, but you're the brains."

She raised her eyebrows. "You got that on the way from the airport?"

"I got more than that. You put up with him, but you're getting tired of it. He only listens when you're talking about business . . ."

"That's amazing."

"No, it isn't, that's what you told him. *I* listen. But I think there's more to it. You kept telling him you're tired, I think you're tired of what you're doing. *You* feed and he scores the points, makes all the money."

"You're close, but that's not it." Those gentle, knowing eyes stayed on him and she seemed about to say more, perhaps confide. But she eased away from herself, saying, "You don't sound quite—

well, like a man who wears a chauffeur's uniform."

"One of the help. No, ordinarily I'm self-employed. I'll try this another week or so."

"You don't like to drive?"

"I don't like to wait for people."

"I don't either. What do you usually do?"

"Well, I sold cars for a few years. Used ones. I drove a truck now and then . . ." He said, "What I wanted to ask you—that time at Chucky's a couple weeks ago, you only saw me for about a half a minute . . ."

"Yeah, about that."

"How did you recognize me today?"

She said, sounding a little surprised, "That's a good question, you don't even look like the same person. But I knew you as soon as I walked up to the car."

13

CORNELL LEWIS WAS SITTING IN a pair of red briefs watching television, his bare feet up on a chair he'd pulled over. He didn't look up as Stick came in.

"What's going on?"

"Chuck Norris, man. Look-it him do it to the gooks."

"I mean what's going on *here*?"

"Nothing—resting up for the evening. I'm off, man."

"There some kind of a producer gonna be staying here?"

"Next week he's coming. Monday, I think."

"Movie producer?"

"Look-it Chuck. Shit, huh? Yeah, the producer gonna show the man and some of his friends how to get into showbiz. As I understand it. Gonna have a few people over for the day."

"We just picked up a girl at the airport—"

"Yeah, Kyle. She's nice, huh? That Kyle is the

only reason I know of I'd ever want to be white and I don't even think she'd care."

"She work for Barry?"

"No, she work for herself, like an advisor. Tells the man how to invest his hard-earned bread."

"She didn't seem too anxious in the car. Or she was tired."

"Man bugs her. No, see, she specializes, tells the man what different businesses he should go into. But, see, he's in *every*thing. You know, with his stocks and bonds? You know what I'm saying? See, she *knows* all that stock-market shit better than he does, even though it's not what she specializes in. So he like *uses* her every chance he can."

"Yeah, that's what it sounded like."

"Ah, you listening, huh? Look at this one, man." Nodding at the TV set. "Hawaiian Punch, with little Donny and Marie. They cute, you know it? Look-it 'em."

"She live in New York?"

"Who, this girl?"

"Kyle McLaren."

"She live in Palm Beach. I think she used to be in New York when she was a stockbroker. First time she come here she was telling me all about it. She's got a brother that's in the FBI."

"Jesus, you kidding?"

"Not here. I think in New York. Look-it little

Donny and Marie. Yeah, baby, I give you a punch. Shit, I'd punch him too, he's so cute."

"Why's she staying here?"

"Who's that?"

"Kyle McLaren." He liked her name.

"Man wants her to be here for the producer, the showbiz pitch and then spend some time with him. But not the way you thinking. I seen the man, he's half in the bag one time start to hit on her? No deal. She put him down quick, but very nice about it. No strain, no pain. Man say she don't take no shit offa *any*body. One of these millionaires—don't matter who it is, she don't like him she don't do business with him."

"She married?"

"I don't believe—no, she live by herself. Got a condo up there on Lake Worth."

Stick took off his coat and tie, walked into his room to drop them on the bed and came out again.

"How's Aurora doing?"

"What are you, the question man? She still out'n the boat. Man run in and talk to her on the phone soon as you got back. Could almost hear her yelling from outside. Got this voice sound like she crying."

Stick said, "So they'll be going out for a cruise."

"Uh-unh, not today. Mama fixed him, she called some people and made a date to meet at the club for cocktails and dinner . . . little dancing to that ricky-tick club jive. Yeah, they gonna have *fun*, man. Big evening at the country club with all the beautiful folks."

"I guess I drive, uh?"

"Said tell you the black suit."

He watched Chuck Norris lay out several Orientals with chops and kicks but without changing his expression. He was surprised Chuck Norris was a little guy. Chuck and Chucky . . .

Chucky and Barry and all the hotshots who made it look easy. He said to Cornell, "What's the most you ever made on a job? Before you got sent away."

"You mean in my other life?"

"Yeah, what's the most you scored?"

"Was from a liquor store. I had a piece I picked up on a break-in one time? I went in there . . . had to do speed to get me in the door. I took eleven hundred and sixty dollars and could never do it again sky high. Why you asking?"

"I was just thinking," Stick said, "that making a phone call to your broker in the backseat of a Cadillac doing sixty miles an hour with the air conditioning on is an awful lot easier than going in someplace with a gun, isn't it?"

Cornell looked away from the television screen for the first time. "You just finding that out?"

"I got a few things to learn," Stick said.

*   *   *

The chauffeurs were not watching with purpose, though they were looking out of darkness toward the source of the music, across flower beds and shrubbery to the club patio strung with paper lanterns where ladies in long skirts danced with men in blazers and pastel trousers to medleys of show tunes: some barely moving, some moving as though they were following footprints, some of the ladies discoing with studied abandon while their men, with glazed expressions, glasses reflecting the lantern glow, hunched their shoulders and sometimes snapped their fingers.

The sound of elevator music filled the night. Stick had never seen a country club dance before.

He'd dropped off the Stams and Kyle McLaren an hour ago, raced up to Southwest Eighth Street to find a bar and had several bourbons over shaved ice while Cubans stared at him in his black suit. Or would have stared at him anyway. Stick didn't mind. He was free, taking a time-out; he bothered no one and they left him alone. Now he was back at Leucadendra.

Harvey saw him, adjusted his chauffeur's cap and came away from the others: a half-dozen drivers over there, along the edge of light coming from a window in the working part of the clubhouse. One of the drivers looked like Lionel Oliva, but it was too dark here to be certain. Faint moonlight through the palm trees, the sound of a kitchen fan blending with the melodic rush of the five-piece dance band, *The Man I Love* turning into *A Stranger in Paradise* as Harvey, chauffeur's cap cocked like a fighter pilot's, came over to him.

"How's it going? Or should I say, what do you hear from the backseat these days?"

"That heavyset guy over there," Stick said, "his name Lionel?"

"That's him, the Cuban." Harvey turned his back to the group, standing in close. "Says his boss's been in there in the locker room rolling Indian dice since this afternoon and Lionel ain't had his dinner yet."

"Why doesn't he leave and come back?" Stick wasn't sure if he wanted Lionel here, or if it mattered.

"He'd drive off and there'd be Mr. Gorman looking for him," Harvey said. "Don't you know that's how it works?"

Stick said, "I guess I'll learn, if I stay at it long enough." The bourbon was glowing inside him and Lionel's presence, he decided, didn't matter. Though it gave him something else to think about: still another chance of running into Chucky Gorman. He had walked into a new, tight little world down here and had not yet walked out the other side. But he was learning a few things.

Harvey was holding back, trying to appear casual. He said, "Look at all that money out there dancing. Not a care in the world."

It seemed enough of an opening. Stick said, "On these stock market tips you mentioned? . . ."

Harvey said, "Yeah, how we doing there?"

"Well, I wondered if you have a certain procedure you follow." He saw Edgar coming over now.

"You tell us what Mr. Stam's playing," Harvey said. He shrugged, hands in his pants pockets.

Stick waited. "That's it?"

Harvey said to Edgar, "He wants to know is there any procedure giving us, telling us about any interesting stocks he might've heard about."

"What procedure?" Edgar said.

Stick said, "What if I give you a good one and you pass it on and then come back and tell me your boss already has that stock? You know what I mean? How do I protect myself?" He saw Harvey and Edgar catch each other's eye as he looked off toward the strains of *Alley Cat*, Jesus, hoping they'd rush it faster than the others or he'd have to get out of here. It was the only song he knew that made him want to break something.

Edgar said, "You mean like if Mr. Harrison accepted the tip but told me he already had it?"

"I'd be out of luck," Stick said, "wouldn't I?"

"But Mr. Harrison would never pull anything like that."

"How do I know? You guys say it, but, hell, I don't know Mr. Harrison." He shot a glance at Harvey. "Or Miz Wilson. You know as well as I do rich people can be funny. They're not always generous." Stick shook his head, tired. "Boy, he was on that phone with his broker all the way from the airport. His financial advisor—you know who I mean? . . ."

Harvey said, "Miz McLaren?"

"That's the one, yeah. She was with him, see, telling him what to buy and then he'd pass it on to his broker. On the phone the whole time. See, she just come in from New York and I guess she had all these hot tips."

Edgar said, "Yeah? What were some of 'em?"

"Well, that's why I asked about a procedure," Stick said. "I got these companies"—he patted his side pocket—"fact I wrote 'em down right after we got back so I wouldn't forget. I remember you mentioning somebody did that."

Harvey said, "Over-the-counter stocks, huh?"

Stick said, "Well, I suppose you could say that." Not having any idea what Harvey was talking about, though he had heard it before. *Over the counter*. Harvey was squinting at him and Stick said, "I got one they say is about to take off and hit the moon and it's only seventeen bucks at the present time."

"Jeez," Edgar said. "Gonna take off, huh?"

"When they get done driving it up," Stick said. "It'll go at least to fifty, you can bet on it. Probably higher."

Harvey said, "They gonna drive it up, uh? What kind of stock is it?"

"You mean what kind of company?"

"Yeah, what do they do? What's the product?"

"Something for the military. I guess it's one of those top-secret deals, you know . . ."

Edgar said, "Musta heard about a big government contract, what it sounds like. That's the way you make it, get the inside poop. You in?"

"You better believe it," Stick said.

Harvey said, "I thought you never play the market."

"I do now," Stick said.

"How'd you make a buy on Saturday?"

"Well, I haven't actually done it yet, no. But I called this friend of mine, bartender, plays the market all the time. He'll take care of it first thing Monday. I told him buy all he can. This mother's gonna fly."

Edgar said, "Going from seventeen to fifty? That's—"

"Thirty-three hundred dollars a hundred," Harvey said. "About a three-hundred-percent kick," Harvey said. "I don't know, sounds fishy."

Stick edged out on unfamiliar ground. He said, "Not when you take into account the P-E ratio."

Harvey was staring at him hard. "Figure twenty to one," Stick told him, eye to eye. "Based on"—shit, he dug in his mind for the words—"you know, what they're making, the profit."

"Earnings per share," Harvey said.

"That's what I said. See, forecasted up to like three and a quarter. So what's that tell you?"

"Jeez," Edgar said. "What's the stock?"

"We're back to procedure," Stick said. Christ, they were still bouncing relentlessly through *Alley Cat.* "I gotta go." He started off.

"Whatta you mean you gotta go?" Harvey said. "Wait a minute."

"I got to move around. I stand in one place too long—I got a bad knee, an old basketball injury starts acting up."

"We can walk with you," Harvey said. "Where you want to go? How about the men's locker room? I think we can promote us a cup a coffee in there."

"I was thinking of going for a drive," Stick said. "Mr. and Mis Stam oughta be a while yet."

Harvey said, "Wait now, you can never be sure; they're liable to come out any minute. Let's talk about this procedure idea, how you see it might work. Say just for this stock you mentioned."

"The seventeen-dollar one going up to fifty?"

"That one," Edgar said.

"Only way I see it," Stick said, "is cash up front.

Two bills gets you the name of the stock. Monday the price goes up to three, and if I see the stock take off right away the price might go up even higher. How's that sound to you fellas?"

Harvey said, "You're crazy, or you think we are."

Stick said, "Then forget I mentioned it. You want to take your money home to bed with you, Harve, that's up to you. I personally believe money should never sleep . . ."

One A.M. the drivers brought their cars out of darkness now to gleam in lamplight, creeping them up the circular drive to the front entrance. One-twenty, Barry appeared like a playboy with a girl on each arm, his wife and Kyle. Stick got out of the car, came around.

But Barry wasn't holding them; they were guiding him along, keeping him in check. Barry was drunk, glassy-eyed. His mouth looked wet. He did not appear to Stick to be a fun-loving drunk. He looked, right now, like a high school kid ready to fight. He pulled his arm free of Diane's grasp, roughly. She smoothed the gauzy, peach-colored material of her dress, layers of it, touched her pearls. Barry pulled open the front passenger-side door and said to Stick for all to hear, "Get inna car. I'm gonna drive."

Stick tried an easy smile. "You sure you want to?"

"Get inna fucking car, will you?"

Diane seemed paler than usual, face drawn. She turned as though to walk off, saw the dressed-up club members standing on the steps watching and turned back to the car again, not knowing where to look. Kyle, still holding Barry's arm, said, "If you drive, buddy, I walk."

Barry said, "Buddy? What's this buddy shit?"

"I mean it," Kyle said.

"Then walk, for Christ sake. You want to walk, walk."

Stick touched his boss's arm. "Mr. Stam?" Still pleasant. "I'm the one with the driving suit on."

Barry stared up at him with his boozy eyes, pink shirt open, necktie gone. He said, "Stick? Shit, I know why they call you that. Got nothing to do with Stickley, huh?" Barry getting a shrewd-drunk look now, crafty eyes. "You stick people up is why they call you Stick. Isn't that right?"

Stick made a gun of his hand, pointing it at Barry, saying, "Yes, sir, you got it right," crowding him into the front-seat opening, staying close, jamming him, so that Barry was forced to get in, Stick's head and shoulders following. Now with his back filling the doorway, in there with Barry, away from everyone outside watching, Stick said, "You little fucker, you say another word I'll punch you into the backseat. I drive. You can fire me tomorrow, but tonight I drive. You got it?" He waited. Barry stared straight ahead, rigid. His face bore a strained expression now that made his nose appear larger, vulnerable. But he didn't move or make a sound.

Stick came out of the car. He opened the rear door, turned to Diane and Kyle and said, "Ladies . . ."

Barry's expression had turned to stone. He refused to speak. He walked with exaggerated care along the hallway, brushing the wall with his shoulder, turned into his bedroom and fell across the bed. Stick looked in from the hall at Barry in his brown-canopied sultan's bed, a royal tent, the sides gathered up with gold roping. The poor little guy.

He waited for Diane to come out. "I'll undress him if you want. Put him under the covers . . . tuck him in."

She said, "He'll be all right," not smiling but calm once more, brown eyes impassive. "But if you would, please, go down to the boat . . ." She hesitated. "I want to be sure the key isn't there."

"I'll be glad to."

"If you don't mind." The voice so quiet and soft.

Not wanting to leave he wondered what would make her smile. Or show any kind of emotion. Her eyes seemed to daydream, looking at him and giving him the feeling he was in the dream. Letting him look at her . . . at the pearls lying against her skin, lips slightly parted and the eyes again, reflecting . . . what?

"Is there anything else I can do?"

Hesitant. "I don't think so . . ."

"Can I get you something?" He said it knowing it made little sense. Yet she seemed to accept it without question. He felt that if he took her by the hand and led her through the house and out the garage, to his room, she would follow along without a word, without making a sound. Her gaze lulled him.

"Well, if you need me . . ."

He turned to go and she said, "I'll be up for a little while."

He paused. He nodded. He couldn't think of anything else to say. "All right . . ."

She turned the light off in Barry's room, looked at him once more and walked past him and across the hall to a bedroom door, pushed it open and went in. A slanting patch of light appeared on the hall floor. The door closed. He didn't hear the lock click. A narrow line of light remained on the polished marble. It took him several moments to move away.

Kyle was waiting on the terrace, holding her arms—her brown arms and shoulders bare in the blue cotton shift—looking up at the sky. She turned as Stick approached, coming down the steps.

"Is he all right?"

"He passed out."

"What did you say to him in the car?"

The pool lay behind her in light green illumination, darkness beyond.

"I told him to behave himself."

She narrowed her eyes—for fun, it didn't matter. "I'll bet."

"You want, I'll walk you home."

"Fine." And started off, as though she was expecting it: crossed the patio toward the walk that led to the tennis court, Kyle telling him Barry was a terrible drinker and knew it and didn't get smashed very often. Booze wasn't that important to him.

"Like making money," Stick said.

"Barry's last day on earth he'll spend on the phone with his broker," Kyle said, "but not because he wants to make more money . . ."

"He just likes to talk on the phone."

"No—he gets his thrill playing with the money, risking it. He's got more than he'll ever be able to spend, but when he plays the market and *wins*, then he's outsmarted the game and that's his satisfaction, his accomplishment."

"But if he loses," Stick said, "what's he out? It's not like betting the farm. Is it?"

She said, with realization, "I should be telling you about taking risks . . ."

Stick said, "Oh," with his own sense of realization, that Barry had been talking about him. "I forgot I'm one of his exhibits now."

"You said you sold cars . . ."

"Used ones."

"You didn't mention you stole them first, and you were about to take off in Barry's Rolls when he came out and caught you."

"Is that how he tells it? He caught me? No, I helped him out, that's all, and he took a liking to me."

"I'm never sure when you're serious." They walked along the white squares of cement. "You want to know what he said?" Her tone changed to a mild street-sound imitation of Barry. "Jesus Christ, I got Aurora on the boat and Diane pacing up and down on the terrace and I got a new driver who was in prison for armed robbery and I don't know which one of my cars he's gonna steal . . . This was before we left for the club, waiting for Diane. She takes longer to get dressed than anyone I know."

"He say prison?"

"No, you're right. He said, in the slammer. Then at dinner he started in again, about you. Diane seemed interested and kept him going . . ."

"She did?"

"But you don't have to urge Barry when he's on.

Which is almost all the time. The way he was drinking, I think it was for dramatic effect, so I'd think he's pining for Aurora. Or he wanted Diane to ask him what was wrong and he could say, oh, nothing. But she didn't. So he talked about you—you're right, with all the words—because he can get into the part and sound tough."

"He sounds like the Bowery Boys at Miami Beach," Stick said. "Why's he do that?"

They had crossed the tennis court and were following the walk that led to the front of the guest house. He saw the pale length of the cabin cruiser, windows dark—wondering if Diane wanted him to find somebody aboard and come running back to tell. Or if she wanted him to report back, tell her no, the key wasn't in the ignition. But no hired skipper was going to leave the key and she'd know that.

Kyle was saying that maybe Barry acted tough because he was insecure. "Maybe as a kid he was a little smartass and got beat up all the time. Barry loves to start fights in bars."

"He does?"

"Yes, but only when he's sure somebody'll stop it. You know, before they come to blows. Barry's got a problem."

They were coming to her front steps now.

Stick said, "Well, I've done some dumb things, I guess, trying to do it the hard way, but I haven't been in a fistfight since about the eighth grade."

"You sound just like my brother."

"You kidding? The Fed?"

She turned to him in the amber glow of the light by the door. "Barry tell you that?"

"Cornell. He says he'd change color for you."

"God, he's funny. I wish he were a client, instead of most of the ones I have. I could listen to him all day." She meant it, too, her eyes smiling. "No, you remind me of my other brother, the stockbroker. He used to pitch for the Red Sox."

"Jim McLaren, that's your brother?"

"Ah, you're a baseball fan."

"Sure, I used to watch him, when the Sox came to Detroit. He was always accused of throwing spitters. Right?"

"Or, as they say, doctoring the ball with a foreign substance. Jim used to say sweat isn't foreign, it's mine."

"What'd he do on a cold day?"

"Well, his pitch, he had a forkball and a gorgeous slider that broke down and in on a right-handed batter. Otherwise, Fenway Park, he could've gotten killed."

"That short left-field porch," Stick said. "So Jim McLaren's your brother, that's something. I always admired his nerve—the skinny southpaw with the high leg-kick. He isn't very big, is he?"

"About your size. He's heavier now."

"That was about, what, ten years ago."

" 'Seventy-one was his last year. I was going to school in Boston, so I got to see him all the time."

"Lemme guess—Harvard Business School."

"Nope, I was at Boston U. In sociology, then I switched to speech therapy. But I left school, decided not to fight it and got a job as a market analyst. My dad's a stockbroker, he was pushing me toward Wall Street as far back as I can remember."

"You don't have to have a special degree?"

"No . . . You can't be dumb, but just selling stock you're usually no more than an order-taker anyway. You learn the words. I sold options for a few years, then got into commodities . . ."

"I don't understand any of that."

"Well, in that end of the market the next stop's Las Vegas. I got out of trading, came down to Palm Beach, the big bucks, and opened an office as an investment counselor. Anyway, you remind me a lot of Jim."

"When he's throwing spitters or selling stock?"

"You sound like him. But I didn't think of it till this evening, when Barry was talking about you. That's why I remembered you, I guess."

"You have fun at the club?"

"It was all right. Except for the music. As soon as I heard them swing into *Alley Cat*, God . . ."

Stick said, "Yeah? . . ."

"I was going to get up and leave. I can't stand that insipid goddamn song."

Stick said, "How about *Climb Every Mountain* and *You Light Up My Life*?"

She began to smile, those knowing eyes looking right at him. "How about a nightcap? We've got scotch, champagne and Gatorade."

"You drink with the help?"

"I'm help, too, aren't I?"

He said, "I have to do something for Mrs. Stam. How about if I come right back?"

Her expression didn't change; though the amused look in her eyes seemed different somehow. She said, "Well, if you make it, fine."

She went inside, leaving it up to him.

14

HE WASN'T SURE IF HE should sneak aboard the docked cruiser or make noise. Either way he could scare hell out of the poor girl, probably waiting below. *A Prisoner of Love.* Perry Como, 1950-something. His mom's favorite. He had the feeling, ducking into the main cabin, even the guy's boat was bigger than any house he'd ever lived in. There was a light on below . . . down a short ladder . . . he felt his way along and came to a stateroom with—he couldn't believe it—a double bed. The spread—a blue, red and yellow rainbow design— was mussed, the rainbow pillows pulled out from beneath the cover. He heard a noise, a pumping action, water running . . .

The girl came into the room with her head down. She wore a man's turtleneck sweater and was holding the bottom of it with her wrists, bunched up, while she buttoned the waist of her white shorts, rings on all her fingers.

Stick said, "Aurora?"

She jumped with a strangled sound, drawing back.

"It's okay. I'm a friend."

"Who *are* you?" All eyes.

"I work for Barry."

"Where is he?" About to cry, she seemed so frightened. "Did he tell you to get me?"

"He's in bed."

"In *bed*!"

"Shhhh. You don't want to wake up his wife."

"The hell I don't! You know how long I've been on this fucking boat?" She had the eyes of a cat now, a mean one.

"I know. I dropped him off yesterday to meet you. I'm his chauffeur."

"You're not Cecil."

"I wouldn't want to be. I'm the new one."

She seemed suspicious, but got over it right away. "Good. You can drive me home. That son of a bitch, I'm telling you . . ."

"I'm supposed to see if the key's here."

"What key?"

Was she scowling or pouting? Her lower lip stuck out.

"The one you start the boat with. Is it here?"

"How would I know? I don't want you to drive me home in *this*. I don't want to ever see this fucking boat again as long as I live. I mean in a car."

"I don't think I can do that."

"Why not?"

"I mean unless he tells me."

"You're driving me home," Aurora said. "I don't give a shit what Barry says. All I do is wait for him."

"You too, huh?"

She didn't hear him. Aurora was pulling the sweater up over her head and he was staring at her bare breasts. Two round red eyes staring back at him as she fought the sweater, trying to work the snug neck past her chin, her breasts swaying, bouncing up and down, big ones. When the sweater came off it left her hair sticking out in all directions. She was the wild woman of Bal Harbour now, the cat woman of Biscayne Bay.

"You too, huh?"

"What?"

"You said all you do is wait."

"*Wait*? You don't even know."

"Yes, I do," Stick said. He couldn't take his eyes off her breasts as she smoothed her hair now, not looking at him. They were beauties. They were show breasts. "I wait around till he wants to go out, then we go someplace and I have to wait around again, hours sometimes."

"The big shit," Aurora said. "Why does he have to be so mean?"

"Well, that's what he is," Stick said, "a meany. I'll tell you something though. I'd never make you wait." No, *sir*.

"You wouldn't?" She looked at him, caught him staring, hypnotized, but didn't seem to mind. "I've been all by myself since last night. Not *any*body came to see me." She was unbuttoning the shorts now, pushed them down, stepped out with one foot and kicked them across the bed with the other. She stood with hands on hips in narrow bikini panties, looking around the stateroom. "I don't know where I put my clothes."

Stick didn't know where to look. At her tiny white panties between tan tummy and thighs or at her big white breasts. It was better than a cellblock dream, beyond imagination. She came to the foot of the bed, bent over, aimed her can at him and picked up a pair of designer jeans, turned then and sat down on the bed with the jeans in her lap.

"I don't know what to do." That lower lip quivering a little, pushing out.

Stick knew what he wanted to do. He wanted to bite that lip off. First. He walked over to her, reached out carefully and put his hand on her shoulder. There, there. She didn't spook, draw back. He said, "Don't worry, I'll"—what?—"help you out. If I can." And saw those kitty eyes raised, peering out from among long dark lashes. He eased down on the bed, arm moving around her back. The poor little thing. She snuggled against him, laid her hand on the tight material across his thigh.

"He doesn't care about me. How I feel." Yes, she

anted to be comforted—this little girl all by her-
elf. He brought his hand past those beauties to her
are arm and stroked it gently, saw her face raise in
he lamplight, her sorrowful eyes. "I feel so lonely."

"I know . . ."

"Will you be nice to me?"

"I'll try—I mean I *will*. I'll be nice as can be to
ou."

She slid up around his black suit, cat turning to
nake, arms going around his neck, acrobatic tan
ighs twisting, uncoiling to straddle him, feeling
er pushing and letting himself be pushed over to
e on the rainbow-design spread, her mouth com-
ng down on his now, murmuring, "Will you take
ne home after?"

His mouth on hers made mmmmm sounds, like
e was humming.

)id he sleep? Maybe for a minute, fading out and
ack again, opening his eyes to her lazy gaze, a tan-
le of dark hair spread over the rainbow pillow.

She said, very softly, "Boy, you're good. Who-
ver you are." She said, surprised, but still softly,
You still have your tie on." She said, sounding
rowsy, eyes closing, "Would I love a glass of
nilk."

It sounded good, an ice-cold glass. But he chose a
an of Bud instead, closed the refrigerator, light

gone from the kitchen again, and popped the can.
Aurora could have her milk in the morning, when
she woke up. He wanted a cigarette. He hadn't had
a cigarette in almost four years but he wanted one
now. He could live on simple pleasures. Every once
in a while accept one not so simple. When the
sound came from the hall he thought of an animal;
it was like a series of grunts, low snuffling sounds.
Close.

He placed his beer on the counter and stepped
over to the doorway to listen. Mrs. Hoffer, snoring.
The cook's room was right there, a wing off the
kitchen. The maids went home to Little Havana
when they were through. Barry said they went
home every night and brushed their hair, a hundred
strokes, then they'd do the other leg.

A voice said, "Oh . . ."

He turned to see a figure in the hall, faint light
from a window far behind telling him it was Mrs.
Stam, a silhouette within a sheer cover that reached
the floor.

"Did you hear something?" Her voice a whisper.

"I think it's Mrs. Hoffer."

"No, I mean outside."

"It could've been me. I just came in."

"No, it was something else. Would you look,
please?"

She turned and he followed her, hearing bare feet
pat on marble. She brought him out to the morning

room past fat chairs finished in canvas and over to one of the arched openings. They stood at a border of flower pots, Stick behind her, hunching a little to see out past the awning at eye level. They looked out at the terrace in clear, cloudless moonlight, at the sweep of lawn beyond the pool, the bay like a little ocean and there it was in the night sky. He felt a warm rush, an irresistible urge and had to say it.

"Shine on my love and me."

Diane's head turned, chin to her shoulder, so that he saw her profile in soft illumination and caught the expensive scent of her perfume. She said, "What?"

"Moon over Miami," Stick said. "It's true. There it is."

She said, "Oh." After a moment she said, "Yes, it is." She stood without moving.

He said, "What are we listening for?"

"Wait." Quietly, a hushed tone.

She turned then very slowly, staring out at the terrace. Her shoulder touched his chest. She remained this way until her face came closer and she said, though not looking at him, "I'm frightened."

"Of what?"

"Would you walk out by the hedge?"

"What am I looking for?"

"I'm not sure. Whatever it is . . ."

"Whatever what is?"

"Please . . ."

He ducked under the awning, walked across the flagstones to the low hedge that bordered the top level of the terrace, looked across at the tiers descending to the pool. Looked the other way, past the sloping lawn to the turnaround by the garage. He came full circle, slowly, until he was facing the house again.

Diane stood within the oval arch, facing him in moonlight, waiting . . . that picture out of early memory more than thirty years ago of a bare naked lady with a bush of hair between her legs and it hadn't changed one bit, it was true and beautiful as ever, as real as that moon over Miami and he was a boy again in a grown-man's chauffeur's suit with the lady of the house ready to go for a ride . . . on fat canvas cushions on the floor, as it turned out. She nearly killed him she was so much moving female telling him to do it, do it, saying oh, God, oh, God, do it, that quiet woman set free, Stick wondering what kind of glittering phase of his life he was going through this woman so pleased she couldn't believe it, breathless the way he stayed with her and never let up till she was wrung limp and Stick was soaring to his own stars and said to her, cocky, "Now it's my turn . . ."

Kyle said, "You've changed. Good."

He followed her into the yellow living room

softly lighted, set to music he couldn't identify but good stuff that had a George Benson sound with subtle percussion rimshots rocking it along. He had changed into his lime green knit shirt and laundered khakis, and brushed his teeth, and washed up here and there.

"I hope I didn't take too long. I was afraid you'd be in bed."

"No, I'm wide awake. You're the one looks tired."

"Been a long day," Stick said. And not over yet. "They keep me jumping, when I'm not waiting around."

Was she looking at him funny? She wasn't as tall as before; barefoot now, but still wearing the dress with little thin straps. Her tan skin glowed in the lamplight. The whites of her eyes seemed whiter. When they settled into the deep sofa with the scotch she poured, Kyle sat low with her legs stretched out, bare feet crossed on the cocktail table. She was a cushion away from him. He thought of her in the car this afternoon and said, "What's float mean? And P-E?"

She said, "Is that what you want to talk about?" The way she had sounded when she told Barry she was tired.

"No, but tell me some time. There a lot of words you have to learn?"

"No more than if you wanted to be a croupier.

Or a car salesman. You probably know a lot of words I don't. So there you are." Now she sounded more relaxed than tired, her head turned against the cushion, looking at him.

Stick said, "I wondered—you don't mind I was in jail? It doesn't make you nervous?"

"No, it surprises me, you lived that kind of life. I know you're smarter than that, just talking to you."

"It looked easy," Stick said. "What do you have to know to steal a car? Get in and start it."

"What about the risk, was that part of it? The excitement?"

"I was making a living. I'd drive a cement truck, a transit-mix for a while, then go back to it. I don't know—maybe I thought I was getting away with something. I was a lot younger and dumber then. I did a little time for cars; then I was picked up again and thought I'd be going away for quite a while. But at the pretrial exam the witness got on the stand and said he made a mistake, he'd never seen me before. I couldn't believe it. Till after, I find out he has a plan of his own. Did Barry mention Frank Ryan to you?"

"Was that your partner?"

Stick nodded. "I never said a word about Frank, but he knew all about him, like somebody read him my sheet."

"Barry has a friend in the Dade State Attorney's

office," Kyle said. "That's his source. His friend called the Detroit police."

"That's what I thought. Anyway, Frank Ryan was the witness. He was a car salesman. I mean a real one. So after I was let off Frank took me aside and told me his plan—his ten rules for success and happiness in armed robbery—and we went in business together."

"You're kidding."

"No, he had ten rules. I remember he wrote 'em down for me on cocktail napkins."

"Were you successful?"

"For about three months."

"Happy?"

"When I wasn't scared to death. It was a lot different than picking up a Cadillac and selling it down in Ohio for parts, but there was a lot of money in it too."

"What were some of the rules?"

"Well, like, always be polite on the job. Say please and thank you."

"You serious?"

"Keeps everybody calm. Never call your partner by name, when you're in the place. Never use your own car. Never flash money. Never tell anybody your business . . . Like that, just common sense. They worked, too."

"Then why'd you get caught?"

"We broke rule number ten. Never associate

with people known to be in crime. We teamed up with some guys that Frank knew and . . . well, it didn't work out."

"Where's Frank? Still in prison?"

"He died in Jackson. Cirrhosis. He got hooked on moonshine they made out of potatoes. Toward the end his stomach was out to here, his liver . . . Dumb shit. I told him, he wouldn't listen. He never learned how to jail. You know, live in a place like that. So, he died."

"Were you good friends?"

"Well, we were together all the time. We had a nice apartment. Sometimes, it was like we were married, the kind of arguments we had. Over little picky things that didn't matter. But we had a good time for a while. It was different, I'll say that."

"What're you smiling at?"

"Nothing, really. I can hear him bitching, like an old lady."

"Do you miss him?"

"Do I *miss* him? No, I don't miss him, I remember him, you know, I suppose we were pretty close at that. But it was a different kind of life and it's over."

She said, "Didn't you feel you were doing anything wrong? Stealing?"

"Sure, I knew it was wrong. And I knew I'd have to pay for it if I got caught. I accepted that. And that's what happened and now it's over with. Done.

Now I'm going to get in the stock market, become a financial expert."

She said, "You probably could"—still with her head against the cushion—"if you wanted to. Why not? We could trade places. I'll get a designer chauffeur uniform."

"What's the matter with what you're doing?"

"I don't know—I'm tired of it."

"I think I mentioned that this afternoon."

"I know you did. But I'm not tired of it—as you implied, because I tell my clients what to do and they make all the money. Money doesn't have anything to do with it. I'm tired of this middle position, advising. There's no tangible satisfaction. What I'd like, I *think*, is to run a manufacturing business. Produce something, an end product, and not just deal in paper."

"How about portable water tanks?" Stick said. "I understand, you sell to the military there's a lot of money in it."

She said, just barely smiling, "You're kind of a show-off, aren't you? But very subtle. 'Do you see anything you like?' And before Chucky knows it he's your straight man, 'No, I guess not,' and walk away. You're an actor, aren't you?"

"Nope. I'm a very simple soul."

"What's the name of the water tank company?"

"Ranco Manufacturing."

"What're some other good buys?"

"Automated Medical Labs. Kaneb Services. Firestone, maybe, if there's a takeover."

"You're scary."

Stick eased over to rest his arm on the cushion separating them, leaning closer to her. "But I still don't know what a float is, or options."

She said, "I have a feeling you could learn everything there is to know in about two days."

"You want to teach me?" He touched her hand lying in her lap, fingertips tracing fine bones.

She said, "I don't know if I'm ready for you," though she turned her hand over, felt his calloused palm and slowly laced her fingers into his, still with her head against the cushion of the backrest, eyes mildly appraising, perhaps curious. "I think I'm out of practice. I deal with people who read balance sheets and play business golf and go from the club to board-of-directors meetings."

"You don't have any fun?"

She said, "I have friends—we go to polo matches, we go sailing, we play tennis . . ."

"Yeah? . . ."

"When I'm home, but I travel quite a lot."

"You going with a guy?"

"No, not really. I see the same people most of the time . . . I go to dinner parties and sit next to recently divorced men, most of them very wealthy . . ."

"Yeah? . . ."

"And listen to them talk about themselves. Or real estate."

"You get to laugh much?"

"Politely. Nothing's that funny."

"It sounds like the whole show is."

"Yeah, if there was somebody else, you know, to nudge and say, God, listen to that pontificating asshole; but I feel like I'm alone, I don't fit in."

Stick worked up closer to her, laid his head against the cushion to face hers, only a few inches away. He said, "You poor little girl, you could be having fun and you're stuck with humbuggers. You need somebody to play with." Meaning to volunteer and wondering seriously if this was the evening he'd go for the hat trick.

Three goals, three different girls, this one with blue eyes becoming sad and a soft powdery scent—this one a giant step beyond the other two, a girl he could talk to and nudge and they'd give each other knowing looks. He was confident with the feeling he had engraved himself on her and she was attracted to him, for whatever reason.

She said, "I'm not sure what to call you."

What difference did it make? He said, "Ernest. That's my real name. I don't think of it much one way or the other. Stick I'm used to, it's all right. But now *Kyle*, that's a winner."

She said, "You want to know something?"

He said, "Uh-oh. What?"

"I made it up."

"Come on—you did?"

"You want to know my real name? . . . Emma."

He said, "Emma," rolled it around in his head and began to nod, slowly. "Emma. Emma Peel. What's wrong with it?"

"It sounds like enema. That's what kids used to call me."

He said, "But you're grown up now, Em," and raised his head enough to place his mouth on hers, kissed her with meaning while holding back a little, showing her he had restraint and was in control of himself, and so he would not look awkward if she twisted away. But she didn't. Her mouth began to work on his, gradually getting more serious about it—Stick keeping up, with no more glimpses of those other two, no more comparing or counting goals—until Kyle said, "I want to go to bed with you . . ."

He recognized Herbie Hancock working away in the living room now, the chorus telling them *Give It All Your Heart*, with drive, determination, but something had happened to his timing and across the bay the moon was gone, down behind Miami.

He said in the dark, "I don't know what's the matter."

She said, "It's all right. Let's go to sleep."

"I guess it's just one of those things. You never know."

"No, you don't."

"What does that mean?"

"I'm agreeing with you. It's just one of those things. Don't get mad at *me*."

"I'm not mad . . . You think I'm mad?"

"Why don't we go to sleep? All right?"

"Fine . . ."

15

THE FIRST THING STICK'S FORMER wife Mary Lou said to him after seven and a half years was, "Do you know what time it is?" Holding the door open with one hand, her robe closed with the other. She had three pink curlers sitting squarely on top of her head.

"It's about nine o'clock," Stick said. "Can I come in?"

"It's ten minutes of," Mary Lou said. "You woke me up—you know what time you woke me up?"

"I think it was about eight," Stick said.

"It was seven-forty. Because I looked at the clock. I could not imagine who could possibly be calling at seven-forty on Sunday morning."

Stick said, "What happened, I got a car to use right after I talked to you, if I'd drop somebody off in Lauderdale first. So I had to do it right away. Otherwise I'd be thumbing half the day and still might not get here."

She was looking past him toward the street. "That's the car? It's pretty old, isn't it?"

"A Rolls-Royce, Mary Lou, it doesn't matter how old it is." He glanced around at it, sitting out there on a street of cement ranch bungalows, bikes and toys on front lawns, where no Rolls had ever been before: Pompano Beach, a block off Federal Highway.

She said, as he knew she'd have to, "Did you steal it?" She had not changed one bit, still with that drawn look about the nose, like she was smelling her own bitter aura.

He said, "It's my boss's. We gonna stand here and talk or can I come in and see Katy?"

"She's sleeping," Mary Lou said, lowering her voice, but let him into the living room of shiny maple and blue-green plaid, Stick remembering living rooms like this, though not this particular one. He hadn't seen this maple set before. Or the electric organ. Or the grandfather clock. Mary Lou saying, "You didn't expect her to be up, did you?"

Stick said, "You go on with whatever you're doing. I won't bother you any." With a drawl to his voice he hadn't heard in years; as though being in the presence of this woman caused him to revert and he should go out and fix her car seat that was always slipping when she stopped.

She said, "I'm not going back to bed with you

here," clutching that pink robe around her—more of the past coming back—like he might have a quick Sunday morning jump in mind. No thank you. He thought of Kyle and his spirit dipped. He would have to work his way back up and show her he was ordinarily fit and dependable. It was pride; but he was also fascinated by her and maybe a little bit in love. Really.

He said, "You sleep in curlers now?"

She raised her hand partway up but didn't touch her head. She turned and went out of the room.

Stick sat down to wait, careful of the crease in his pressed khakis. Looking around—there wasn't a piece of furniture or flowery print he recognized, here or in the dining-L. Everything looked new.

Mary Lou took till almost nine-thirty to return, wearing slacks now and a sleeveless print blouse, her dark hair combed blown up in a bouffant, cheeks rouged. He said, "Katy still asleep?"

"I didn't open her door to see."

"Why don't you wake her up?"

"Because she needs her sleep."

"You getting along all right?"

"You mean are we making ends meet without any help from you? Not one cent in over seven years? Yes, thank you, we're doing just fine."

"I sent you a couple hundred from Jackson."

"You sent a hundred and eighty-five dollars. Mr. Wonderful."

"I'm going to help out," Stick said. "In fact"—he dug out his wallet—"I got paid this morning. I even got a raise. I thought I was going to get fired for something I did, he gave me a raise. So I can let you have . . . here's three hundred. How's that?"

"In seven years," Mary Lou said, "I'd say it's pretty shitty. What would you say?"

He knew this would happen. "I'm going to give you something every week now, for Katy. Or every month." He laid the bills on the end table.

"You bet you are," Mary Lou said. "At least till you go to prison again. When do you think that'll be?"

It was hard not to get up and walk out. Stick said, "Not ever again. I've changed."

"Does the man you work for know you're a convict?"

"I'm an *ex*-convict, Mary Lou." The thought came into his mind that Mary Lou would make a pretty good hack at a women's correctional facility. Or even a men's. He said, "Tell me how your mother's doing."

She said, "Mama's dead." Giving him a withering look, as though he were the cause of it.

"I'm sorry to hear that, I really am."

"Why, 'cause you got along so well? You never said a kind word about mama in your life."

"I couldn't think of any," Stick said, seeing that

tough old broad squinting at the Temptations on
Ed Sullivan, saying, "Is that niggers?" Ready to
turn off the set, miss her favorite program if they
were. There was a twenty-four-inch console color
TV set now. Plus the organ, all the new furniture . . . Looking around the room he said, "You
must be doing pretty good over at Fashion
Square."

She said, "Oh, you're interested in how we're
getting by?"

He said, "Your mom left you fixed, didn't she? I
know the last time I saw her she still had her First
Communion money." It wasn't a good subject to
stay with. He got off of it asking, "You dating
anybody?"

She said, "I don't see that anything I'm doing is
any of your business." She looked toward the front
door a moment before Stick heard it bang open and
there was his little girl:

Skinny brown legs and arms, coming in yelling,
"Mom!" and stopping, looking amazed as she saw
him on the sofa. He didn't want to say anything
dumb. He smiled . . . She knew who he was, he
could tell. But she glanced at her Mom for confir-
mation; got nothing. Mary Lou wasn't going to
help.

When he stood up and said, "Katy?" she came to
him, into his arms and he felt her arms going

around his middle, the top of her head touching his
mouth. He felt her clinging, meaning it. Heard her
say against him, "I got your letter . . ."

But now Mary Lou was giving them a furious
look.

"Where have you been!"

It pulled them apart. Katy said, "I told you I was
staying at Jenny's." She seemed surprised. "Remember? And we're going to the beach today?
They're waiting for me, I just came home to get my
towel and stuff."

"Well," Mary Lou said, showing she was helpless, "your father finally comes to see you and you
run off."

Katy said, "But I didn't know . . ."

"It's okay," Stick said, "go on. I just stopped
by—I'll be around here, we'll get to see plenty of
each other." He saw gratitude in the girl's eyes—
more than that, recognition that they were in tune
and would be at ease with one another. He said,
"You look great. You're all grown up . . . How's
school?"

"It's okay." She didn't seem anxious now.

"You like it?"

"Sorta. We go back, God, in two weeks. I can't
believe it."

Mary Lou was moving to the front window.
"Who's out in the car?"

"Just some kids. Jenny and David. And Tim. I told you we were going."

"Who's driving?"

"Lee." Surprised again. "I told you, his dad's letting him use the car."

"I thought his license was taken away."

"He got it back two months ago." She looked up at her dad, smiling. "How've you been?"

"Fine. I'll call you real soon, we'll go out for dinner. School's okay, huh?"

"It's all right." She was edging away.

"What's your favorite subject?"

"I guess typing."

"Typing," Stick said. "You any good?"

"Pretty good. I gotta go, okay?"

He watched her hurry out of the room, into the hall. "She spends the night out," he said to Mary Lou, "and you don't even know it?"

"I work. You should try it sometime."

"You work last night?"

"I was at services. You going to give me the third degree now? You should be quite good at it, all the experience you've had. Come out of prison and have the gall to start criticizing . . ."

She glanced away and Stick looked over to see Katy with a beach towel and a plastic bottle of suntan lotion, her expression vague, lost. Then came back into character with a look of innocence.

"I gotta go, okay? They're waiting." She came

over and kissed him on the cheek and he kissed hers.

"I'll call you in a couple of days." He could see a reflection of himself in her, a little-girl version of his nose and mouth. More than anything he wanted to know what she was thinking. He watched her give her mother a peck on the cheek and start for the door.

Mary Lou said, "You have your towel, your lotion, you have your suit on?"

Katy pulled out the neck of her T-shirt and peered in. "Yep, it's still there."

"Don't stay in the sun too long."

"I won't."

"You'll get skin cancer."

"I won't."

"And don't be late. What time're you coming home?"

"*Ma*-om, I gotta *go*." She looked at her dad again, said, "See ya," and was gone.

Mary Lou remained at the window, sounds outside fading. He studied the round sag of her shoulders in the print blouse and felt a sadness and hoped she wouldn't say anything more to him. Her belly showed in the slacks, worn high, her hips broader than he remembered them . . . He would tell her she was cute as a bug and she would wrinkle up her nose at him and sometimes slap his arm . . . He was aware for the first time that she had no sense of style or color. He didn't want to talk to her anymore and still he asked, "How can she be out all night and you don't know it?"

Mary Lou turned from the window. "You've got a lot of nerve."

"We're not talking about me, we're on you for a change. Just tell me that one thing and I'll get out of your way."

"I knew she wasn't home," Mary Lou said. "I forgot for a minute, that's all. I went to services last night and when I got home her door was closed—it's always closed, I never know if she's in there or not. She's either in her room or on the phone."

"Services," Stick said. "You don't go to mass anymore?"

"I suppose you do?"

"Not too often."

She said, "Well, I attend the Church of Healing Grace now, since I've become acquainted with Reverend Don Forrestall . . ." Letting it hang.

So that Stick had to say, "Acquainted?"

"We're seeing each other. Reverend Don Forrestall has asked me to join his ministry as a healing assistant and I'm now studying for it. As soon as I heard him speak," Mary Lou said, "I had absolute certainty for the first time in my life."

A lie. He could never remember her being uncertain. She knew everything.

"I felt waves of love, which you would not understand, but it happened to me as he laid on his hands and Reverend Don Forrestall told me I had received the gift. He said, 'All things thou has seen the Lord do through me now shall be done through thee unto His praise and glory.' "

"He said that?" Stick said.

"In front of the congregation. I opened my mouth then and my fillings over here on this side"—Mary Lou hooked a finger inside her cheek—"had turned to pure gold. He's done it many, many times. Reverend Don Forrestall has cured thousands of severe toothaches, he's filled cavities with gold or silver, usually gold, he's corrected overbites, does wonderful things through laying on his hands and saying, 'In the name of Our Lord Jesus, let this mouth be healed that it may shout thy praise and glory.' It's all he has to do."

Stick said, "You mean Reverend Don is a dental faith healer?"

"Ailments of the mouth," Mary Lou said. "He does cold sores, fever blisters and inflammation of the gums also. Wisdom teeth . . ."

Stick said, "You had gold crowns put in there in 'Seventy-two. They cost a hundred and twenty-eight dollars."

"I never did. It was regular fillings and now they're gold, through the healing ministry of Reverend Don Forrestall."

"How much you give him?"

"Nothing. He doesn't *charge*, he does it in praise of the Lord Jesus."

"How much you contribute to the Church of the Healing Grace?"

"None of your business."

As soon as Aurora got home she called Pam at Chucky's, talked to her for almost a half hour about her experience and how she was going to tell off Mr. Barry Stam, the creep, who didn't think of anyone but himself. She said she wouldn't care if she never saw his big boat and his little pecker ever again.

Pam jumped on Chucky's bed, got him bolt upright and told about Barry's new driver taking Rorie home at eight o'clock in the morning for God's sake after being cooped up on Barry's boat for like almost two days. Chucky asked Pam what the new driver's name was and she said Aurora didn't know but she thought he was cute. Chucky called Moke, told him it would be worthwhile to go out and look for a gray Rolls returning to Bal Harbour, license number BS-one.

Moke sat in the blue Chevy van at the east end of Broad Causeway from ten-thirty to eleven-fifteen Sunday morning, wearing his brand-new forty-dollar Bullrider straw he'd bought with his own money. He smoked weed to help him wait and listened to WCKO playing nigger gospel. He said, "A-man and A-man," when he saw the gray Rolls come out of the chute past the twenty-cent toll gate. He followed after, turned in at the Bal Harbour shopping center and watched Stick get out of the Rolls and go into the drugstore. No suit on this morning, wearing khakis and a blue shirt, but it was the guy, no doubt of it. He had said to Chucky, why not call this fella Barry and ask him about his new driver? But Chucky said if they aroused suspicion the guy might take off; no, let's ease up close, Chucky said, not let on. Moke watched him come out of followed behind again and watched the son of a bitch drive in past the Bal Harbour gatehouse guard, giving him a wave.

Moke crept past in the van. Now should he call Chucky back, listen to him piss and moan? . . . Or call Avilanosa and get her done. Bright and clear, it was too nice a day to sit around smoking weed.

16

STICK PULLED INTO THE TURNAROUND wondering what Kyle was doing, wondering what he'd say to her. Cornell was standing by the open garage door.

"You have a nice time with Rorie?"

"She never shut up all the way to Lauderdale." He pulled the Rolls into the garage and came out.

Cornell said, "Love the scene, sneaking her off the boat this morning. Man so hung over he could barely see to walk."

"Aurora says she's going to tell him off," Stick said. They were moving across the cobblestones toward the lawn.

"He's heard it," Cornell said. "Man will put up with just so much, then she be looking for another daddy. Speaking of—the lady was looking for you." Stick's gaze swung toward the pool and Cornell said, "Not that one, the lady of the house. I told her it was your day off. But she's gone now, went to the club to fool around, have a few salty dogs. How come you're back?"

"Why would I want to leave this," Stick said, his eyes moving across the slant of lawn again to the swimming pool: to Kyle on a lounge, motionless, long brown legs shining in the sun. Her suit, wide blue and white stripes, was cut high on the sides, almost to her hips. He wanted to walk up to her—say something to Barry first. Barry sat at the umbrella table with a pile of Sunday papers. Looking at Barry he felt sorry for him, or else it was a twinge of guilt; or an awareness that he might feel guilty if he thought about it long enough or hoped to be seduced again by the man's wife. But there would never be another night like that one. He'd keep it to bring out and look at now and then, close to his vest, knowing his amazement would be shaded with remorse once he got to the part with Kyle. Not because he'd failed but because he'd tried, because he'd included her in his personal record attempt. Dumb. Still, he could forgive himself. It wasn't that dumb. He didn't know on the guest-house sofa he was going to have a knot in his gut thinking of her the next day. There was no one to tell to get a reaction. All he could do was start again from scratch—something he'd had a lot of practice doing—and this time hope she'd feel he was worth waiting for.

Cornell said, "Was a man name of Harvey stop by, look like he was gonna be sick he didn't find you. Gave me a number said for you to call soon as you got back. Hey, you see your little girl?"

"I sure did." It picked him up, like that, thinking of her arms around him, saying close to him, *I got your letter* . . . It reached deep into him. He felt a sadness even while he smiled, telling Cornell about Katy, and asked, "How 'bout you, you have a good time last night?"

"Fell in love," Cornell said. "Again. Yeah, while you doing the chores."

"They keep you humping," Stick said.

"Man got good and smashed, uh? I hear him say he don't remember nothing. That's safe." Cornell looked off. "I think he's waving at me. Wants a bloody." Cornell walked to the edge of the grass, watched Barry beneath the umbrella waving his arms, gesturing. "No, don't want me, wants you."

Stick walked across the grass slope with his magazines and aftershave and toothpaste in the sack trying to get words ready and found he didn't have to. Barry was into the stock market again, throwing questions at Kyle lying motionless a few feet away, sunglasses covering her eyes, arms at her sides.

"How do you like Biogen? Raised forty million for research, their objective"—glancing at the newspaper—"to become the IBM of biotechnology."

Kyle said, not moving, "You're already into biotechnology."

"With what?"

"Automated Medical Labs."

"I want to cover my ass," Barry said. "This"—looking at the paper again—"recombinant DNA, you understand that?"

"Gene splicing."

Barry waited, Stick watching. "That's it, uh? Gene splicing?"

"Transplanting genetic characteristics from one cell to another. Cloning . . . mass-producing human hormones . . . all that stuff." She sounded sleepy.

"How do you know that?"

"You sound like Aurora," Kyle said, still not moving.

Barry looked up at the terrace, his gaze monitoring the area before settling on Stick. "Hey, buddy, how you doing?"

Kyle didn't look over. Stick said to Barry, "What can I get you?"

"Not a thing. Listen, I hope I didn't give you a hard time last night. I don't remember a goddamn thing from the time we walked outta the club. How was . . . my friend? She give you any trouble?"

"Not a bit. She was fine."

"Last time I got that drunk," Barry said, "years ago, I didn't know any better, I pick up a broad someplace—I mean I must've 'cause I wake up the next morning and there's this broad laying there. We're in a motel, that Holiday Inn over on LeJeune.

I've got my arm out like this and the broad's laying on it with her head turned away from me? I lean up to get a look at her—I don't remember a goddamn thing from the night before—and, Jesus, I can't believe it. This is the ugliest broad I ever saw in my life. I mean that's how drunk I was. This broad was so ugly . . . Ask me how ugly she was."

Stick said, "How ugly was she?"

"She was so ugly I actually considered chewing my arm off rather than wake her up. You talk about an ugly broad . . ."

Stick glanced over. Kyle didn't move. Now Barry was looking at his newspaper again and Stick wondered if he was dismissed. He didn't want to leave, he hadn't learned anything yet.

Barry said, "I think Enzo Biochem's looking good. Up from six and a quarter to twenty-three." He turned to Kyle. "What do you think, babe?"

Kyle said, sleepy or bored, still without moving, "Nothing in the field of biotechnology has been brought to market. You're trading in names and numbers. They could be making cat food or you could be playing Keno for all it has to do with product." She said, even more slowly, "You don't need me for that."

Barry lowered his sunglasses and ducked his head looking over them. "Babe? What's the matter?"

"Nothing."

It seemed that was all she was going to say.

Stick said, "I heard about a dental faith healer, he straightens your teeth and fills cavities with gold in the name of Jesus. That come under biotechnology?"

Kyle opened her eyes.

"You're putting me on," Barry said. "Come on, you serious? A *dent*al faith healer? The age of specialization, man."

"At the Church of the Healing Grace," Stick said. He watched Kyle get up from the lounge.

"That's where you've been?" Barry said. "You get your teeth capped or what? Lemme see. Babe, you hear this? . . . Where you going?"

"Home."

"You mean *home* home?"

"No, my room"—waving him off with a tired gesture—"I'll see you later." Not looking at either of them as she walked around the deep end of the pool and headed for the tennis court. They both watched her. Barry said, "Look at those lovely long legs. They go right up to her brain, without any stops along the way."

Stick didn't say anything.

Kyle put on shorts and a tennis shirt and left the guest house with no purpose but to walk, feel herself doing something physical. She walked past hedges and walls that enclosed the wealth of the kind of people she counseled, walked east to the Atlantic Ocean, a neutral ground, and took off her sneakers to wander an empty stretch of shoreline.

She had said to her dad, "The money's great, but there's no satisfaction. I want to *do* something, see tangible results." He told her to drop her start-up companies going public and get back on the Board quick, for the upswing. She said to her dad, "Do you know what I wanted to be when I was little? A cop . . . No, not ever a nurse or a nun." She had played guns with her brothers and baseball in Central Park and at school in Boston, the boys amazed she didn't throw like a girl. She side-armed snowballs at cops in '69 demonstrating on the Commons, knit scarf flying, nose running, perspiring in her pea-coat, drinking beer after and smoking pot; into living. Now: "There's no excitement anymore. I watch. I'm a spectator."

Her dad said get married, raise a family. When she felt like trading, pick up the phone.

"Who do I marry?"

Lot of bright young guys on the Street to choose from, share a common interest.

Like dating sociology majors at school: have something to talk about. Except that textbook conversations ran out of gas and when they took the Orange Line to Dudley Station and prowled through Roxbury she found she could not study "real people" statistically: they were in a life that made hers seem innocent make-believe. Still, she was drawn to the street, fascinated, feeling a rapport she didn't understand.

Kyle had brought that home from school and her dad said there was the Street and there was the street. One was neither more real nor unreal than the other. Kyle said, except one was concocted, invented in the name of commerce; while the other was concerned with existence, degrees of survival. She would talk about social and economic inequalities and watch her dad doze off in his chair.

Today there was still a distinction in her mind. Comparing her Street with the ghetto street—or with rural, suburban or industrial streets, for that matter—she felt insulated, left out of life. She dealt in paper, in notes, contracts, certificates, coupons, with a self-conscious feeling of irrelevance.

On her recent trip home Kyle said to her dad, "I think I want to get into manufacturing, make something."

"Like what?"

"I don't know, it's down the road. Maybe something in genetic engineering."

"Pie in the sky. You want to be realistic, buy a stamping plant in Detroit and go out of your mind that way."

"Or get into a service business that deals with people who need help on a survival level."

"The public defender complex. I thought you got over that in Boston."

"You've got an answer for everything, haven't you?"

"I hope to God I do," her dad said. "But if you're serious, why don't you make a lot of money in the market, then open a home for cute little nigger kids the Junior League ladies can dress up and take to the zoo? Would that make you happy?"

Her dad had not been entertained by the Chucky stories. Or, he'd refused to accept the fact his daughter had a drug dealer as a client, put it out of his mind without comment. Now, if she told him she'd gone to bed with a man who'd served seven years for armed robbery . . . (The failure to bring it off with skyrockets was beside the point.) On second thought her dad might accept Ernest Stickley the ex-con—once he knew him—and still disapprove of their sleeping together. It wasn't a subject you discussed with parents, at least not comfortably. She had lived with a premed student in Boston for a year and a lawyer on and off in New York for a year and a half; her parents had been aware of both, without a word of comment.

Getting involved with Ernest Stickley, Jr., from Norman, Oklahoma, by way of a state penitentiary—God—previewed what could be an entirely new experience. She liked him. She liked to talk to him and felt good with him. At this moment she missed him. He appeared to be predictable, but wasn't the least bit. The dental faith healer . . . She had left because she was tired of hearing Barry's voice and was certain he'd take over and do all the dental-faith-healer possibilities to death, without restraint. Which was one of Stick's strong points, his control, patience, without—thank God—putting on a show of being cool. They had been natural together in bed, both at ease, in sort of a dreamy nod. It was great. Until, *maybe*, he began to think too much and his male ego got him worrying about performing, being a star, instead of simply letting it happen. Her dad might call it the unfortunate stud syndrome, self-emasculation through anxiety. But that's all the analysis she was going to give it. Feeling good with him and close to him was enough for the time being. The boy-girl aspect would take care of itself.

What might require work would be getting him out of that chauffeur's uniform and into a business suit. But why not? He had the potential, he certainly caught on fast enough. Why not help him get started? Not think of it as rehabilitation, like she was going to straighten out his life. Though it was an intriguing idea: from armed robber to investment counselor. Forget the gun, Stickley, there's an easier way to make it. No, just help him out, gradually.

Her dad would call it latent motherhood.

Crossing Collins Avenue on the way back she

noticed the van parked off the road by a clump of seagrape, standing alone. She could make out a man's head and shoulders through the windshield, a cowboy hat, and thought of Chucky's unbelievable friend Eddie Moke.

Kyle began to jog, just in case: in past the gatehouse and for several blocks, letting the perspiration sting her eyes, thighs aching now as she turned the corner and came along Bali Way. It was not until she saw the black limousine that she broke stride and slowed to a walk, catching her breath. The car stood at the entrance to Barry's driveway, a figure hunched over next to it. As she approached, the figure straightened, looking toward her. It was Stick. The car started up and came past her, a uniformed chauffeur at the wheel, alone in the car. Stick waited, starting to smile.

"You run in weather like this, Emma, you know what happens?"

"What?" She touched the sleeve of her T-shirt to her forehead. *Emma*. She had forgot about that part of last night.

"You die," Stick said. They started up the drive together, the blacktop soft underfoot. He said, "I just made nine hundred dollars. Not all from that one. The word's gotten around. He's my third customer; they call and stop by."

"I'm afraid to ask what you're selling."

"Guess."

"Not dope . . . Are you?"

"I never was into that. No, tips on the market. I'm a Wall Street tout, unless there's another name for it."

She said, "*Nine* hundred dollars?"

"Two hundred up front for a hot one about to take off, like Ranco. And I sold some over-the-counter stuff for fifty bucks each."

"*Nine* hundred dollars?"

"Cash, flat-rate deal, Em. I haven't figured out yet how to charge a percentage or if I should."

"Well, first you need a license." She was aware of the trace of amazement still in her voice. Now it was *Em*, like last night, familiar.

"I think I could even make up names of phony companies, they'd buy 'em. They've got that much faith in Barry. They think he's a wizard, up from boy wonder. They think you give him inside information, but he's the one who picks the winners. And you know what, he loves it. He said sell 'em anything you want."

They passed from sunlight into the shade of malaleucas and hibiscus lining the drive, the black-top hard and firm now.

"So I guess what it comes down to," Stick said, "selling's pretty easy if you have what people want. Is that it?"

She was recovering. "They don't even have to want it," Kyle said. "They only have to believe they'd be fools to pass it up."

Barry called to them as they were crossing the terrace, walking away from the house. "Hey, where you going with my driver?"

He appeared out of a dark archway of the morning room—where his wife had stood in moonlight. Stick saw her again with a wince of guilt, a minor tug that was losing its edge.

Barry came out to the grass. "Stickley, I got a favor to ask. Guy's coming in from New York, five something. You want to go meet him?" Barry stood with one arm raised straight up, wrist bent, finger pointing somewhere beyond Biscayne Bay.

"It's my day off."

"I know it is. I'm not *telling* you to pick the guy up, I'm asking you."

"What if I wasn't here?" Stick said.

Kyle took a few aimless steps away and turned back, to be able to watch both of them.

"If you weren't here," Barry said, "then I'd have to pick him up myself or get Cornell, but you're here. I can see you, you're standing right there." Barry pointed. "That's you, isn't it?"

"Since it's my day off," Stick said, "I think it

should be the same as I'm not here. Otherwise what good's a day off?"

"Jesus Christ," Barry said, "all I'm asking you to do is go to the fucking airport and pick somebody up. Take you maybe an hour and a half. Here—" He stepped back into the morning room and reappeared holding a rectangle of white cardboard, a shirt stiffener, that said in black Magic Marker MR. LEO FIRESTONE. "You hold this up as the passengers come off the flight. You don't even have to say anything."

Stick looked at Barry holding the sign against his chest. "I don't think I could do that."

Kyle said, "I couldn't either."

Barry said, "Whatta you mean you don't think you could do it? You don't *do* anything, you hold the fucking sign up, that's all."

Stick said, "You asking me if I want to do it?"

"As a favor, yeah."

"If you're giving me a choice," Stick said, "then I pass. I think you should handle it as if I'm not here. Okay?" He turned to Kyle. She shrugged and they started off across the terrace. Barry yelled at them, "I don't believe it!" but they kept going.

Kyle said, "Instead of trying to get fired, why don't you just quit?"

"I'm not trying to get fired." Stick seemed a little surprised. "You know him—he eats that up.

Gives him something to tell his friends, act it out."

She said, "You're right, he'll work it into an I-don't-get-no-respect routine. But it's still chancy, meeting him head to head like that."

"You give in too easy. He picks your brain to pieces and you let him. You have to act like you don't need him."

"I don't," Kyle said, "but I like him. I'm not sure why exactly . . ."

"Well, you're in a position you know what you're doing, you can afford to let him take advantage of you. I'm still feeling around, learning a few things . . ."

"Fast," Kyle said.

"Doing some thinking . . ."

"Maybe I can help you."

"I bet you can, Em. Who's Leo Firestone?"

A horn blared loud behind the van parked in the seagrape and Moke jumped, lifted the curled brim from his eyes to check the outside mirror.

Nestor's car, the Fleetwood Caddy.

Well, now they were getting someplace. Moke got out and walked back on the driver's side, away from the road, hunching as the Cadillac window went down fast, automatically, and there was Avilanosa, with no expression but an odor of garlic that hit Moke in the face and he tried not to breathe.

"We going to take flowers," Avilanosa said.

"Shit," Moke said, "bust through the gate. All they got there's a rent-a-cop."

"We going to take flowers," Avilanosa said. "Nestor talk to Chucky, Chucky say he talk to the man lives there. He say the man is going to leave pretty soon."

Moke straightened, restless, fooled with his hat and hunched over again. "Why don't we just go *in*? Me and you."

"Listen to me," Avilanosa said. "The guy will be there alone he thinks, in the garage where he lives. We take him away from here to do it. They have business. You understand? So they don't want police to come and bother them."

"*Business*? Jeez-us Christ, what's business got to do with it?" He saw the window start to rise. "Wait! You bring my piece?"

The window stopped for a moment. "I give it to you later," Avilanosa said, "when I come back."

17

KYLE GAVE STICK THE PROSPECTUS to look over while she showered, telling him, "This is what a film offering looks like. It describes what you have to invest to become a limited partner and how you share in the profits, if and when."

"They all do it this way, make movies?"

"The independents do. Then they go to one of the major studios and try to make a distribution deal."

He sat on the guest-house patio turning pages, trying to get a quick idea of what it was about. There was a story synopsis—he read some of it— also names of actors he recognized; but most of it looked like a legal contract or a subpoena, or the kind of words you'd see in a small-print money-back guarantee and skip over.

The prospectus was spiral-bound, the size of a nine-by-twelve notebook with about sixty pages in it. The embossed plastic cover read:

FIRESTONE ENTERPRISES
PRESENTS A
LEO NORMAN FIRESTONE PRODUCTION
"SHUCK & JIVE"

He was interested but the legal tone stopped him and he didn't feel like concentrating. He would look off at the bright expanse of Miami—a post-card picture with sailboats and seagulls—but aware of Kyle's bedroom, its sliding glass doors right behind him. Kyle in there now where they'd been last night. Coming out of the shower, slipping on her skimpy white panties . . . Neither of them had mentioned last night. Everything seemed to be moving along fine, so he sure wasn't going to bring it up. The best thing to do with failure, put it out of your mind.

Kyle didn't take long. She came out in a sun-dress, barefoot, with a tray that held a bucket of ice, a bottle of Dewar's and glasses—this girl didn't fool around—and placed the tray on the patio table. She asked him what he thought of the movie deal, beginning to pour drinks.

"This isn't the tire company—buy now and look for a takeover, is it?"

"No, no relation. This is Leo Firestone, Hollywood film producer. It says. His credits are in there."

"I saw them. I mean I saw the list, but I must've missed the pictures when they came out. I never heard of any of them."

"You didn't see *Gringo Guns*? About five years ago."

"I was in prison."

"You were lucky. He did one of those, too. *Big House Breakout*. But he's best known for *The Cowboy and the Alien*."

Stick turned to a page in the prospectus. "This *Shuck and Jive* . . . 'the hilarious escapades of a couple of undercover narcotics agents' . . . is he serious?"

"Two and a half million," Kyle said, "that's fairly serious. It's also zany, with riveting suspense and sizzling love."

He turned a few more pages. "Mostly, all I see is a lot of legal stuff."

"It describes the company, who the general partners are and their background, the risk factors, a budget estimate, a distribution plan . . ." She handed Stick a drink and sat down in a canvas director's chair with her own. "You'll see a tax opinion that runs about ten pages I think Leo Firestone's brother-in-law must've written. The story synopsis—you saw that—and some of the Hollywood stars Leo expects to sign."

"What you're telling me," Stick said, "this isn't your idea. You didn't bring Leo in."

"No, Barry ran into him somewhere, I think Bimini, and now Barry wants to be in the movie business. He thinks Leo is an extremely talented guy."

"Have you met him?"

"Not yet, but I can hardly wait. I told Barry
months ago I'd shop a film venture for him if he
was interested; they come along all the time. But
the way Barry operates, he decides he wants to go
now, he goes. He told Firestone he'd round up as
many investors as he needed, with their checkbooks, and sit them down for the pitch. Leo
must've kissed him."

"So if Barry goes in the others will too . . ."

"It's quite likely."

Stick turned to the first inside page. "It says a
hundred and seventy-five Limited Partnership units
at fourteen thousand two-eighty-five each . . . minimum purchase five units. That's . . . seventy grand
to get in. Is that right? To raise two and a half million."

"You're close," Kyle said. "See, the offering's
limited to thirty-five qualified investors. So the minimum you have to invest to get in is exactly seventy-
one thousand four-hundred twenty-eight dollars
and fifty-seven cents."

"And what does that get you?"

"Wait. That's the original prospectus you have,"
Kyle said. "Firestone, Barry says, is going to simplify the first couple of pages for the meeting tomorrow, sweeten the deal. Now the offering will

call for ten investors to put in a hundred thousand each. A million bucks. Then Firestone will take that to the bank to leverage another million and a half on a note payable in five years. The limited partners put in a hundred thousand each for twenty percent of the picture, but they each get a tax write-off of two-hundred fifty thousand."

Stick said, "I'm not sure I understand that."

"How the tax law applies?"

"I don't think I'm ready for it," Stick said. "But the way it works here, Firestone makes his pitch and they walk up and they each hand him a hundred grand?"

"Right."

"How do they know he's gonna make the movie? Or if he does if it's gonna be any good?"

"In there under *risk* it states you should seek the counsel of an independent tax advisor," Kyle said. "Which these guys may or may not do. As I mentioned, if Barry goes in, the rest of them will probably follow."

"All that dough," Stick said, looking at the cover again, "for this."

"At least the title works," Kyle said. "I think the whole deal's shuck and jive."

Avilanosa made a U-turn, came around toward the van and pulled in behind it. Once he had backed into position the trunk of the Cadillac was only a few feet from the van's rear doors. Moke was out waiting, fooling with his Bullrider hat, setting it loose on his head. He looked at the Cadillac trunk as he heard it pop open but didn't touch it. Avilanosa, his belly sticking out of his summer-plaid sportcoat, came back and raised the lid, not looking at Moke. The trunk held a half-dozen pots of begonias.

"What'd you get so many for?"

"This is from Nestor and Chucky. I have the card," Avilanosa said. "Did the man leave?"

"Wasn't more'n a few minutes ago. Had his nigger driving him in the Rolls-Royce." Moke turned aside to spit into the sand. "Looks like an old woman's car."

"All right," Avilanosa said, his dark features closing in a squint as he looked off across the road, down the beach side of Collins Avenue. "What is that, what it says?"

Moke turned to look. "That's the Singapore Motel."

"Sing-apore," Avilanosa said, studying the sign.

"It's a place in China," Moke said.

"I know where it is," Avilanosa said. "All right, I'm going to leave this car over there." He looked up and down Collins, then reached into the trunk behind the red-flowering plants and brought out, wrapped loosely in a chamois, a 9-mm Beretta

Parabellum that held fifteen rounds, blue steel with a wood grip. He raised the skirt of his coat and worked the automatic into the waist of his trousers.

Moke said, "Where's mine?" Avilanosa nodded to the trunk. Moke stuck his head in, felt around behind the flowers and came out with a High Standard 44 Mag Crusader with the long 8⅜-inch barrel, a dull blue finish. Moke said with a whine, "Shit, I wanted my pearl-handle Smith for this one, my favorite."

Avilanosa pushed him, getting his attention, and said, "Put it under your clothes. And take off your hat. You don't look like somebody that brings flowers wearing that hat."

Stick said, "But there were some funny things that happened, too. There was an Armenian guy that owned a party store . . . That story Barry told about wanting to chew his arm off reminded me. You hear him tell that or were you asleep?"

"I've heard it before," Kyle said. "Barry calls it his coyote story."

"The guy, the Armenian, had thirty-eight bucks in the cash register and absolutely refused to tell us where he hid his money. This place had to be worth eight to twelve hundred, a Saturday night. So Frank sticks his gun in the guy's ear and tells him *I'm* gonna rape his wife if he doesn't get the dough out, quick. The wife's this dark, bent-over little old lady with a mustache I'd put in the bathroom. I want to say to Frank, not me, man, you do it. The guy, the Armenian, didn't say a word, nothing. Frank threatens to shoot him, counts to three and now the guy says, 'Kill me! I don't care—kill me!' So we left. And you know what? We forgot the thirty-eight bucks."

"You're right," Kyle said, pouring them another Dewar's, "you were in the wrong business. What you could do, though, maybe, is give Leo Firestone a pretty good story."

"Another time we're sitting in a bar, we're just about to make the move—a guy comes out of the men's room with a shotgun and holds the place up. Does it all wrong. Still, he got the dough. We waited till he was about to walk out and took it away from him. So we locked him in the storeroom where they kept the booze supply, cases stacked up—the guy and all the patrons that were in the place. The next day we read in the paper they were in there six hours. The cops open the door, everybody's smashed, having a great time and the holdup man, it said, appeared to have suffered a severe beating. I think he was in the wrong business, too." Stick shook his head. "I remember the guy was wearing a gold satin athletic jacket with *Port Huron Bullets* on the back."

She said, "Daring holdup pair get away with—how much on that one?"

"I don't remember. Our career only lasted a hundred days and it was over for good."

"But exciting, huh?"

"I'm not sure that's the word."

"I knew a couple of guys who sold commodities options, which is illegal, but not exactly dangerous," Kyle said. "And, I had a client who lost a hundred thousand in a real-estate swindle. I advised against getting into it and he said, 'But look who's investing, and named a very prominent local businessman. It turned out the *name* that lent so much assurance to this very shaky development was part of the scheme and the investors lost nine million dollars."

Stick said, "Without having to point a gun at anybody."

"You go to the same prison though," Kyle said.

Stick nodded. "That's the truth."

What it came down to every time if you lost: dirty drafty place with broken windows, awful food and dumb people, few you could talk to . . . far from Biscayne Bay sipping Dewar's on ice, watching the gulls and sailboats, the first red streaks of sunset. He felt at home here. He had felt at home down on South Beach, too, in that cheap retirement hotel. Strange? He hadn't liked that place any less. Maybe he didn't know where he belonged.

He said, "You know who else is from Norman? My old hometown?"

Kyle said, "Wait, let me guess."

He watched her thinking about it, that beautiful nose raised in the air, the delicate line of her nostril . . . looking at him again with clear blue eyes, interested.

"Is he a famous outlaw?"

"Uh-unh, James Garner. I wonder if they could get him for *Shuck and Jive*. My first choice would be Warren Oates, but he's gone."

She seemed surprised. "What happened to him?"

Stick didn't answer; he looked off, listening. "You hear a car door?"

"It's probably Diane," Kyle said. "Barry would be gone by now." She watched him get up, walk away from the patio.

Now Kyle got up. She followed him across the front of the guest house to the corner. It was nearly a hundred yards from here to the garage turn-around—beyond the tennis court, the palm trees, the terraced front yard—but they were able to make out the shape of the van, blue metal in the cavernous shade of old trees. A figure appeared from behind the van, carrying something that obscured him. Then another figure appeared. They were unloading plants.

Stick felt Kyle's hand touch him, stroke down his back. She said, "More customers for you?"

He shook his head. "I don't think so."

"If it's the same van," Kyle said, "it was parked out on the beach road when I came back. But there was only one person in it. This looks like a delivery."

"Did you get a look at him?"

"Not really. He was wearing a cowboy hat and reminded me of somebody. A very creepy guy who's a friend of Chucky's. If Chucky isn't creepy enough for you—" And stopped as Stick came around, taking her arm and she was moving with him back to the patio.

He said, "Put some shoes on."

18

FROM THE OFF-SIDE OF the guest house they walked out toward the road, crossed the front of the property through stands of acacia trees and came all the way around to the driveway. Kyle asked questions and he told her to wait, not now. He told her to stay in the trees, he'd see about getting a car, if he could sneak one out of there.

But when he came to the corner of the garage and saw the van right there, the rear doors open, six pots of flowering plants standing on the cobblestones, he thought of taking the van and liked the idea. He didn't see Moke or the guy with him until they came out of the morning room and stood on the lawn to decide where they'd look next: go down to the cruiser tied up at the dock or over to the guest house. After a few moments they walked off toward the tennis court: a heavyset Cuban-looking guy, big hands hanging empty; Moke holding a long-barreled revolver at his side, but not wearing his hat.

The hat was on the driver's seat in the van. Stick reached in for it and saw the key in the ignition. He took the hat—glancing inside the crown to see the inscription, *Bullrider*, but no toilet paper in this one—and placed it behind the left front wheel, against the tire tread. He got up in the seat then and watched through the windshield. As soon as the two figures, way off now, walked around the front of the guest house and were no longer in sight, Stick turned the key. He let the engine idle low, backed up slowly, got the van turned around and looked out the window at Moke's Bullrider straw squashed flat on the cobblestones before heading down the drive, past the house to the trees in front. When Kyle got in she said, "When can I ask you what's going on?"

"While we're having dinner," Stick said. "Look in the glove box and see if there's a registration."

She said, "You like to know whose car you're stealing?" They followed Bal Harbour Drive to the gatehouse, followed the exit lane out and Kyle said, holding a plastic-covered registration, "Charles Buck, an address in South Miami."

Stick said, "Does that tell you anything? How about Chucky Gorman a.k.a. Charles Chucky Buck?"

They left the van in Bayfront Park, walked to a restaurant in Coral Gables, a favorite of Kyle's, where they dined in the seclusion of the garden patio and Stick told quietly how Rainy Mora was murdered.

Kyle did not interrupt. She seemed awed. When he had finished the story she asked questions, in turn, quietly. There was no hurry and she wanted to understand it and how he felt about it. They sipped wine, they ordered avocado and crabmeat . . . What was most difficult for her to understand was why he hadn't gone to the police.

Stick said, "The first thing you have to realize, the police aren't my friends." He said, "You're not only the best-looking girl I've ever known you're the smartest, by far, and I respect your judgment *but*—two things. Rainy's dead. He knew what he was doing, he knew what could happen to him, and it did. The other thing, I've already been to a correctional institution, I'm not going to put myself in a position like I'm asking to go back. I go to the cops with my record, tell my story, the first thing the state attorney'll do is try to get me to change it. He'll take the position, the only reason I'm talking to him I was working with the Cubans, but we had some kind of disagreement, so now I want to cop. The state attorney won't ever believe I was along for the ride or to keep Rainy company and make a few bucks. Why would I do that? I'd have to be crazy, guy with a record. But if I'm not, then they give you that business—if I'm smart I'll accept a plea deal, accessory or up as high as second degree, like they're doing me a favor, if I tell who pulled the trigger. Now I think I'd get off. But only after six months to a year in Dade County with a bond set around a quarter of a million."

"I know several good lawyers," Kyle said.

"Well, if they've had any experience along these lines they'd want ten up front and another fifteen if we go to trial. But even if I had the money I wouldn't give it to a lawyer."

"Don't worry about that part, the money."

"I appreciate it," Stick said, "but it's got nothing to do with lawyers. See—if I can explain it—you know Chucky deals, you know what goes on around here, the dope business. But you have to look at it from the inside maybe to understand what I'm talking about. I wasn't an innocent by-stander, I was *there*. Rainy was there, too, but he didn't make it."

She said, "Don't you *feel* anything? How can you remove yourself from it?"

"You mean do I feel anything emotionally?"

"Yeah. How can you be objective?"

"Well, the only emotion that enters into it is fear—you see a guy with a submachine gun . . . I don't think I'm explaining it right. Am I *mad* at any-body?" He paused as though he had to think about it. "Yeah, I am. I'd like to kick Moke's teeth in. But then I think I would anyway, just knowing him. The guy with the machine gun, I don't know who he is but, yeah, I think the cops should take him off the street, for the good of mankind. Chucky, you know he's a bad guy—you want to see him go to jail?"

She said, "But he seems so harmless . . ."

"Does it have to be something personal? Like he kills a friend of yours? He didn't kill Rainy, he sent him to *be* killed. And me with him because I walked around his house and told him I didn't see anything I liked. Or maybe—give him the benefit—he told them to take me instead of Rainy because he didn't know me. But he sent the two guys in the van to Barry's house, we're pretty sure, because it's Chucky's van. And if they put me against the wall and you happened to be there, a witness . . . you see what I mean? That's your weird client you imitate and your dad doesn't think is very funny. I tend to go along with your dad. So, you want to turn Chucky in? What's he done you can give the state attorney to make a case?" He smiled at her. "I haven't had anybody to talk to before this. I keep going 'round and 'round."

She said, "I don't know how you've kept it in. You must think about it all the time."

"For a while I did."

"Why didn't you run, get as far away as you could?"

"I thought of that, too."

"But you stayed," Kyle said. She gave him an appraising look, thoughtful, as though to see into him and discover something he didn't understand himself. "Why?"

"I don't like to keep bringing it up," Stick said, "but I was into some heavy stuff and did time for it. I've met a lot of people with poor manners and ugly dispositions. Guys that chew with their mouth open. So it isn't like I'm new in the life. Something like this happens, the first thing you do is hide. Then you peek out. Then you come out a little way, look around. Come out a little farther. Finally you come all the way out, and in this particular situation a strange thing happened. Nobody recognized me."

"I did."

"Except you. I got to the point I was going to leave because I couldn't see myself going up to the top floor of Chucky's building, fifteen stories with a rail this high on the balcony, and demand anything. Like the five thousand for delivering the suitcase . . . Which he still owes. Then I go to work for Barry and find out he and Chucky are buddies, they double-date out on the boat. What's this, a sign? Maybe I should hang around, see what happens."

"What you're really saying," Kyle said, "you're not looking for a warm, safe place, are you? You like the action."

"I was in Las Vegas once," Stick said, "I was driving from L.A. to Detroit and I stopped in Las Vegas because I'd never seen it. I walked around all afternoon to the different hotels, lost twenty bucks, went back to the Travel Lodge and slept for a couple of hours. I went back out that evening, made the rounds again, had a warmed-over roast beef dinner at one of the hotels, lost forty bucks . . . Nothing had changed from the afternoon. The same people were playing the slot machines, there was the same litter and dust. There was a longer line now for the show at the Frontier, see Wayne Newton in his out-fit. The place is all colored lights and chrome, red carpeting—you know what it looks like—but it's dirty, like a circus. Everything looks soiled. I couldn't get out of there fast enough. I drove straight through the night and most of the next day to Vail, Colorado. From all that phony glitter to Vail, where even the Holiday Inn sign is carved on a log; you have to look to find the name of the place. I go in a restaurant there, now it's all crepes and patty melts. People at the next table are ordering claret and soda, talking about the Woody Allen film they're going to see. And you know what? I walked around there half a day, the place bored the shit out of me, I had to get back to Detroit . . . You been to Vegas?"

"Couple of times."

"You like it?"

"How about cheap perfume covering up b.o.?"

"There you are. You been to Vail?"

"Once, in the summer."

"You like it?"

"It's all right. I wouldn't want to buy a place there and have to go all the time."

"Good, you know what I'm talking about," Stick said. "Could you live down on South Beach?"

"Well, it's an interesting area—yes, I could live there for a while."

"But you like Palm Beach."

"It's clean," Kyle said.

"See, I don't have a goal 'cause I don't seem to know what I want. Money, yeah, you have to have money. But I wouldn't want to be Barry, I wouldn't trade with him, live the way he does . . . You think I'm looking for action?" He seemed intent, wanting an answer.

"No, I said you like the action. You seem to."

"Maybe I do, to a certain extent. People race cars two hundred miles an hour, climb mountains . . . I tend to get in the way of people who carry firearms. Or I put myself in the way."

Kyle hesitated, staring. "I hate to ask, but, . . . it's happened before?"

"As a matter of fact, twice."

"People have tried to kill you?"

"Well, two guys tried to mug me one time. One had a gun, the other a knife . . ."

"Yeah?"

"I shot 'em. I didn't feel I had a choice. The other time, two guys that Frank and I were doing business with set us up. We had a meeting, it was suppose to be a payoff; but they came out with guns instead of money, so . . . I shot 'em. I've shot four people. I'm not the least bit prejudiced, I don't know if you happen to know that, but I'm not. But I've shot four people and all four happened to be colored guys. I mean it just happened that way. My closest friend in the can, outside of Frank, was a black guy. I get along great with Cornell Lewis, he's black . . . It's very strange."

Kyle said, carefully, taking her time, "Is there anything else you'd like to tell me? About yourself?"

"I think we're up to date now," Stick said. "I told you about my daughter . . ."

"A little."

"I hope you can get to meet her sometime."

"I'd like to."

"The only thing I haven't told you about is the tornado I was in when I was nine years old, in Norman. That was the scaredest I've ever been in my life, see a house blow away, gone . . . It was before we moved to Detroit."

She said, again carefully, "You accept what happens to you. You have the ability to detach yourself, look at things objectively."

He frowned. "You mean after or during?"

"I'm trying to find out what moves you."

"I thought I told you—being with you. But you don't believe me."

"You want to sleep with me, that's all."

He stared at her face in shadowed light, wanting to touch her.

"You're smarter than that," Stick said. "I know you're smarter than I am, that doesn't bother me. If I were the money whiz and you were, say, a bartender, you'd still be smarter only it wouldn't be as obvious. It doesn't matter who's what, we can talk without beating around. I could tell you I'm in love with you and you can be glad to hear it or you can clutch up and want to run, but there it is . . . What do you think?"

She hesitated. "Are you being romantic now?"

"I'm trying to tell you how I feel without exposing myself. You know what I mean."

"Playing it safe."

"I guess. I don't know." She said, "I have a feeling you don't see us walking off into the sunset."

"In a way, that's what I *do* see," Stick said. "They kiss and it says The End. What happens after that is the part that's kind of hazy. Me coming home with cement dust all over my work clothes and pulling my pickup into the garage next to your Porsche."

She said, "Why not sell investments? I know you have the talent and I could help you get started."

"Well, it'd be better than you learning a building trade. And I would appreciate your help and pay attention. But I'd also be a little, well, uneasy."

"Why?"

"I'd be afraid—don't laugh, but I'd be afraid you'd try to make me over, into somebody else."

She didn't laugh; she was surprised. "Why would I do that?"

"I don't mean intentionally, I don't think you'd be aware of it. I think it's an instinct girls have, some girls, anyway. Like wanting to have a horse when they're around twelve. Young girls write to guys doing time; they think they can bring out the good person that's inside this mean, miserable son of a bitch that hates everybody. Or I'd start wearing suits and change on my own, become somebody else. You'd look at me and think, who's this guy? What happened to that nice, simple boy from Norman?"

She smiled a little as he did. "The nice, simple boy from Norman. That's how you see yourself? Come on, tell me the truth."

Stick shrugged. "Raised on an oil lease."

Looking right at him she said, "You know what you are, Ernest? You're a snob. You love the idea of living by your wits. Why would a slick guy like you want to work and lose your independence? Isn't that about it?"

He smiled again to see if she'd smile back. She did, staring at him with a glow in her eyes he would accept as mild admiration. They were having fun. He said, "You think I'm slick, huh?"

"*You* think you are."

"Uh-unh, I look in the mirror I see what's there, nothing else. But I learned in prison I can get along with myself and have a pretty good time without breaking my neck, or joining a club where you have to listen to *Alley Cat* . . . Rich people sure have fun, don't they?"

"You'd love to have money," Kyle said. "Don't tell me you wouldn't."

"Some. How 'bout you? How much you make a year?"

"Why?"

"Come on, how much?"

"I average better than a hundred thousand."

"And you live in Palm Beach 'cause it's clean."

"Don't oversimplify. I'm not tied to where I live or *how* I live. I can be as independent as you believe you are."

"But you're tired of helping people make money who don't need it and I come along, I look like a worthy cause. Help the underprivileged."

She raised her eyebrows and said, "That's not bad, Ernest, you may be right," and looked at him thoughtfully. "The deserving free spirit, just a regular guy, rehabilitated after a couple of trips to prison, and now . . . What's your game, Ernest? Tell me what you have in mind."

It surprised him. "You think I've been putting you on?"

"No, no, I think basically you're a straight-shooter—within your own frame of values . . ."

"I've told you things I've never told anybody."

She was nodding. "Yes, I know you have. Past things. But you haven't told me your plan."

"What plan?"

"How you're going to get Chucky to pay the five thousand he owes."

Stick let a silence fill in space between them, a pause while he smiled and admired those knowing eyes. When he felt time was up he said, "You got any ideas?"

They took a cab back. They walked through trees roundabout to the guest house and slipped inside while torches burned on the patio and faraway sounds drifted across the yard. Later, when they heard the door-chime and Barry's voice call "Babe?" they held each other without moving. They heard him bump something on the patio and held their breath.

Much later Kyle opened the draperies covering the glass doors and they had the bay and the night-time sky to themselves. They whispered.

"There's nothing wrong with you, Ernie."

"Thank you."

"My polite lover."

Still later they heard doors bang, faint voices in the adjoining wing of the guest house. "Mr. Firestone," Kyle said. "It seems he's not alone." She left the bed and put on a light wrap.

"Hold a glass to the wall," Stick said. "You can hear what they're saying."

Kyle left the bedroom. A lamp went on in the living room. Stick lay without moving, neck bent against the pillow. Kyle came back. She stood in the doorway with a folder in her hands, looking at a sheet of paper that was attached to it.

"What's that?"

"The revised prospectus." She didn't look up. "And the guest list for tomorrow. Barry must've dropped it through the mail slot."

"I guess I'd better sneak off to my own room." Stick rolled out of bed and began looking for his shorts. "I'm suppose to help serve tomorrow, if you can picture that."

He heard her say, "You can't . . ." On his hands and knees looking under the bed.

"I'll try not to spill anything on you."

"No—you can't be here tomorrow."

Her tone brought his head up to look at her across the rumpled bed. "Why not?"

Kyle held out the sheet of paper. "Chucky's coming. Both of them, Chucky and his friend, Nestor Soto."

19

LEO FIRESTONE TOLD BARRY HE was a genius setting the morning room up for the conference: the long tables pushed together covered in bright yellow—dynamic color—the directors' chairs—very subtle—and right outside across the bay, Miami. "Where it's all happening," Firestone said with his glasses up on his bald head. "A cinema verité backdrop for the presentation. You weren't so fucking rich, Bare, I'd hire you for my art director."

As Stick and Cornell stood by Barry said, "It's your baby, Leo, but I do feel some responsibility. If the deal's got legs I don't want to see it crash and burn on account of something I neglected to do. Now how about the bar? You want it?"

Firestone began nodding with enthusiasm. "Yes, absolutely. I think the tone, the ambience we want should be very relaxed. I'm not making a pitch, I'm presenting a creative venture to a group of highly successful, intelligent men. I want them to understand they can let their hair down, say anything they want."

Stick watched him, fascinated. This was a Hollywood producer. This guy in the cowboy boots and tan cords, shirt hanging out: a strange, loose-fitting, ethnic-looking white shirt that some poor but clean peasant might wear, now on a fifty-year-old hipster. The guy's hair, brown and gray, hung from the circular edge of his bald, freckled crown almost to his shoulders. Stick had the feeling the guy liked the way he looked: tan, slim, not tall but with enough confidence he could slouch and not worry about his shoulders rounding on him.

Barry gestured to Stick and Cornell, waiting. "So bring the bar up. Set it in the arch there, be out of the way." He took Firestone down to the patio for coffee and Danish.

Kyle was at the umbrella table with Firestone's assistant, a tall, good-looking girl with dark hair cut short and hardly any breasts, though the ones she had were right there poking at her thin tank top. She wore her sunglasses up on her head, too. Cornell said her name was Jane, twenty-one years old. "The kind of girl you drop her off anywhere, I mean in the world, she'll find the man in charge and get next to him."

Stick said, "That mean you like her or not?"

"Means I have great admiration for the lady. I

watched her last night serving them drinks and before that driving the car—thanks a whole lot . . ."

"It was my day off, he could've driven. Why
didn't he pick 'em up?"

"Man was putting on his show. Called home
twice, nobody answered. You and Kyle go someplace?"

"Went out to dinner."

"You walk?"

"Got a cab."

Cornell seemed to want to ask him more, but he
said, "You watch this girl Jane. She still a baby,
but that's the kind can go all the way, be a big
name out'n Hollywood . . . While me and you
gonna go down there and carry up the bar, get
sweaty. Man, it's a bitch, ain't it, knowing enough
to slip by, but not enough to make the run that
will set you free."

"I don't think that way," Stick said.

Cornell said, "Yeah? Wait till I get you your
white coat."

While they were setting up the bar, stocking it with
bottles and glasses, Mrs. Stam came out with a bag
of Jelly Bellies. She nodded to them. Stick watched
her to see if she'd glance over, give him some kind
of look. He hadn't seen her since they were both on

the floor of this room early Sunday morning, a few feet from where she was pouring Jelly Bellies into a crystal jar. She was wearing a pale green sundress. Her legs from the knees down, Stick noticed, were straight but thick through the ankles; her instep seemed to puff out of her medium heels. When she was finished with the Jelly Bellies she asked them to come outside with her. Stick walked behind, watching Cornell talking to her, smiling and getting a smile back, watching her can roll from side to side. She wanted them to move the pots of begonias out of the drive, line them up along the edge of the grass overlooking the terrace. When they had finished she thanked them and walked away.

Stick said to Cornell, "You have any trouble talking to her?"

"Not too much."

"She looks at you," Stick said, "like she expects you to tell her something, but she never says anything."

Cornell said, "You got to say what she wants to hear, my man, then she'll talk to you."

"Got to push the right button, uh?"

Cornell said, dreamy, wise, "Got to find out where her interests lie, what activities please her most."

Telling the new man, the white boy.

"You could've fooled me," Stick said. "I thought all she liked to do was get laid."

* * *

He had on his white coat now over a white shirt with black tie and black pants. He believed he looked like a middle-aged busboy, a guy who had missed or blown whatever chances he'd had in life and was now on the way down. Which might not be bad. He certainly didn't look like a threat to anyone. He was at the bar slicing limes when Kyle came over. She surprised him.

She said, "I don't believe it." But without sounding serious, concerned.

"I don't either," Stick said, "but Barry'd rather have me over here than spilling stuff on people."

She said, "You know what I mean. You're still here."

"I think it's safer than out there somewhere, looking over my shoulder. If they're doing business with Barry they're not going to mess up his house, or get him involved. At least I hope."

"You might be right," Kyle said. "What're you going to say to Chucky?"

"Ask him what he wants to drink."

"Maybe you could poison him."

"Whatever anybody wants outside of whiskey and plain water they're taking a chance. I got limes, olives, cherries—what else do I need?"

"Balls," Kyle said. "But I guess you've got those, too."

The paring knife slipped on the tough skin of the lime Stick was holding, nicking the tip of his thumb. He said to her, "You're making me nervous."

By twelve-thirty the turnaround and upper end of the driveway resembled a Mercedes used car lot. There were six of them, the expensive BMW and two Cadillacs. Lionel Oliva and Avilanosa were the only drivers. They stood in the shade for a while, then wandered into the garage. When Cornell found them they were already inside the apartment, Lionel fooling with the TV set, Avilanosa looking around. Cornell said, "Oh." He said, "I spilled cocktail sauce on my pants, have to make a quick change." Lionel was tuning in a soap. "You all help yourself to beer and pop in the fridge, okay? But don't go in the bedrooms, if you don't mind, gents. Those are private quarters." Lionel said okay, sitting back, watching the soap. Avilanosa, looking into Stick's room from the hallway, didn't say anything.

Most of them were dressed casually and could be going out to play golf; two older men wore business suits. They all seemed to know one another, standing in groups, talking in loud, confident voices. Stick, behind the bar, decided the Cuban-looking guy wearing sunglasses and a brown silk suit that glistened and looked metallic was Nestor Soto. The man's expression never changed and he seemed to barely move his mouth as he spoke to Chucky. They stood apart from the others, Chucky waving the maids over to spear shrimp and hot meatballs from their trays. Stick saw Chucky glance over, chewing. Then Nestor was looking, staring at him.

Cornell, with a round tray, appeared before Stick to block his view.

"Two bloodies, a mimosa, two vodka tonic . . ."

"Wait a minute. What's a mimosa?"

"O.J. and champagne."

"Orange juice?"

"You got it. Two vodka tonic, then I want a Campari and soda . . ."

"Jesus Christ."

"That's the red one, underneath. And a salty dog."

"I quit," Stick said.

"Be cool. Tell me something—what did you mean, all she like to do is get laid?"

"Who, Diane?"

"Who we talking about? She come on to you?"

"Not in so many words." Not in *any* words. "No, I was kidding, I just think she's a little weird."

"She more like, formal about things . . . Listen, I make the salty dog. You make the bloodies, everybody will be happy."

"What do you put in it, tomato juice, what else?"

"Oh, shit," Cornell said.

After Cornell had moved off Stick saw Chucky looking over again. Chucky said something to Nestor Soto and started this way, coming around the conference table. But now Firestone's assistant, the girl in the tank top, stepped up to the bar.

"I guess Perrier."

Stick said, "Yes, ma'am," and poured her one. "Lime?"

"No, that's okay. It doesn't help it much."

"You don't like it," Stick said, "why do you drink it?"

She looked at him directly for the first time. Boyish from a distance this girl was a beauty up close, clean, precise features, perfect teeth. She said, "I thought all the cheeky help worked in L.A. Don't tell me you're an actor."

"I'm a chauffeur."

She looked at him for another moment, deadpan. "Well, you're not a comic, if you feel that's your gift."

Chucky stepped up next to the girl, laying a dozen used toothpicks on the bar. He said, "Honey, let me talk to this boy a minute, okay? Take your wah-wah someplace else."

The girl turned to Chucky with a pleasant expression, offering her hand. "Hi, I'm Jane, Mr. Firestone's assistant. You're Mr. Gorman, aren't you?"

Chucky took her hand. He said, "Jane, you want to be in show biz you ought to do some exercise, build up those pectorals."

Stick watched the girl smile as she shrugged, a nice lazy move. She said, "I work behind the camera, Mr. Gorman, so it really doesn't matter if I have tits or don't have them, does it?" She said, "Very nice meeting you," and walked away.

Chucky said, "How 'bout that?" looking past his shoulder. "That's a spunky girl, you know it?" He came back to Stick. "And you have to be some kind of spunky fella, hanging around here. We been looking all *over* for you."

Stick said, "How come?"

"Well, we thought you might be confused, what happened to Rainy . . ."

Barry's voice said, "Gentlemen, if you'll take a seat, we'd like to get started."

Stick leaned on the bar. He said, "Chucky?" and waited as he glanced around at Barry and then at Nestor. Chucky seemed anxious now. "I did time, twice, and made it, no problem."

"I heard that," Chucky said.

"Doesn't it tell you anything? Am I gonna go to Metro, give 'em a statement? They punch a button my sheet's on the screen. I say I was *there*, they gonna believe I was just watching?"

Barry's voice said, "Gentlemen . . . Chucky, hey, come on!"

Chucky said to Stick, "I'm not your problem, man. Nestor wants to talk to you."

"That's fine," Stick said. Chucky started to turn away and Stick said, "Hey, Chucky? I'm not a problem long as you pay what you owe me."

Chucky frowned at him. "You talking about?"

"Five grand," Stick said. "The suitcase was delivered, wasn't it?"

Chucky stared; he seemed about to say something, but Barry called his name again and Chucky walked over to the conference table.

Barry introduced Leo Firestone, who rose and said, "Gentlemen, when you're making love to a Jewish woman, you know how to tell when she reaches her climax?" He looked down the long table of impassive faces. "My dear wife Roz, the original princess, mother of two fine boys, Scott and Sherm, always blushes becomingly when I get to the punch line. Okay, from the top. You're making love to a Jewish woman—you know how to tell when she reaches her climax?" Firestone snapped his fingers. "Cue the blush from Roz. Punch line: she drops her emery board."

Barry raised his eyebrows. "It's true, believe me."

Firestone said, "What I want to do here is get you guys to drop your emery boards and realize this isn't another dry, boring investment proposal. It's an opportunity to have some fun for a change around a conference table. A profit opportunity to get those twenty million or more people who go to the movies every week to drop *their* emery boards, buy tickets and contribute to your financial stability. You with me so far?"

Jesus Christ, Stick thought.

From what he could see, behind the bar, Barry was with the guy. The others down the table seemed patient but that was about all. Each one of them had a prospectus at his place; some were open. Chucky leaned toward Nestor and whispered something, maybe translating; Nestor's face immobile, carved from dark wood. At the foot of the table Kyle sat next to the girl in the tank top, Jane; Kyle looking at the prospectus, Jane staring out at Biscayne Bay.

Firestone said, "I'm not going to go over the figures with you. It's all in the offering circular and you guys know far more about how limited partnerships are structured than I ever will, doing my number over on the creative side. But I want to mention something that's not in the prospectus I'll explain in detail later. And that is, even if this project doesn't get off the ground for one reason or another, I'll give you a tax write-off of two and a half times your investment. Gimme shelter is still the name of the tune, when you can pull it off."

Stick saw Kyle paying attention to that, making notes. The girl in the tank top was still looking out at the bay.

Firestone said, "So what we've got in Starsky and Hutch . . ." He grinned. "Testing you, see if you're paying attention. What we've got in *Shuck and Jive* are a couple of laid-back undercover operatives privy to, if you will, all the shit, all the scummy stuff going down in the Miami area. These guys might look like hippie bums to you gentlemen, but I want to relate to that vast fourteen to twenty-four audience out there. We'll see them cleaned up, too; but what I want to emphasize, these guys are pros. All the collars they've made down in Little Havana, I mean if you handcuffed them all side by side, lined them up, you'd have a spicket fence."

Stick watched Firestone, the dumb shit, look out over the audience. The man's gaze met Jane's and Stick saw her shake her head, twice, and nod toward the table where Nestor was staring at Firestone with his trancelike expression.

"If there's anyone here of Hispanic persuasion," Firestone said, "that's a bit of harmless levity along the lines I like to have a little fun with my Jewish ladies, God love 'em. No, we've been fortunate since the Bay of Pigs to receive into our land, our hearts, a great number of highly respectable and successful Spanish-speaking people. No, what we're talking about in *Shuck and Jive*, the film, is another element entirely. The garbage that has washed up on our shores, the gangsters, the murderers, who traffic in the sale of controlled substances with no regard whatsoever for human life."

Stick kept watching Nestor Soto. If he knew the guy and was sitting next to him, he'd give him a nudge with his elbow. Beautiful, sitting there listening to the bald-headed asshole from Hollywood.

"You read every day, I'm sure," Firestone said, "about the cocaine busts, the boatloads of marijuana confiscated, the gangland-type killings and murders. But, gentlemen, let me assure you it's only the tip of the iceberg you read about. If the papers even printed half the facts I've uncovered in my research it would literally curl your hair." Firestone patted the top of his head. "Fortunately I'm immune. I can look at the raunchy underbelly of the dope business, look at the vermin that live there with the eye of the artist and select its most dramatic elements for portrayal in a major motion picture." He held up the palms of his hands to the table. "But you ask me my source I'll plead the Fifth, so don't, okay? Believe me, you would not want to know these people."

Barry said, "Leo, let's move on to casting, okay?" Barry wide eyed, trying to appear innocent and interested at the same time.

Stick counted heads at the table. He believed Firestone had already lost three of his prospective investors—Chucky, Nestor and the guy who ran Wolfgang's, Gabe something—and might have to run for it before he was through. He sure seemed dumb for a Hollywood producer about to make another major motion picture.

Firestone moved to casting and told of several actors who had read the property and "flipped" and were under serious consideration. "You know," Firestone said, "what's his name. Tremendously successful recording star, plays Vegas." He looked down the center of the table.

And Jane said, "Neil Diamond."

"Right, Neil Diamond. He's perfect for the part of Jive, who plays cocktail piano as his cover . . . For Shuck we're considering . . . I have to tell you Sly Stallone turned it down—okay, that happens— due to commitments, but . . . what's his name, the guy that rides the motorcycle, the cop . . ."

"Erik Estrada," Jane said.

Jesus Christ, Stick thought. Warren Oates dead, you bonehead, could play it better than Erik Estrada.

"Erik Estrada is a real possibility." Firestone held up crossed fingers. "We're considering Laurence Olivier—Sir Laurence, I should say—for the role of Domingo, the wise old Cuban who turns snitch. It's a beautiful little cammie, could win Larry another best-supporting nomination. And for the female lead we're seriously considering . . . she was an answer on *Tic Tac Dough* the other night. The one that's emceed by my good friend Wink Martindale, reaches millions . . ."

"Linda Blair," Jane said.

"That's the girl, Linda Blair. Tremendously successful in . . . you remember, the kid throws up the pea soup?"

"The Exorcist," Jane said.

Firestone extended his arm, pointing to the back of the room. "My lovely assistant, Jane. If you wonder what I'd do without her . . . Listen, I'm going to open this up to the board of directors in a minute, you guys, and ask what you think of the story and what film stars you like that we might consider. There are a number of cameos I wouldn't be surprised one or two of you gentlemen"—looking at Chucky and Nestor—"might not fit perfectly. And don't tell me you'd turn it down. We're going to do this picture our way, gentlemen. Sell off foreign rights, TV, cable, which will more than recoup your investment before the picture is even released. Then let the majors bid for domestic distribution. I wasn't going to tell you this—but since I've got a handshake on it—listen up. Wherever David Begelman locates—and I know in my heart he'll be back in the thick of the action any day now—we'll cut a distribution deal. Take my word."

Stick poured a Jack Daniel's and stooped down to straighten the shelf beneath the bar while Firestone talked about bank loans and tax benefits, words that were hard to understand because they did not offer things to picture. By the time Stick finished his drink and stood up, Barry was saying, with his head cocked, "Yeah, I think I like it. I wouldn't mind seeing more broads in it. I think we could lighten the story up, show that *many* of the dealers are good guys that're only giving the public what they want. But on the whole I have to say, yeah, I think I like it very much."

Chucky said, "I think you're going to have to lighten it up considerably. I think you might even have to turn a few things around . . ."

Firestone winked and said, "That's the kind of input we want. Listen, we can write in walk-ons for any pretty faces you gentlemen might consider star material."

Barry said, "Okay, any questions about the investment itself, the risk, the tax angle? Anybody? Kyle, how about you? You have any questions?"

Stick watched her, seated with a pad of paper and the open prospectus on her lap. The girl in the tank top was watching her too, closely.

"Or any comments?" Barry said.

"Just one," Kyle said. "It sounds to me like a tax fraud."

Firestone pretended to do a double-take and then smiled, leaning over the table on his hands.

"I beg your pardon?"

Kyle said, "You want to raise a million here, a hundred thousand from each investor . . ."

"Very good," Firestone said, animated.

". . . take it to the bank and leverage another million and a half . . ."

"I think you've got it."

". . . and allow the investors to write off the bank loan even though they're not obligated to the bank. You are, but they aren't."

"By Jove, I think she's got it," Firestone said.

What an asshole, Stick thought. He wanted Kyle to let him have it. The girl in the tank top was sitting up straight, giving Kyle her full attention.

"I'm teasing you, sweetheart," Firestone said, "but you're right. We sign a recourse note to a bank payable in five years. So the guys each get to write off two-hundred and fifty thousand. Their hundred grand investment plus their share of the note, another hundred and fifty grand. *But* . . . here's the sweet spot of the deal. I give them each a signed memo that states they're not responsible for the bank loan. They've already written it off. And by the time the note comes due, in five years, the statute will have run out and the IRS won't be able to touch them. Now I think that's pretty cute, if I have to say so myself."

"Adorable," Kyle said. "Except the statute of limitations has nothing to do with it. When you forgive them a note that's due in five years—which they've already written off—then five years from now each investor will be a hundred and fifty thousand dollars ahead. Which is the same as income, and they'll have to declare it and pay tax on it. If you don't believe me, ask the IRS."

Firestone stared at her, half-smiling. "You serious?"

Kyle didn't answer him.

"Well," Firestone said, playing to the audience, giving the rich guys a palms-up, what-can-I-do shrug, "what it comes down to, really, is that age-old entrepreneurial question . . . who's to know?"

Kyle gave him her nice-girl smile and said, "I will, Mr. Firestone. That's why I say it's fraud . . ."

"Your interpretation . . ." Firestone said.

". . . and why I would advise any one of my clients to run if they ever see you coming."

Stick began to clap—four times before deciding he'd better knock it off. Kyle was smiling at him.

Cornell came over to the bar. "Three scotch, two vodka tonic. You learn anything?"

"Never open your mouth," Stick said, "when

you're fulla shit. What happened—they're ordering regular drinks?"

It was interesting, everybody talking now, getting into it among themselves. Stick saw Kyle and the girl in the tank top in close conversation, the girl on the edge of her seat, nodding as she listened. While at the other end of the table Barry, shaking his head with a solemn expression—What can I tell you?—seemed to be finishing Firestone off, denying a reprieve.

Stick turned to watch Kyle and found Chucky standing at the bar, directly in front of him.

"Nestor's ready to talk to you."

20

THEY STOOD IN ACACIA SHADE among expensive automobiles, Nestor looking him over, making no pretext of doing anything else, in control, letting Stick know it would be up to him.

Stick was not going to push him. There was a ritual of respect to be observed here, at the least a show of deference to the man who could order your death if he wanted it. Still, the way Stick saw it, he wasn't going to wait forever.

He said, "How long's it been? Three, four weeks? If I told Metro you'd a heard from them by now. Don't you think?" Trying not to get a plea in his voice. But the Cuban was not an ordinary-looking Cuban made up of black and Spanish parts going back four hundred years. This was an Indian-looking Cuban with a mask face he must have practiced for some time and could use now when he needed to scare hell out of people without saying a word. Who was he? What did he do on Sunday? Did he let his wife yell at him?

"What else can I tell you?" Stick said.

Chucky said, "You can tell me where a blue Chevy van's at for openers."

"Last seen in Bayfront Park," Stick said, "or impounded. You think I was gonna wait and talk to those guys? Moke's got his gun *out*, in his hand. The other guy, he didn't look like he even needed one. I left, that's all." He said to Chucky, "What would you do?"

Nestor kept staring at him.

Stick felt like pushing the Cuban. Let the Cuban take a swing and then belt him, crack the mask. He felt his stomach getting tighter and knew he would have to think, take his time before he said anything. But what was there to say? You didn't tell this guy anything, you listened. It tightened him up even more to realize that.

Nestor, staring, said, "I don't know . . ."

Stick asked him, "What do you want me to do?"

Nestor took his time. "You in the business?"

"No, I'm driving for Mr. Stam. That's all I'm doing."

"You were with Rene."

"That's right, I was with him, that's all."

"Got some action going, I understand," Chucky said, "selling tips on the stock market. I mean this is an enterprising guy," Chucky said to Nestor. "He came right out and asked me . . . You won't believe this. The suitcase Rainy had? He tells me he wants five grand for making the delivery. Right here, while he's working the bar."

"Well, it was delivered," Stick said, "and that's what you told us you'd pay."

Nestor's eyes moved, a momentary look of interest, mild surprise.

Stick saw it. He said, "What am I doing? Am I down at the state attorney's office? I'm standing here talking to you."

Nestor said, "You ever been to that office?"

"I don't even know where it is."

"By the courts, Northwest Twelfth," Nestor said. "They put a wire on you?"

"You want to feel me?"

"No, I don't feel you," Nestor said.

"He's not wired," Chucky said. "They wouldn't wire him for something like this, listen to all the bullshit. But he was a friend of Rainy's. How good a friend, that's what I want to know." Talking tough in front of Nestor.

Stick began to wonder which one was the problem, getting right down to it. Maybe it wasn't Nestor. Maybe he could talk to Nestor, but not in front of Chucky. It was a feeling and did not come from anything Nestor said or the way the man stared at him. It was like trying to decide who you would rather talk to: a man who might shoot you in the back, or a man who tells you to your face he's going to kill you?

This was in his mind now as he said to Nestor, not to Chucky, "I gotta go back to work. You want to talk to me sometime, give me a call. I'll be right here." Stick walked away.

It was Chucky who yelled after him, "Hey! I'm not done with you!" So he kept walking.

Chucky found Lionel and Avilanosa. While they were moving cars like parking attendants to work Nestor's Cadillac out of the turnaround, Chucky said, "What do you think?"

Nestor said, "It don't sound like *The Godfather.* I don't think this movie would be very good."

"I mean the guy," Chucky said, "Ernest Stickley. What do we do with him?"

"What do you want to do with him?"

"You were the one, I remember correctly, was so anxious to find him."

"Yes, and we did," Nestor said. "Now I don't worry about him so much. He ask a good question, what do you want him to do?" Nestor brushed at a fly close to his face, hand limp, diamond ring giving off a faint gleam. "He's here, he's not talking to nobody. I think what bothers you is what he wants *you* to do, uh? You promise Rene five thousand dollar?"

"I might have. Yeah, I probably said five to hook him. But you and I know it wasn't that kind of deal.

Rainy's not coming back I'm not gonna pay him, am I?"

"Well, you made a deal and somebody come back."

"I didn't make it with *him*."

Nestor smiled, a slight easing at the corners of his mouth. "He say to you, it was deliver, wasn't it?"

"See, that's what I mean," Chucky said. "Guy acts like he's got it coming. I didn't hire him, I hired Rainy."

"Yes, you keep telling me that. But it was deliver . . ."

"You think that's funny?"

"I think you can believe him."

"I'm not gonna give him five grand . . . Why would I give him anything?"

"I don't know," Nestor said.

"You think I should?"

"It's your business, not mine."

Chucky said, "But if I don't . . . I'm thinking out loud. A guy like that, you don't know what he might do. I mean something crazy. You know?"

"Then pay him."

"I don't owe him a fucking thing."

"Then get rid of him."

"What would you do?"

Nestor looked up at Chucky through his tinted glasses. "I don't know what I would do. I have no feeling about it, it isn't my business."

"I could argue that one with you. You're the one got the delivery. You were the other end of the deal."

"But I only promise to kill the delivery man, whoever it is," Nestor said. "And I keep my promise." He walked over to his car, Avilanosa holding the door open, and got in.

Big help . . .

Somebody had tossed his room. Emptied the drawers on the floor, pulled the bed covers apart, turned the mattress cocked half off the box spring. His magazines were still on the dresser. And the original prospectus Kyle had given him to read. The one in which thirty-five investors put in seventy-two thousand and something each and didn't involve the tricky bank loan part that Kyle said was a fraud. Stick took the prospectus over to his one bedroom chair—green plastic that was supposed to look like leather—sat down and began reading the film offering again, understanding most of it now and wondering why Firestone hadn't brought it out when Kyle shot down the other scheme. Except the story wasn't going to sell anyway. Christ, Shuck and Jive. Were they really that dumb out there?

Cornell said, "Oh, man," sadly, from the doorway. "I was afraid something like this might happen. Wasn't nothing I could do."

Stick looked over. "Who was it?"

"Nestor's man, his father-in-law. The big moth-erfucker looks like the bouncer at a live-sex show. He found out what he was looking for? Or shouldn't I ask?"

"Wasn't anything to find," Stick said. "Less he's trying to tell me something."

"Well, you cool about it. Didn't mess up your stuff too much?"

"No, it's okay." Stick wasn't interested in Nestor's father-in-law. He said, "The guy wasn't too quick, was he? Mr. Firestone."

"Man should be parking cars. He went to pack, gonna leave. Him and his little girl having an argu-ment about something."

"She seemed pretty sharp."

"Has good instincts, but a few things to learn. I told you, she still a baby."

Stick straightened, smiled, and Cornell glanced over his shoulder at Kyle standing behind him and got out of her way so she could look in.

She said, "I don't know why, I thought you'd be neater than this."

"Somebody looking for the microfilm," Cornell said. "Did you know this man was a secret agent?"

She seemed concerned for a moment, but said, "I know he has secrets." Giving it a light touch.

They went into the sitting room, Stick telling her she was a star while Cornell popped open cans of beer. They put their feet up and did quick Leo Firestone sketches, recalling memorable moments—Firestone dumping on Hispanics right in front of Nestor—Stick saying he wouldn't have believed it if he hadn't seen it. Cornell saying, man, we should make the movie, put some real life in it.

"Chucky had the best idea," Kyle said, "but I don't think anyone heard him. He said lighten up and turn it around. I remember a story in the *Herald* about customs agents finding two hundred and thirty-six pounds of cocaine in a cargo jet—I think it said with a street value of a hundred and forty-seven *million*; but there wasn't anyone they could prove had knowledge of it. So all that coke's sitting in some storeroom."

"The Feds licking their lips," Cornell said. "I like the one, the customs plane chases the smuggler from Bimini, the man running out of gas and has to ditch, so he lands at Homestead, man, of all places, right at the customs *base*, where they keep their airplanes, and while they running around looking for him he goes in the office and steals the names and addresses of all the customs dudes. You dig it? Wait. Then—listen now—the man sends an announcement to all the customs dudes saying he's made it, he's quitting and, listen, invites them all to his retirement party in Nassau."

Stick liked it. "They go?"

"Would have to quit their jobs or sneak over to

do it. No, the man said he would even send a jet plane over, pick 'em up. But the fools—you know what I mean? They could have gone over there, talk to the man drunk out of his mind celebrating and learn all his tricks. But no, the man in charge of the customs dudes won't let 'em go."

Stick said, "Instead of the guy taking the names and addresses—no, the one guy, Shuck, takes the names and addresses and Jive finds the two-hundred and thirty-six pounds of coke . . . Except how's he going to lift it?"

Cornell said, "It ain't all in one cake, man, it's in bags. See-through baggies inside of burlap sacks; you know, inside something. They take it out, make two trips each, do it easy."

Kyle said, "I think the names would definitely have to go. Shuck and Jive. How about . . . Stick and Cornell?"

"Frank and Ernest," Stick said. "But it doesn't have any punch, does it? Just lays there."

"Can't be too real," Cornell said. "Yeah, has to have some zip. Zip and Punch . . . Sock and Piz-zazz."

"Sacco and Vanzetti," Kyle said. "How about Ron and Rick at the Seashore?"

"No, you know what the title is?" Stick said. "The two dopers rip off the Feds, walk away with a hundred and forty-seven million dollars worth of coke? Scam."

•

"That says it all," Kyle said.

"Yeah, Scam," Cornell said, grinning, dragging the word. "You want to hear a true story maybe we can work in? The gardener that comes here twice a week? Man's Colombian." Cornell still grinning. "You know what's coming, don't you? I had him put in a patch over the other side of the guest house among the hibiscus. Ain't Santa Marta, not the same kind of soil, you know? Won't make dreadlocks grow out of your head either. But it's fine domestic weed. What I'm saying, who wants some?"

Barry appeared. At first he looked surprised. Then sad, left out. Then waved his hand in front of his face and clutched his throat as though he couldn't breathe, wanting to be one of them. Brow furrowed, helpless, he said, "You know how far away you can smell this party you're having?"

Cornell, grinning: "Tell us, Mr. Stam."

"The Coast Guard station. I just saw a boat coming up from Government Cut . . . Gimme a hit."

Barry put his feet up with them. He said he should've held the meeting in here, get everybody zonked and decadent on a strong stone, get them good and banged—using all the words he knew—then present the movie deal. He said, "Leo Norman Firestone Presents told the emery board one, he should've started with the one, You know how to stop a Jewish broad from screwing? Marry her." He said to Cornell, "You like that one, huh? Little ethnic humor? You know how they know Adam was white? . . . You ever try to take a rib from a jig? I would've said black gentleman but it doesn't work as good. Okay?" He said to Kyle, "You ought to change your name"—Kyle and Stick giving each other a look—"to Hernia. Hernia, the ball buster. I say that, you understand, with affection, with deep admiration. Hernia McLaren. Try and con me, pal, I'll take your nuts home in my purse." He said to Stick, "Since this is not your day off, Stickley, and you're supposedly on the job I believe? Could I ask you to do something for me, if it's not too much trouble?"

Stick said, "It depends what it is."

Barry said, "He's not kidding. He makes it sound like he's playing along, but he isn't. I don't know— I think the help around here has more fun than the . . . whatever the fuck I am. Sometimes I'm not too sure."

Cornell said, "You the master, Mr. Stam. The head dude."

"Thank you," Barry said, and looked at Stick again. "If you have time and it doesn't interfere with your plans too much . . ."

Even with a buzz Stick was getting tired of smiling.

". . . would you mind driving Leo Norman Firestone and his flat-chested assistant to the airport in about an hour?"

When Stick hesitated Barry said, "What're you doing, thinking it over?"

Stick said, "Mr. Stam, it sounds easy enough," and stared at him, straight faced. "But there's a mile of wire in a screen door."

He watched Barry nod with a thoughtful expression. It was good dope.

Eddie Moke picked up the black Cadillac, BS-2, coming out of Bal Harbour, identified Stickley driving—his window down as he went out the gate—but not the people in the backseat. Moke followed the limo all the way crosstown to Miami International . . . goddamnit, where he had to be wide awake in all that airport traffic, not get faked out. It was coming on dusk, which was good, but made keeping the limo in sight harder.

Moke was operating on his own this trip, needing no orders or plan other than his will to get Mr. Stickley in a fix and shoot holes in him. He hoped then to find 105 dollars in Stickley's wallet. Forty for the Bullrider straw Stickley had run over and 65 for what he'd had to pay to get the van out of the Miami city pound. Chucky had asked him one time, "They ever let you out of the chute?"

Fat turd. There'd come a time he'd settle with

Chucky. Most likely be told to and he'd take pleasure in it.

But this one now had become personal.

Wait till Stickley was alone going back. Run him off the road . . . Or cut past him and open up, *yeah*, with the nickel-plate Mag and blow the sucker right out of his Cadillac saddle. If the chance didn't come he could always slip into that garage where he lived. Do it late at night.

Go on over to Nestor's after and tell him about it. Say, what else you need done? Nestor would be lost somewhere in his head or not believe it and him and Avilanosa would start laughing and speeling in Cuban and that's when he'd take the fellas ears out, wrapped in a hanky, and drop them on the table like a couple of dried apricots.

"You believe me now, señor?" Moke said out loud, looking through the windshield at the Cadillac parked with its trunk open, five cars ahead and two rows over in the traffic, by the Eastern sign. Then squinted and said, "The hell's going on?"

The man was walking away with his suitcase, shaking his head at a skycap. But now the skinny girl in the red undershirt was getting back in the car . . .

21

JANE SAT IN FRONT WITH Stick on the way back to Miami Beach. He drove in silence, letting her come back down after the yelling match with Firestone all the way to the airport. The guy accusing her of not preparing him for the meeting, the spics. The girl actually telling him if he hadn't opened his mouth so ridiculously wide he wouldn't have been able to put his foot in it. Stick had kept his eyes on the mirror most of the way there.

He would still look at the mirror from time to time. They were on 112 heading east when Stick told her he'd kept waiting for the guy to fire her.

"He can't afford to," the girl said.

Whatever that meant. Did she have something on him?

She seemed relaxed now. She said, "You told me you were a chauffeur—remember, this afternoon? I thought you were trying to be funny."

"I don't think it's funny," Stick said, "at all."

"Well, some people are what they say they are,"

Jane said, "but not many. Especially in the industry. What they do, they talk on the phone, they take meetings and go to screenings and put down everything they see. They make wry, supposedly clever comments, but too loud and dumb to be clever. Because—you know why? They don't like pictures. If they didn't happen to be in the industry they wouldn't even go see them, ever. Bunch of fucking lawyers and business types . . . You know any lawyers that see pictures, actually go to a theater and buy a ticket?"

Stick said, "I've only known two and they didn't do me much good."

"The lawyers and the business types answer to the egomaniacs running the conglomerates that own the majors and none of them knows dick about film or has any kind of feeling for it," Jane said. "You want a development deal now you have to bring them a story that takes place on a giant pinball machine with a lot of flashing lights. Special effects, that's the name of the game. You don't have ten million bucks worth of special effects in the script you're fucked. You see *E.T.*?"

"Not yet."

"Mary Poppins goes electronic. Flying bicycles and Valley kids talking cute-dirty. I'd rate it right up there with that Velveeta cheese commercial, everybody's trying to promote a slice of cheese off this little boy and he won't give them any."

"I'll wait'll it's on TV," Stick said. He looked over at her sitting close to the door, tan bare shoulders slumped. She looked worn out. "Firestone a lawyer?"

"It's grossing three million a *day*. No, he's not a lawyer. Leo's problem, he doesn't have any talent. He makes rotten pictures. Did you see *The Cowboy and the Alien*?"

"I missed it . . . How come you work for him?"

"Because at least he makes pictures and I felt I could learn *some*thing, just being around. You ever read John O'Hara?"

"I might've."

"There's a character in one of his stories, an actor by the name of Doris Arlington. She works hard, she makes it, the studio finally gives her a contract that reflects her ability. Doris signs it, puts the pen down and says, 'There. I'll never suck another Jewish cock.' She isn't showing prejudice. She's saying she'll never again submit to people who have no understanding or feeling for her art. Well, I'm still submitting. I'll work on a picture I know is a piece of shit, because at least I'll be working."

"You like movies."

"I love them. I want to produce my own."

"Not *Shuck and Jive*?"

"Jesus . . ."

"How about—call it *Scam*. The two guys're dopers now. They walk into customs in the middle of the day and con them out of a hundred and forty-seven million dollars' worth of top-grade cocaine."

"Starring Elliott Gould and George Segal," Jane said. "I saw it. Make it twenty-million dollars' worth. Even with inflation it's a lot." She paused and said, "Considering some of the investors I think even Leo would've had a better chance of selling it."

"You think so?"

"He really blew it."

"How do you know some of those guys're into dope?"

"Nestor Soto? He practically wears a sign. And the pudgy one, Chucky. Barry hinted around he's a dealer."

"You like Barry?"

"I know a hundred and ninety-nine Barrys. They come with interchangeable one-liners."

"You think he deals?"

She turned enough to face Stick. "Is that what you're trying to find out? You're not really a chauffeur, are you?"

"Not in real life," Stick said, his gaze on Miami Beach in the distance, pale structures against the darkening sky. "Firestone said the Eden Roc, right? We natives call it just the Roc."

"What were you in real life?"

"That's a hard one. I'm still trying to decide what I want to be when I grow up."

"How about a cop?" She seemed to have hold of something and wasn't going to let go.

"Why do you say that?"

"You ask questions like a cop. Slip them in, no hurry, very patient. What're you, a narc? . . . Well, it doesn't matter. You're not going to tell me if you are."

"Nobody's ever accused me of that before," Stick said. "Jesus, a narc . . ."

"I worked for a casting company when I first started. I'd make you any day as an undercover cop."

Stick thought for a minute, getting a glimpse of Biscayne Bay now, the little ocean before the big one. He said, "If I look institutionalized it's 'cause I just finished doing seven years for armed robbery. You want references, call the Detroit Police or the Oakland County Sheriff's Department. I'm not proud of it, but there it is."

She said, "Wow. Really? What was it like?"

"It wasn't like the movies, I'll tell you that."

"Did you get raped?"

"No, I had friends in the yard."

"Tell me about it."

"I have a feeling," Stick said, "if I was a narc you wouldn't be as interested."

"Probably not," Jane said. "What's the narc's motivation? It's a job. But an ex-con armed robber driving a limo for a millionaire who thinks he's a stand-up comic is something else. I mean if you do it straight though, not as a comedy."

"You think it'd sell?"

"I like it so far."

"Would you like it more if I told you we were being tailed?"

She turned half-around to look back over the seat.

"The van, blue Chevy. He's been on us since we left Bal Harbour."

"Who is it? Do you know him?"

"I have a good idea."

"But why is he following you?"

"I think he wants to kill me."

"Come on . . . Why?"

"I wrecked his cowboy hat. Two of 'em, in fact."

She sat back again to look straight ahead. They were on the Julia Tuttle Causeway now.

"I thought you were serious."

Stick said, "I've found that real life is weirder than the movies. But I like movies better, they're safer. You ever meet Warren Oates?"

"Yeah, once, at Dan Tana's. I was with a friend of his and he joined us for dinner. Why?"

"I just wondered. Was he a nice guy?"

"Yeah, I liked him. He was all right."

"How long you going to be at the Roc?"

"I guess a few days. I'm supposed to wait till Leo gets back from New York, but I'm going to make a few calls to L.A. and if I can find anything at all, *any*thing, I'm gone. If I have to hitchhike. Leo, the son of a bitch, hasn't paid me in over a month."

"Why you supposed to wait here?"

"Leo took a suite to use as a production office—he was so confident we'd be in business. It's cheaper to leave me here than take me to New York. While he makes another pitch and gets all the names wrong." She bit at her thumbnail, not so much anxious as impatient. "My problem, I've got plenty of self-esteem but no credits. I meet somebody like Kyle—very pro, a super lady—and it makes me want to *move*, get going . . . I loved the way she handled Leo, led him along with the questions—the asshole, with that condescending 'I think she's got it'—and then zapped him. It was a beautiful set piece, just beautiful."

"She knows what she's doing," Stick said.

Jane stared at him. "You've got something going with her, haven't you?"

Stick took his eyes from the causeway, the pavement rising gradually ahead of them. "I tell you I'm just the chauffeur . . ."

"Yeah, well, I caught a few looks passing back and forth between you," Jane said. "That's why I was sure you weren't *just* the chauffeur. Then I thought, Jesus, maybe *she's* a narc, too. Listen, the relationships around here are so weird I'd be willing to believe anything . . . starting with the butler, what's his name, Cornell, and the lady of the house. Is she in a nod all the time or what?"

"Yeah? You saw something there?"

"I could be wrong, but I'd bet even money they're fucking."

"Real life," Stick said.

"Yeah, you're right."

She looked around again as they came off the causeway and turned left onto Collins Avenue.

"Jesus, I think you're right. He *is* following us."

Stick cranked the wheel, pointing the Cadillac up and around the circular drive that rose to the Eden Roc's main entrance. He popped the trunk release as the girl opened her door. Then dug into his pants pocket before getting out and walking to the rear end of the Cadillac. A bellman came out, lifted the bag and tote from the trunk. Stick closed it, turned to see Jane looking down the ramp toward the street.

"He's parked back there. What're you going to do?"

"Maybe I can win his respect," Stick said. "Don't worry about it."

Her hand was extended now. "Well, it was fun. And I wish you luck."

Stick took her hand in both of his and saw her expression change, the lines through her jaw harden.

"What's this?"

"One-way fare to L.A. Or close to it."

She looked at the folded one-hundred-dollar bills in her hand, three of them. "For what?" With that hard edge, suspicious.

"You remember Chucky . . ."

"What about him?"

"The one told you to do breast exercises?"

"I know who you mean. Fatty."

"Suppose he calls you—"

"Bullshit—what're you *doing*? I thought you were a nice guy."

"Listen to me a minute, will you?" Standing here in his black suit arguing with a girl in a tank top, the liveried help watching. "What's the number of your suite?"

She hesitated. "Why?"

"Come on, just tell me."

"Fifteen-oh-three."

"When somebody calls, they want the production office, how do you answer the phone?"

"I say hello. What do you think?"

"What if you—just for the next couple of days when you answer, what if you said . . . Norman Enterprises? And sounded, well, happy and optimistic about it."

She said, "Norman Enterprises? . . ."

"Yeah. You like it? Good morning, Norman Enterprises. No, I'm sorry, Mr. Norman isn't in right now. You want to leave a message?"

She began to smile and looked like a little girl. She said, "Oh, wow," and sounded like a little girl.

"I'd really appreciate it," Stick said.

A cabdriver came along the street toward the van, stocky old guy about sixty, pointing to the sign that said TAXIS ONLY, shaking his head. "You can't park here. Move it out." He didn't look Cuban to Moke, probably Italian. Wise-ass guy come down here from the Big City.

Moke had tied a lavender bandana around his head like a sweatband. He had on his old comfortable leather jacket that fit the bends and creases of his body, nothing under it but sweat and his big Smith & Wesson 44 Mag. It hurt, the better-than eight-inch barrel digging into his groin and thigh but felt good, too. Moke rolled his window down, felt the rush of warm, humid air, rested his elbow on the sill.

He said, "Papa, you want to bleed out your ears? Keep talking to me."

The old guy stood his ground in the street but kept his mouth shut now, Moke getting a kick out of the geezer trying to give him an evil look. The next thing, Moke was sitting up straight, slipping the Hurst shifter into gear, ready to pop the clutch—and that old man better get out of the way.

Then got a surprise. The Cadillac had eased down the ramp and stopped, waiting for traffic to pass on Collins. Moke was sure it would turn right and head up to Bal Harbour. But the Cadillac turned *left*, came past him going south and Moke had to U-turn away from the cab stand to get on its tail.

Stickley had not looked at him going by. At least he hadn't seemed to, though it was hard to tell with those no-glare windows. Moke tailed the Cadillac back toward the causeway, then got another surprise when it turned left on Alton Road, staying on the island, crossed the narrow bridge over the inlet and now drove along Bay Shore Golf Course, darker in here with all the foliage, though the sky was still showing some daylight. When the Cadillac turned in at the club entrance Moke braked and held back. What was Stickley going in there for? It was a public course, they'd allow him, but it was sure too late to play any golf.

Moke drove past the entrance, scouting, saw rows of cars in the parking lot still. Two hundred feet down the road he turned around, came back and nosed the van into the lot past high shrubs and trees. The parked cars were scattered around. There was the Cadillac in the second row from the front, facing toward the clubhouse. There wasn't a soul around. Moke kept to the back of the lot be-

fore coming up slow behind the Cadillac, letting
the van coast in neutral. He braked gently to stop a
row behind.

Still nobody around. He rolled his window
down. All he heard were crickets. He could sit and
watch that Cadillac with its goddamn dark-tinted
windows and Stickley might be in the car and he
might not. He would have had time to get out and
go into the clubhouse. Maybe have some drinks.
Maybe he knew a waitress in there. Or he could be
in that car waiting for somebody to come out,
maybe picking up a waitress after work. If he *was*
in that car, sitting there . . .

There was another car close on the driver's side
of the Cadillac, empty space on the other.

Moke raised his door handle, pushed with his
shoulder and slipped down off the seat. He pulled
his 44 Mag, gleaming in the dusk, and his jeans felt
loose on him. He did not have to check the loads;
he was ready. Tiptoe up on the passenger side of the
Cadillac . . .

Which he did, concentrating on his game. Got all
the way to the right-side door, eased in close,
pressed his headband against the glass . . .

Empty.

The son of a bitch must have gone inside the
clubhouse. It gave Moke little choice. He walked
toward the clubhouse, looked over the near
grounds, out at the fairways getting dark. Shit. He

walked back to the van, got up behind the wheel and slammed the door. What difference did it make? Son of a bitch. He'd sat in here all day Sunday—his butt'd be growing into the seat pretty soon. He bent over and laid the Mag on the floor between his boots, handy.

It was when he straightened up again that the cord or whatever it was came over his head and around his neck—Christ!—yanked him back tight against the seat, making him gag, the cord or whatever it was digging into his throat, slick plastic-coated, and when he tried to pull it free his head was yanked back by the hair—Christ!—pulling his scalp, pulling his eyes open wide as they would go looking at the van ceiling.

Stick's voice, close, directly behind him, said, "You got a problem, son. How you're gonna hand me your gun without strangling to death."

22

BARRY WAS GOING TO KILL HIM. The car telephone was still attached to one end of the cord. But he'd rather have Barry threaten and try than Moke, any day.

One fist clenched in a stringy handful of hair, the other twisting, pulling on the cord, keeping it taut, Stick did not want to let go. But he would have to give Moke some slack.

He said, "You think you can do it?"

Moke gagged, managed to say, breathless, "I can't breathe."

"I believe you," Stick said. "I want to see you reach down and pick up that piece by the barrel . . . Go ahead, try it." He rose on his knees, extending his arms to stay with Moke, saw the revolver, the clean mother-of-pearl grip. Stick let go of the telephone cord, took the solid weight of the Mag in his right hand and felt a world better. He pressed the tip of the barrel into the back of Moke's neck.

"Now your other one."

"I don't have no other one," Moke said.

Stick tightened his grip in Moke's greasy hair, yanked back hard and Moke screamed. Stick raised enough to look down into Moke's upturned face, into wide eyes rolled back, mouth open.

"You're gonna be bald-headed or dead, one. I want the piece you had Sunday."

"It's down underneath the seat."

"Let's see you bring it out the same way."

Moke found it, handed back the High Standard, and Stick released his hair to take it. He hefted the two revolvers; they felt of equal weight.

"Around eight pounds of heavy metal. You put on a show, don't you?"

"You gonna kill me?"

"I could. Save you doing time."

"Well, get her done."

Stick almost hit him with the gun, staring at the headband where he'd lay the barrel across Moke's skull. He put the High Standard down next to him, grabbed hold of Moke's hair again and got a howl from him as he yanked back as hard as he could.

He said, "Are you that fucking dumb? Is there something wrong with you?" Staring down into Moke's face, into those round dull eyes that knew nothing about him. "You think I wouldn't do it? I don't have the nerve? . . . I've *done* it."

He felt himself shaking. He had to let his body relax, sit back on his legs. He had to make a con-

scious effort to open his fist, release his hold on
Moke's hair. Strands of it came away, twisted between his fingers.

Moke said, "Owww," a whine, and pulled himself up slowly, hunching, looking over his shoulder
at Stick.

"We're going to get in the Cadillac," Stick said.
"You're going to drive. You're going to take me to
see Nestor."

Moke said, "Jeez-us Christ . . ."

"But don't open your mouth," Stick said. "I'm
afraid I'd shoot you through the head, and I don't
want us to have an accident."

Nestor dreamed of a jaguar that had walked down
the deserted main street of Filadelfia, the town
where he was born in the Chaco region of Paraguay.
The street was deserted because of the jaguar, the
people watching the wild animal from windows and
from doors that were open a few inches. This jaguar
was very likely the one that had killed several cows,
a goat or two and an old horse; but no one threat-
ened the life of the jaguar because of the wonder of
seeing it in the street, in civilization. Walking past a
truck, sniffing. Turning to look at a dog barking
from a porch. Sniffing its way along the dirt street
from one end to the other. Nestor was a small boy
the day the jaguar came to town. He was there, but

he wasn't certain now if his dreams came from what he had actually seen or what had been told to him many times and was able to see in his mind. It was winter, the dry time, and they said the jaguar was thirsty. They marveled at it and held children up to look at it. Then the men of the village—not the Mennonites who farmed here, but the men of the country who spoke Guaraní more times than Spanish—followed the cat out into the lifeless desert and on the second day the men shot it twenty times with their rifles and held a drawing, a lottery, for its skin.

Nestor dreamed occasionally of other places. He dreamed of Barranquilla in Colombia, of filth in narrow streets and the smell of fish. He dreamed of Cuba, of black smoke rising to the sky, fields on fire, the men going out to do battle with the cane. He could remember the fires clearly as well as dream about them.

But he dreamed most often of the jaguar in the Chaco, a place he could not recall from memory except for a few glimpses and smells. So if the jaguar was in his mind, coming uninvited as it did, it must be a sign.

Yes?

He told it to Stick on the backyard patio of the walled home in South Miami, the big revolvers lying on the stone table between them, the grass illuminated like a polo field, for security, the *santería* shrine against the cement wall, off in a corner, an altar to African gods that resembled an outdoor barbecue. Moke was gone. Sent home. Avilanosa brought them beer and left without a word. Nestor offered cocaine. Stick shook his head.

He said, "I wish I had a dream like that. I fall down steep, narrow stairs."

"What does it mean to you?"

"It means I'm not getting anywhere fast."

"Or there is danger up those stairs, uh? The sign being you shouldn't go there."

Stick thought about it. "Don't overreach. Don't bite off more than you can chew."

"Yes, of course."

"Or sometimes I see myself in a dream. I'm on a busy street, or I'm in a church . . ."

"Yes?"

"And I don't have any clothes on. I'm naked."

"It means you have nothing to hide," Nestor said. "I think it's good you tell me that. It's the same as with the jaguar dream. I see I don't have to worry about you. You come here . . . I see you, ah, isn't it something very unusual to see? How many men would do it?"

"But"—Stick wasn't sure how to say it—"the people of the town went out and shot the jaguar . . ."

"Yes, because it was their enemy again. The sign was over, the sign that you take with you and . . . *Como se dice, aplicar?*"

"Apply?"

"Yes, you apply it in your life to other things. I apply it to you. I think already I don't have to worry, you tell me you not going to the police or to the state attorney. All right, this afternoon I sleep, I have the dream. This evening, finally you come. Well, it's very clear to me then. You see it?"

"But if you never had the dream? . . ."

"I don't know. Shit. I get tired thinking. The dreams make it much easier to know things."

"Did a dream tell you to shoot Rene?" He said it quickly to have said it. Then knew it was all right.

Nestor smiled. "I wait for that. No, it was my intelligence told me. It was too bad. I know Rene, but he was the one Chucky sent. So, if I want to stay in the business, huh? . . . Not be ripped off, take to a cleaner . . ."

"I want to take somebody to a cleaner," Stick said.

Nestor smiled again. "The jaguar came looking for water. Now we find out what you come for."

"Permission," Stick said.

"How do you know to do this?"

"I was in prison. Or I just know, I'm not sure."

"You want that money from Chucky he promise you. Five thousand, uh?"

"Maybe more."

"Why not? If you can do it."

"But not if you say no. It wouldn't be worth it."

"It's your business with Chucky," Nestor said. "Only if you going to turn him in I say no. Because Chucky, they lock him in a room he start talking. He's very crazy, you know that. You give him to the police then I have to go to Colombia for a year or two and I don't want to do that. I like this place, this country, it's very good place to live."

"Make a lot of money here?"

"Yes, all you want."

"You pay income tax?"

"Some. But it's hard, I don't keep good records."

"Is Chucky dangerous?"

"Of course he is. The people he has, no. They're like waiters to him. He's afraid to have strong people, they throw him out, see they don't need him and take over his business. But Chucky himself, yes. Don't let him walk behind you."

"That's what I thought."

"If you know that, well . . . But he's not sitting there waiting to go to the cleaner. You have to know he would like you dead."

"He sent Moke to get me?"

"No, no one sent Moke. He like the shoot-them-up business. He wants everyone to think he's very bad. Sure, so Chucky, he try to buy Moke. And Moke, he's so stupid, from the country, huh? You can buy him for a cowboy hat. But he has no honor in remaining bought. Do you understand?"

"But you keep him around."

Nestor smiled. "Of course. Who knows when I have to send a—what is it, a *maleta*—a bag to someone in payment, huh?" Nestor shook his head, relaxed in his high-backed cane chair, hands hanging limp, diamond reflecting a cold spark of light. "I tell you, in this business, it's very difficult to find people of honor. Or people who have the custom of being generous. Chucky say you're . . . what is it? Enterprising. You sell information about the stock markets. You must be intelligent yourself to do that."

"It's only what I hear."

"Yes? What is it looks good these days?"

"Well," Stick said, "let me see. You know Chi-Chi's, the fast-food chain? It's at eighteen and a quarter. They say it should go up to thirty. Another one, Wendy's, looks good . . ."

Nestor took a pen from his shirt pocket, reached for an envelope among his mail lying on the stone table next to the two revolvers.

"How does it look, that one, McDonald's?"

"I think it's around seventy-five," Stick said.

"Yes, seventy-five and five-eights this morning."

"Yeah, well, I understand it should be up over a hundred pretty soon."

"I don't think so," Nestor said.

"Well, I got a thousand bucks, or will have," Stick said, "thinks it'll be a hundred or better by January."

He watched Nestor mark it down on his envelope.

23

STICK WROTE ON TABLET PAPER: *Although Buck and Charlie are famous and experienced ~~trafficers~~ dealers, they are able to ~~get~~ be believed to be government agents, because of all the confusion there is among the different state and U.S. law enforcement groups that are falling all over each other ~~and~~ not telling each other what they are doing in their work of trying to stop the ~~trafficing~~ dealing in controlled substances and apprehend the alleged . . .*

Jesus.

It was hard.

Why didn't he just say: *Since none of the feds know what the fuck they are doing, they believe that Buck and Charlie are . . .*

Cornell came out of his bedroom, sleep in his eyes. "You doing, writing to your mama?"

"Yeah, got to let her know I'm all right."

Cornell scratched himself idly, down to the bulge in his low-slung briefs. "I didn't hear you come in."

"I made a stop on the way home. Figured no-body'd be looking for me."

"They going out in the boat today. You suppose to meet them up in Lauderdale. I believe the man say five o'clock."

"What suit do I wear?"

"Didn't tell me that. Why don't you surprise him? Wear the tan suit with the black car and see if it freaks him any."

Stick thought of the telephone in the Cadillac, the cord ripped out of the box. He could see Barry picking it up his look of amazement . . .

He said, "Or the gray suit with the tan car?"

"Whatever your imagination tells you," Cornell said. "The maids call early this morning. You hear it?"

"Not a sound."

"They call *me* to tell the madam they don't have a ride today. The car won't start, like they know it ahead of time. Monday, the cook's day off . . . gonna be quiet around here. You got any plans? You could probably go someplace, you wanted to."

"You trying to get rid of me?"

"Man, free time, take it when you can."

It sounded good. Stick wrote two entire pages while Cornell made coffee and had his breakfast. When Cornell went into the bathroom Stick picked up the phone and dialed a number.

"Mary Lou? Hi, it's me . . . Come on—I want to

talk to Katy . . . You sure? . . . The only reason I ask, the last time you thought she was sleeping she wasn't even home." He held the phone at arm's length while Mary Lou commented and he caught only some of the words, like, "Boy, you think you're so smart," and so forth along those lines. Stick brought the phone to his face again and said, "Mary Lou? If I have to get a court order I'm going to talk to Katy whether she's sleeping or what." Mary Lou hung up on him. He called her back and said, "I think we had a bad connection." Mary Lou said, "We sure did," and hung up again. Jesus. A lovely person. The mother of his only child. Himself forty-two and not too likely to have any more, unless . . . He dialed the number again. "Mary Lou? Could I ask you a special favor?" He heard her say, away from the phone, "Nobody," and heard his daughter's voice in the background. He yelled, "Katy!" loud. Very loud. He heard her voice in the background say, "But I want to talk to him . . ."

And heard her say into the phone, "Hi. What're you doing?" As though she really wanted to know.

Stick grinned. "Nothing. What're you doing?"

"Nothing."

"You want to do something?"

"Sure."

"You want to do some typing, take you about an hour maybe?"

"Sure. But I don't have a typewriter."

Stick said, "Honey, that's the least of our worries."

Kyle was having breakfast with Barry on the patio.

Stick watched them from the edge of the acacia trees, near the garage. He would like to avoid Barry this morning, but he wanted to see Kyle. He missed her. When he wasn't with her he imagined and believed she had already changed her mind about him. From the good feeling he saw in her eyes to no feeling. He couldn't hold on to the confidence he felt when he was with her. Was it a sign? He hadn't dreamed about her yet. But maybe she was at the top of the stairs he kept falling down.

Ask Nestor.

The cruiser *Seaweed* rumbled in out of the bay, stark, clean white, sunlight flashing on its glass and bright metal. Barry headed for the dock with his newspapers.

And Kyle was looking toward the house, the garage . . . Stick felt his confidence in place again, as though there had been no hollow feeling, doubts of any kind. He walked across the lawn and she was coming toward him now, coming so close he put his arms around her and was self-conscious for only a moment. It didn't matter if anyone was watching, they had to touch each other, renew the familiar feel.

He said, "Well, I got it straightened out."

"How?"

"I saw Nestor. We had a nice talk."

"Just like that," Kyle said. "You make everything sound easy."

She seemed relieved, though with a hint of suspicion, not knowing what he was doing; left out.

"You saw him last night?"

"I thought I might as well get it over with. I went to see him . . . He's scary, but you can talk to him."

"Ernest?" Looking up at him with those eyes. "Are you playing with me?"

"I would never do that. Spooky things're going on around us, but I think we're safe."

"I'm going home Wednesday or Thursday. After that I'll be in Boston a few days."

He said, "How'll we work it?"

She said, "When it's no longer convenient? I don't know, I'm going to leave it up to you."

He said, "Emma? . . ."

She took a moment to answer him. "What?"

"If I make a lot of money, will you tell me what to do with it?"

She said, "Any time. But I don't think you need me." And seemed to smile then, almost, and said,

"I miss you, Ernest, and I don't know what to do about it."

Stick said, "We'll think of something."

He stood with Cornell and waved as *Seaweed* put out to sea. "It's the custom," the houseman said. "Wave some more. Like the man's going out to kill whales and won't be home till Christmas. Bye, bye. Have fun, y'all. Don't worry about us stay-at-homes . . ."

Cornell was watching television when Stick came out of his room, dressed to go, wearing his tan suitcoat, his gray trousers, a pale blue shirt and black tie. Cornell looked over and blinked.

"Gonna freak the man outta his head. What color car?"

"I haven't decided yet."

"Take the green Mercedes, the lady ain't going nowhere. Yeah, gonna freak him good. So where you off to?"

"The bank first. I want to open an account. I think over at Florida First National."

"That's a good one."

"Then I'm going up to Pompano, see my little girl."

"Beautiful. Have a nice day, man."

* * *

Stick felt like he was on display sitting by the big plate-glass window, people going by on Thirty-sixth Street—he felt them watching him as he filled out the application.

The assistant manager said, "That should do it. Now, let me give you a receipt." He counted the four fifties and the three one-hundred-dollar bills again. To make sure, Stick felt, he hadn't palmed one back in his pocket.

"And what type of business is it, Mr. Norman?"

"Mr. Stickley," Stick said.

"Yes, I beg your pardon." Looking at the application again. "Mr. Stickley, yes. And the company is Norman Enterprises. May I ask what you do?" Looking interested, leaning forward on the desk.

Stick said, "No, I don't think you better."

The assistant manager laughed politely and smiled and waited. Stick thanked him and left with his receipt.

Next—a pay phone.

It didn't occur to Stick until this moment that Chucky's number was not likely to be found in a telephone directory. He looked, before leaving the bank, and it wasn't. He tried Information and was told there was no listing. So he'd have to go back to the Stam residence and hope the number was some-where in Barry's den. He said to himself, see? A simple thing like that. He'd have to get in the habit of writing down what he had to do. And then said, what do you mean, get in the habit? This was a one-shot deal.

Wasn't it?

Stick left the Cadillac in the shady part of the turnaround. He felt like a burglar walking into the house, not hearing a sound. It seemed empty and might be, though he had seen no one outside or expected to. Diane wasn't a sunbather and it wouldn't do much for Cornell to sit out there; though he could have deepened his color up at Butler, chopping weeds. Road gang tan. And look at us now—couple of former inmates walking around here where no hack would ever set foot, no probation or parole officer, none of those people on the good side.

He went into Barry's black den, almost all black but for rich touches of red and gold, the blown-up Barry in black and white looking down from the wall, innocent eyes open wide. Who, me?

Yes, you. Showboater.

But a nice guy, basically. If you had to work for anybody for any length of time and didn't want a boss-type boss.

Barry's leather-bound address book, red Morocco, sat on the black desk. Chucky was not among the Gs. No, he was with the Cs. Chucky Gorman on Sunrise, Fort Lauderdale. Might as well do it now.

Stick dialed.

Lionel answered. He said wait.

When Chucky's voice came on it sounded strange, clear but distant, small.

Stick said, "You know who this is?"

"You want to appraise my furniture, my paintings?"

"I'd like to talk to you . . ."

"Yeah?"

"I mean in private. I can't talk here."

"You want to come up?"

"I was thinking someplace else."

"You can't get it any more private. I mean this is *private*, man."

"It's too high up."

"What're we going to discuss? If it's five grand and I were you I wouldn't come here either."

"No, I understand. I thought it was worth a shot."

"One, that's all. So tell me what we're gonna discuss you're afraid if I don't like it I'll drop you out the fifteen-story window?"

"All I can say—I mean over the phone—if you like it, fine. You don't, okay. Nobody's out anything. But it's the kind of deal could interest you. I happened to find out about it . . . I thought, well, I'll lay it on you. You like it, then you know I'm not holding nothing against you."

"You think I give a shit if you are?"

"You know what I mean. I can't explain it, I got to show you."

"You trying to sell me a stock tip?"

"No, it's not like that, but"—he dropped his voice—"it's from that source, if you know what I mean."

"Something Barry's into?"

"You got it."

"Where you want to meet? 'Cross the street?"

"That's fine. How about three o'clock? Around in there."

"I'll think about it."

Stick said, "That's all I ask, Mr. Gorman." Which might have been the most difficult thing he ever said in his life. He hated to lie.

A typewriter . . .

Right there, trim little Olivetti portable electric. He was not disappointed when he could not find the case; he walked out into the hall carrying the typewriter in front of him, and stopped.

What he saw was real. Cornell carrying a silver tray, silver decanter with a long, delicately curved spout, two silver goblets. He had come out of the hall from the kitchen, turned into this main, lateral hallway about twenty feet from Stick—turned before seeing him—and was now walking toward the bedroom wing.

What was unreal, Cornell wore a gold headband around his moderate natural and that was it. Otherwise the man was naked, showing a pronounced demarcation between back and buttocks, burnt sienna over caramel.

Stick followed—he would say he was unable to stop himself—drawn along with the typewriter to Diane's bedroom . . . cautiously through the room to a view of the atrium, the enclosed garden between the Stams' master bedrooms.

Stick remained inside the room, at the edge of drawn gold draperies, with a clear view of Cornell dropping to one knee, head bowed, offering the silver wine service to Diane, who sat on something Stick could not see, hidden by the folds of her transparent white negligee, her pale body naked beneath.

Diane said, "Arise, slave. And as you offer the cup, say how you will delight me with rites of barbaric pleasure."

Cornell rose, placed the tray on a low pedestal next to Diane. He poured champagne into the goblets, bowed as he handed one to Diane and said, "Yes, O Queen. What I am going to perform up one royal side of you and down the other, in the dark and savage land where I come from is called . . . the Freaky Deaky."

Diane said, "Let the rites begin."

Cornell turned and came into the bedroom. He walked past Stick to a stereo system, snapped in a cassette and turned it on. As the Dazz Band came out in full strength, began to funk its way through *Let It Whip*, he turned up the volume, started back to the atrium and stopped. Cornell looked directly at Stick holding the typewriter.

Said, "Come bearing a gift, huh? You want to be a barbarian rapist or a slave that gives pleasure?"

Stick said, "I got to go up the road . . ."

Cornell said, "It's cool. We catch you next time."

24

STICK GOT TO WOLFGANG'S AT ten after three, came
into the dimness, the beer smell, with a thick
manila envelope under his arm. He saw Chucky
and Lionel right away, at a table in back talking to
the guy who owned the place. Stick went up to the
bar and waited for Bobbi to notice him. There—the
big smile. This girl always made him feel good.

"Well, how you doing?"

"Not too bad."

"What're you up to now?" Nodding at his outfit.
"You still working for Barry?"

"Yeah, for a while anyway."

"How's your daughter?"

"I'm glad you asked," Stick said. "You should see
her type." He held up the nine-by-twelve manila envelope, placed it on the bar. "Fourteen years old, she
could get a job in an office. Typed about ten pages
for me, no mistakes. I offered to pay her"—he
seemed both proud of this and surprised—"she
wouldn't take it."

"Well, of course not. You're her dad."

"But I made her. Since I'm about seven years behind in her allowance."

Bobbi said, "Keep your shirt buttoned, Stickley,
your heart'll fall out."

Lionel came over while Bobbi was pouring him a
bourbon. He'd wanted to have a quick one or two
first, but Lionel said, "What you doing? Chucky's
waiting for you."

Stick turned on the stool with his surprised look.
"Yeah? Where?"

Chucky was wearing his fishing cap that had an
extra-long peak, tan cotton with the restful smoked-
plastic visor he could pull down eye level and turn
day to gray evening. He felt no pain or anxiety—he
was moving product, already most of the load
Nestor had delivered—and he did not see his life at
the present time in abnormal danger. If he had to tell
what he felt at the moment—watching Ernest Stickley coming from the bar in sporty tan and gray
attire—he would say curiosity. With a little suspicion
thrown in to keep him on his toes. Living in what
Chucky believed was the rip-off capital of the world
could do that to you. Make you squint at life.

"I'm sorry I'm late," Stick said, holding the envelope to his chest, his drink in the other hand.

He glanced around the room as he sat down.

Chucky noted this and said, "Nobody here but afternoon drunks, a few tourists and maybe a sporty opportunist." Watching Stick closely, testing him with, "I called Barry this morning . . ."

Stick said, "Oh, shit," like all was lost.

"But he was gone," Chucky said, grinning now. He saw Stick nervous, leaning in close to the table, looking so different than he did that first time.

"Jesus," Stick said, "I thought you understood. Mr. Stam finds out about this I'm out of work."

"Well, let's have it," Chucky said. "Whatcha got?"

Stick had the envelope in front of him on the table. He pressed a hand on it as Chucky reached over.

"I don't think you better read it here."

"You picked this place."

"Well, just look at the first part. Okay?" He brought the prospectus out of the envelope and handed it to Chucky.

A familiar feel, familiar words, most of them. Chucky said, "You putting me on? This is the same shit as yesterday."

Stick shook his head. "Look at it good. Norman Enterprises . . ."

"Yeah?"

"You see the title? *Scam.* Turn to the next page. No, the next one. See how it works? Thirty-five limited partners putting in seventy-two five each?"

"Yeah?"

"It's *almost* the same deal. But it's different. They worked on it yesterday, Barry and Leo Firestone, till late last night. They got a different story now. About a couple of dealers named Charlie and Buck . . ."

"You don't mean to tell me."

"They pull the all-time Miami dope scam. Walk in and con the Feds out of forty million bucks worth of pure coke they'd taken off some Colombians. After a lot of action and sex, dirty words— be a minus R—they have a retirement party and invite all the narcs to it. It's a comedy, only based on real life."

"Charlie and Buck?"

"Cool guys. Witty. Barry wants a lot of sex in it."

"Yeah?"

"They did the story fast, you know. Leo says rough but inspired. It sounds pretty good to me."

Chucky flipped through pages. "Say the offering's different now?"

"They took the tax fraud out of it. Now it's a straight deal like any other offering. You put in seven-two five and you and the other investors own half the movie. Not twenty percent like before, half. It's all in there. They put the investment money in Florida First National and if they don't make the picture you get it all back with interest."

"So when's Leo going to pitch this one?" He saw Stick glance around again.

"What do you think I sneaked it out for—give you a peek if you're going to see it anyway?"

"That was my next question."

"He's not going to show it, he's afraid to."

"Who is?"

"Leo Firestone—who're we talking about? He finds out who some of Barry's friends are yesterday, the guy's scared shitless. Won't have anything to do with anybody that's dealing or can't give him an authorized cashier's check on the investment without moving a kilo of flake. I mean the guy's scared to death at how close he came, talking about spics and scum . . . You heard him."

"Man didn't seem too bright."

"Yeah, well, his movies might be shitty but they gross big. All over the world. That's why Barry's so anxious to go in business with him. Have some fun and the dough keeps coming in for years. No risk at all the way Barry sees it."

"Yeah?"

"I suppose he's wrong sometimes, but, I don't know . . . So Barry had to promise Leo okay, he'd leave yesterday's group out of it. Maybe contact a couple of big shooters he knows, that's all. That's why they're using one of Leo's other company names. In case anybody hears about it. It gets in the paper nobody'll see it came out of the other deal."

"Fucking Barry . . ." Chucky said.

"He can't help it. See, Leo came down here as a

favor to Barry, made the pitch. He wanted to raise the dough in New York."

"Leo did?"

"Yeah, so that's what he went back to do. He told Barry—I heard him—get your couple or three guys quick, 'cause I'm going to move on this right away, button it up."

"How quick?"

"From what I understand you got to get in right now. But that's only what I heard. It doesn't say anything about a time limit in there."

Chucky leafed through the prospectus. "It looks like the same one exactly. Most of it."

"Yeah, all the legal and technical stuff. What's changed is the story and the amount you invest. Barry says all the rest is boilerplate."

"Subscription application," Chucky said. "That part's different." He pulled the bill of his cap lower on his eyes, saw Stick in a misty gray wash, most of the tables empty behind him, not many at the bar, the patrons still sober, quiet: a restful atmosphere conducive to clear thinking, spotting false notes and shifty moves. "What else?"

"What do you mean, what else? Read it, see if you want to go in."

"You just said the guy doesn't want me in. The fucker tries to sell a fraudulent deal, but he won't associate with certain types?"

"I think if you hand him the money," Stick said,

"he's not going to turn you down. You know, once he sees he's not going to have any trouble . . . maybe."

"But he won't take cash. Didn't you just tell me that?"

"Write him a check."

"I don't write any in that amount. Seventy thousand."

"Seventy-two five."

"Never put more than nine grand and change in the bank. I'm referring to cash," Chucky said. "And they won't know how much you got."

Stick said, "It was an idea." He said after a moment, "Wait. Firestone's in New York, I took him to the airport this morning. But they have an office in the Eden Roc and I'm pretty sure his girl's there. You know the one?"

"The skinny broad."

"Take her the money, see what she says. The address and phone number are in there. I think the second page . . . Suite fifteen-oh-three, something like that. It's where you send the subscription agreement, Norman Enterprises Production Office."

Chucky leafed through the prospectus another moment or so before he got up and walked around the table.

"Where you going?"

Chucky completed his turn, providing his need for activity, motion, as his mind worked. He sat down again and said, "Something smells. I never heard of raising money and keeping it quiet or leaving people out . . ."

"If you got more people wanting in than units to sell," Stick began.

But now Chucky was saying, "How about Kyle? She know about this?"

"I don't recall she said much."

"These two guys are putting together a deal and she doesn't open her mouth? After she neutered Leo the day before?"

"She must've liked it."

"I better give Barry a call."

"You do," Stick said, "I'm back on the road."

Chucky grinned at him. "You believe I give a shit? I'm dying to know what you're up to."

Stick said, "Let's forget it." He picked up the prospectus. "I made a mistake."

Chucky squinted beneath the plastic bill. "I don't see what you get out of it. *Scam*, that's what it sounds like, all right, but I can't figure the angle . . . You pick up an old prospectus Leo tried to peddle when he was Norman Enterprises? My mouth is suppose to water, envy gets in my eyes, Barry running off with another winner, and for your trouble I let you have . . . what? You're still going for that five grand, aren't you?"

Stick said, "You ever do time?"

" 'Nam. That's time and a half."

"You don't know what you're talking about,"

Stick said. "I'd have gone to Vietnam in a bathing suit. I know you can die in war, but worse things can happen to you in Jackson, Michigan. Sometimes you do favors for people so they don't defile you or piss in your food. Like a peace offering or buying insurance. You understand what I'm saying?" Chucky was looking away. "All I want is to be left alone."

"We'll get it settled," Chucky said.

He was looking toward the terrace at Kyle. She had come in from outside and stood there a moment before she saw them.

Stick said, "You're early. It isn't even four o'clock yet." He had the prospectus in the envelope again and was standing. "I'll get the car."

Chucky said, "Now don't rush off." He was up, pulling a chair out for Kyle.

She said, "We may be a while yet. Barry and Rorie are having a fight. And there's no possibility of it ending because they don't know what they're fighting about."

"Clash of personalities," Chucky said. "Where they, outside?"

"On the boat." She looked at Stick. "You might as well sit down." Then smiled at him. "You look nice." When he didn't smile back her expression changed. She glanced at Chucky, and Stick could see she was beginning to get the picture. Lionel brought Chucky a drink. Kyle shook her head saying she didn't care for anything, looking at Stick again. This time he gave her a weak smile.

Chucky said to her, "Well, how're you and Leo getting along? You make up?"

"He went back to New York," Kyle said. She glanced at Stick and he gave her another smile, on and off.

Chucky said, "Too bad that deal didn't work out. I think if they'd turned the story around, made the two guys like, oh, a couple happy hustlers . . . You know what I mean? Make it a comedy."

"And called it *Scam*?" Kyle said. "How about if they con the customs agents out of millions of dollars worth of stuff?"

Chucky was staring at her.

"And they stage a retirement party somewhere, Nassau, and invite all the customs guys . . ."

Chucky said, subdued, "That doesn't sound too bad . . . Change the offering to get the fraud out of it?"

"I would," Kyle said. "Maybe lower the price of the units . . ."

"Change the names of the two guys?" Chucky asked.

Kyle nodded. "Definitely. You want names that sound fun-loving but have character."

Chucky said, "How about Charlie and Buck?"

"Not bad." She was nodding again, giving Stick a look then as she got up. "If you'll excuse me . . . We've got a dinner engagement tonight and Barry's going to sulk all through it if he and Aurora don't kiss and make up. I'm going to see what I can do." She said to Stick, "You could get the car. Just give me a few minutes."

Stick sat back, watching that wonderful girl making her way through the tables. He was aware of more noise in the place, more people, music playing now.

Chucky said, "I pay her a consulting fee. She's suppose to advise me."

"I think she did," Stick said. "Look, I'm not going to beg you. You want Barry to have all the fun or it's too rich for your blood, forget I ever mentioned it." He pushed the manila envelope toward Chucky. "But if you want in you better move."

Chucky pushed his chair back to get up but continued to sit there. "Keeping it to themselves," he said.

"Trying to."

"I'd have to get them to take cash."

"Tempt 'em."

Chucky got up. He said, "Stay here," and walked out toward the foyer.

Stick went over to the bar and got another bourbon. Looking down the aisle, he could see Chucky out by the front entrance talking on the phone. The tricky part; all Stick could do was wait.

"Broad was very cagey," Chucky said, sitting down again.

Stick acted surprised. "You called the Roc?"

"She said Norman Enterprises and I asked for Leo. She goes, who is this, please? I told her I had spoken to Leo about investing in his new one, *Scam*, and she goes, oh, well I'm the only one here right now and would I like to leave my name. Very cagey."

"You tell her?"

"I hung up on her and called Florida First National."

"You did?"

"It's true, they got an account there."

"They move fast," Stick said.

"I'm thinking," Chucky said, "sign the subscription agreement, get it over to the Eden Roc . . . they see my name they might make up an excuse . . ."

"They might."

"But not if the money's already put in their account."

"Sounds good to me."

"I deposit cash, the bank reports it to the IRS, but it doesn't affect me any."

"I don't know anything about that," Stick said.

They saw Barry coming in now, his arm around Aurora's shoulder, Kyle following them.

Chucky said, "Possessive son of a bitch. Selfish. Spoiled rotten . . ."

They watched Barry walk up to the bar and point a finger at Bobbi. "What's the last thing goes through a bug's mind—"

Bobbi's smile faded; she tried to get it back looking eager, interested.

"I tell you that one? . . . I tell you about the Polack who think's Peter Pan's a wash basin in a cathouse? . . . The difference between erotic and kinky? Erotic you use a feather, kinky you use the whole chicken?"

Stick said to Chucky, "But he sure has fun."

Chucky said, "Jesus, get him outta here." Then said, "Wait a minute. On the subscription agreement? . . ."

"Yeah?"

"What should I put where it says 'Occupation'?"

"Put down Big Shooter," Stick said and saw Chucky actually consider it and shrug. It always surprised Stick, what you could tell people and they believed. Chucky was leaning over the table on his arms. He seemed relieved, as though now everything was all right between them: a couple of friends talking.

"I got to get out."

"I do too," Stick said. He put his hands on the table to rise.

"I'm pushing it now," Chucky said, confiding. "You can't stay in this ten years. Too many people, they start out they want a piece of you, then they want the whole thing."

Stick said, "Well . . ."

"People you deal with, you don't sign anything in this business, a subscription agreement . . ."

"I got to go," Stick said.

"You ask me if I did time? This's doing time, man. Same thing. You can't do what you want, you can't fucking *move*. Try and get some space—you know what I mean? To breathe in? You got to pay for it, buy people . . . I don't get out now, shit . . ."

Stick said, "So get out."

"They don't leave you alone. People like Nestor, Moke . . . I started out, I was quick, man. Now it's like . . . it's hard to explain. I'm still moving but it's like you cut off a snake's head, or a chicken, its body keeps moving, but its head doesn't know what the fuck's going on. It sees the body moving, flopping around, but it can't *feel* anything . . . You see a choice?"

Stick didn't say anything. Looking at him, hearing him, his tone, maybe beginning to understand Chucky for the first time.

"I got no choice. I stay in I get eaten up or I get picked up. Same thing. I get blown away by some crazy fucker like Moke or I get arraigned, sooner or later it'll happen, and they lock me up. You know how long I'd last? I wouldn't ever come up for trial. I wouldn't make it through—what is it, they can hold you like seventy-two hours? I wouldn't make it through the fucking *night*. They lock me up . . . I'd find a way. Bring in the kind of cap, man, concealed on you that'll set you free. There're ways . . ."

"Well, you been lucky so far," Stick said. "You must know what you're doing."

"I been lucky, sure. You got to be lucky. But I been stoking the fire, too, man, all the time stoking my fire . . . Well, it's burning out. I'm tired . . ."

Stick watched him straighten then, pushing back in his chair, his vacant gaze showing a faint gleam of hope.

"So I'm glad you came along," Chucky said. "You might not know it, but you're helping me get out."

Stick kept looking at him. He didn't know what to say. He didn't want to feel sorry for him. It wouldn't make sense to feel sorry for him . . .

He said, "I got to go."

He couldn't understand why people who lived in a place worth a couple million would go someplace else to enjoy themselves. He drove Barry, Diane and Kyle to Leucadendra in the Rolls and brought them home again at eleven, an uneventful trip both ways. When the Stams went inside Kyle walked out into darkness, to the seawall, and Stick followed.

She said, "So Chucky thinks *Scam* is for real. But what happens now?"

"What'd you tell me? Get 'em to believe they'd be a fool to pass it up?"

"You gave him a prospectus?"

"The old one, the one you showed me, but changed here and there."

She looked puzzled. "And he believes the investment's only five thousand?"

"Little more than that."

"How much more?"

"Seventy-two five."

"Seventy-two *thousand*?"

"I had to make it look real."

"My God, I'm helping you commit fraud!"

She was facing him, the lights of Miami behind her and he couldn't see her eyes, though in the tone of her voice there was something more than amazement.

"I thought, in the bar, you were talking about a few thousand, what he owes you."

"Yeah . . ."

"I could see what Chucky was doing, looking for some kind of verification, trying to be sly about it . . ."

"That's right."

"So I played along. What else was I going to do? You're sitting there in the middle."

"How does the amount change anything?"

It stopped her. "I shouldn't have come to the table. I saw you with him, I should've known."

"Sunday you wanted to help me."

"I know I did, but it was different then, exciting. Chucky was the bad guy . . ."

"He still is," Stick said. "He's so bad he'll never miss it."

"That's not the point. You're trying to swindle a client of mine out of seventy-two thousand dollars and I'm helping you."

"I appreciate it, too."

"But I *can't*. He pays me to look after his money."

"Well, he probably won't go for it anyway."

"I'm going to have to talk to him about it," Kyle said, "say *some*thing. Advise against it . . ."

"Why don't we just, for the fun of it," Stick said, "see if it works. If he pays up and you still feel sorry for him—"

"It isn't that at all, it's fraud."

"Okay, whatever the reason. If it bothers you too much I'll give it back. But let's see what happens."

"You promise?"

"On my honor," Stick said.

25

CHUCKY ARRIVED AT Florida First National, corner of Biscayne Boulevard and Thirty-Sixth, a few minutes past one. Lionel, carrying the suitcase, followed him in and waited as Chucky looked from the teller windows to the bank executives at their desks in the fenced-off area. He wondered how they could work, being out in plain sight like that, people walking by outside looking at them.

"We don't want to give it to a teller," Chucky said. "Won't have the right effect."

Lionel didn't know what he was talking about or that he was about to witness one of Chucky's fantasies come to life. Chucky took the suitcase now and Lionel followed him over to the assistant manager's desk, which was by the big plate-glass window.

Chucky said, "I'm here to make a deposit."

He snapped the suitcase open, turned it over as he raised it high, dumped banded packets of currency on the assistant manager's desk, all hundred-dollar bills, and gave him a big smile.

"Seventy-two thousand five hundred dollars, pay to the account of Norman Enterprises. We're in show business."

The assistant manager said, "Oh, really?"

"He wasn't too surprised," Chucky said to Lionel, crossing the Julia Tuttle on their way to the Eden Roc.

"We're in Miami," Lionel said.

They went up to Suite 1503, Chucky with his signed subscription agreement in a plain white envelope, and knocked on the door. He waited and knocked again.

"She's still at lunch," Chucky said. "Though to look at her you wouldn't think it would take long."

They went down to the lounge and had a few, returned in an hour to knock on the door again and waited in silence.

"I'll slip it under the door," Chucky said. "It might even be better if I do it that way."

They stopped at the main desk just to make sure. The clerk went to look, came back and said it seemed the party checked out this morning. Chucky said, "Gone on a trip to the Apple, huh? But they kept the suite, didn't they? The production office?" The clerk said no, checked out and didn't leave a forwarding address.

Chucky said to Lionel, "I want to go home right now."

He needed a secure atmosphere in which to think. Maybe scream, if he had to.

Avilanosa had some fun with Moke when he came to get his revolvers. He said, "Let the man take your pistols, huh? Why you do that?"

Moke would like to have gotten out without seeing Avilanosa today. See Nestor, pick up his guns and leave. But Nestor was resting, not to be disturbed—most likely in a deep nod—and his father-in-law was in charge of the house.

Moke said, "Come on, gimme 'em."

"What, these pistols?" Avilanosa said, offering them, then raising them over his head as Moke reached to take them.

"Come on, don't fuck around."

"Oh, listen to him, the *pistolero*," Avilanosa said, "who lose his pistols. Let them be taken away from him. Here."

Moke reached. Now, as Avilanosa raised the guns over his head, Moke shoved him hard. Avilanosa stumbled against the stone patio table, smiling, not appearing to be angry, playing with Moke. He said, "Here." But now Moke wouldn't take them, so Avilanosa placed the revolvers on the stone table and stepped aside. He waited for Moke to pick them up and work the barrels into his waist. At that moment he stepped toward Moke, chopped him with a back-hand fist that was like a club, caught Moke across the face and sent him sprawling in the grass.

Moke came up with the nickel-plated Mag drawn and Avilanosa shook his head. He said, "You must not be feeling so good, you want to die. You should take some medicine, go to sleep."

Moke lowered the revolver to his side.

Avilanosa said, "You have the truck again you always lose? Man, you lose your pistols and your truck, uh? Get in that truck and go see Chucky."

"What for?"

"Scare him. Time to scare him so he don't forget to pay. You think you can scare him good?"

Moke walked away from Avilanosa, toward the door in the wooden gate that sealed off the drive-way, Avilanosa's voice following him, pushing him: "Try see if you can scare him and not lose your pistols again . . ."

Barry told Stick that morning all four cars were ready for an oil change and lube; take them over to the Amoco station on 125th, he had a charge there. Stick said, "One at a time?" Seeing it as an all-day job.

Barry said, "No, you hook 'em end to end like a

choo-choo, for Christ sake, of *course* one at a time. Get 'em gassed and washed, too."

It sounded like make-work, which could take two hours a car, easy. While Barry and Kyle spent the morning in his den shuffling through papers and doing figures. Stick began with the Lincoln, took it over, brought it back and they were still in there. He couldn't see a way to get Kyle alone. He called the bank around noon, gave his account number and said he wanted to verify his balance. The woman's voice said, exactly five hundred dollars and no cents.

He drove the Rolls over. They were busier now at the station and it took two and a half hours, round trip. He called the bank again, gave his number and said he'd like to verify his balance. A different woman's voice this time said, "Mr. Norman?"

"Mr. Stickley."

"Yes, that balance, Mr. Stickley, is exactly . . . let's see, seventy-three thousand dollars and no cents. Nice round figure."

He said, "Jesus Christ."

The woman said, "Pardon me?"

He had never had a feeling like this before in his life. He was worth at this moment seventy-three thousand dollars. He had thought up an idea with a little help, had talked to a guy for about a half hour selling him on the idea, and he was now worth seventy-three thousand dollars. The same thing they were doing in there in Barry's den, the same kind of thing, making money without working. It seemed the way to do it. He wanted to tell Kyle, but they were still at it.

He wanted to tell Cornell, somebody. But when he saw Cornell he thought better of it and tried to appear calm.

"Well, what're you up to today?"

"Cleaning silver."

"What is this, clean-up, fix-up day?"

"Got to keep us busy, man."

"Slave labor," Stick said.

Cornell grinned at him. "That slave duty can wear you down, man. But you get into it, it's kinda fun. You know what I'm saying? Lose yourself. Be anything you want."

"You do other . . . different things like that?"

"Mostly the queen and the slave."

"What's she the queen of?"

"Queen—I don't know exactly—queen of the afternoon with nothing to do. Queen of the Jelly Bellies. I never seen a lady wished so much she was a queen."

"Well," Stick said, "she looked like a pretty good one."

What he thought of doing, go in the den and tell Barry he was quitting. Except he had to talk to Kyle first. He took the Cadillac over to the station, thought of the movie girl, Jane, as he waited and called the Eden Roc.

Gone.

He hung up with the feeling it had been close. That if the timing hadn't been perfect he'd still be worth five hundred instead of seventy-three thousand. He said the number over and over again. He would like to sit down in a quiet, clean place without distractions, wrenches and tire irons hitting cement, and think about it. Prepare a speech. Hope that Kyle, later, would be in a realistic frame of mind. If she wasn't, deliver the speech: why it would be wrong . . . morally wrong to give dope money back to a dealer so he could buy more dope, corrupt more people and not pay any income tax on it. When on the other hand he would use the money wisely. How? . . . Christ, any way he wanted! Buy things. Buy a car. Buy things for Katy, clothes. Buy a truck, buy a business. Buy Wild Turkey instead of Early Times. There were wonderful ways to spend money that he and Frank had only begun to experience when their hundred days ended, abruptly.

Back and forth, the Stickley shuttle. He wanted to tell the Amoco guy with *Steve* on his shirt, but he didn't. It was nearly six by the time he got back with the Mercedes, the last one. Twenty-four hours since he'd pulled the deal of his life.

The Rolls was not in the garage.

He got out of the Mercedes, walked over to the edge of the grass. Barry was alone on the patio, sitting at the umbrella table with a drink and newspaper. Stick walked down there.

"All through."

"That wasn't too bad, was it?"

"No, sir, not at all." Why was it easier to say having seventy-three thousand dollars?

"I noticed the Rolls is gone."

"I let Kyle have it."

"Oh . . ." Could he ask? He had to. "Where'd she go?"

Barry looked up at him, frowning. "What?"

"I said, where'd she go?"

"That's what I thought you said. She went to see Mr. Gorman."

"When?"

"What's the matter with you?"

"*When?*"

"Little while ago. What *is* this?"

"Did he call her or she call him?"

"He called."

"And she left right away?"

"Yeah, soon after. The hell's wrong with you?"

Stick turned and ran.

Barry stood up and yelled at him. It didn't do any good. Stick was in the Mercedes now wheeling out of the drive.

26

MOKE RODE UP TO FIFTEEN, all the way to the top, thinking: it was big time working for Nestor; but what did he get out of it other than a bunch of shit from Avilanosa? Thinking: if a turd like Chucky could have his own world up here, live how he wanted acting like a weird and nervous woman, then why couldn't Eddie Moke have it too? Or take what Chucky had from him?

Lionel opened the door and Moke opened his worn-out leather jacket to show the pearl grip of his 44.

"You see it?"

Lionel nodded. "You high, huh?"

"I been higher. Climb up another line or two. Nestor's coming to visit. He don't want none of you guys around here."

"It's okay," Lionel said.

"I'll watch Chucky he don't come to harm."

"I better tell him," Lionel said.

"No, I'll tell him. What's he doing?"

Lionel didn't answer. He said after a moment, "You going to kill him?"

It surprised Moke, made him curious. "What if I said that was the deal? What would you do?"

"Go to Miami, see my old woman," Lionel said. "When do we come back?"

"Later on tonight'd be okay."

"There's somebody in there with him. A woman," Lionel said.

"Don't worry about us," Moke said. "We be fine."

He stepped in, bringing Lionel out and closed the door on him. Moke knew the layout, enough of it. He walked down the front hall and turned left at the first door, Chucky's den with the phone deal and the hats . . . but no Crested Beaut or Bullrider hanging up there—the son of a bitch, the man's time was coming. Moke set the white yachting cap down on his eyes, strolled past the balcony glass catching some reflection to the living room door. He stooped to peer through the spy hole.

Kyle said, "Would you sit down? Please. And listen. You haven't heard anything I've said. You've got your mind made up."

Chucky moved. "You haven't said anything

makes sense." And moved back, side to side, sway-ing. "You don't know anything about the deal, but you know what the story's about."

"No, I said it was a misunderstanding."

"Honey, I know when I'm getting fucked, I get this tingling sensation different than my other twitches and tingles . . ."

"Listen to me, okay? Just listen." She began slowly then. "He picked up an old prospectus, it was Leo's original offering, and thought we were going with it."

"Why would he think that?"

"He must've heard us talking about revising the story. It was a possibility . . ."

"You *told* me the story in the bar."

"I thought he was telling you what he'd heard. I was playing along. You know how you take a story and elaborate on it? . . . The way I under-stand it, he was trying to do you a favor, that's all."

Chucky glanced toward the door to his den and back to Kyle. "The first time you came here you said, you want to invest in a movie? You had it in mind *then*."

"A movie, any movie. I wasn't talking about this one. Believe me, Barry's not involved in any kind of film project."

"Then I want to know what's going on . . ."

* * *

Moke slammed the door behind him to get their attention. He said, "I do, too. What're you people arguing about? Chucky, you're not suppose to fight with women." He nodded to Kyle on the sofa. "How you doing?" And looked at Chucky again. "I think you need your medicine."

Chucky said, "Who let you in? . . . You want to see me, wait in the other room. And take that hat off."

Moke adjusted the yachting cap over his eyes. He liked to see the edge of the peak squared straight across his vision. It meant the person had it together and was not prone to accept bullshit of any kind. He said to Chucky, putting his hand in the pocket of his jacket and bringing it out in a fist, "Yeah, it must be medicine time how you're acting." He opened his hand. Two white tablets dropped to the floor from the mound of pills he held.

"Got the real stuff here, the white tabs," Moke said. "Some reds, that bootleg shit . . . What're these blue ones for?"

Chucky started toward him. "Gimme those . . ."

Moke shoved his hand back into the pocket, left it there and pulled open his jacket with his other hand.

"See it?"

Chucky said, "I don't have time for you right now. Come on, gimme those."

"I cleaned out your pill drawer so you won't OD on me, have to take you to the hospital . . ."

Kyle stood up. She said to Chucky, "I'll see you another time."

"Stay there," Moke said. "We like your company." He said to Chucky, "They have to pump you out, man, it'd take a dredge, wouldn't it? Get way down there in your bottomland." Moke was having fun. He liked this smart, good-looking girl as an audience. She looked right at him and listened, as she was doing now. It was fun to act up in front of her. Moke walked over to the glass doors to the balcony, flicked off the catch and slid one of the doors all the way open.

He had their attention.

"Sun going down, starting to cool, huh? Best time of the day."

Chucky said, "Tell me what you want, partner."

"Don't call me that less you mean it."

Chucky edged toward him and stopped. "Tell me."

"I want you to be healthy," Moke said, brought his hand out and looked at the pills. "I don't think you need these no more."

There were two Cadillacs and Barry's Rolls in the high-rise circular drive, Lionel Oliva standing against the first car as the Mercedes came up the ramp toward him. Stick swung in past him and parked on the downgrade.

Lionel waited for him.

"You know Kyle McLaren? She upstairs?"

Lionel said, "You know Eddie Moke?"

Stick hesitated. "What's going on?"

"He's high, man. Got a funny look. He told me to get out."

Stick walked away from him toward the entrance, stopped and came back.

"I think he's going to kill him," Lionel said.

"You're his bodyguard . . ."

"No, it's not my business, this kind of thing."

"You have a key to the place?"

Lionel looked at him but didn't answer.

"Let me use it."

"You're crazy," Lionel said.

"Gimme the key."

Moke showed Chucky the three white tablets in the palm of his hand. "This the good stuff?"

Chucky shuffled, shook his head sadly and looked at Moke again. "You having fun?"

"How'd you know?"

"Take one. Mellow you down so you recognize your old pard."

"I got my old pard by the yang, ain't I?" Moke

said. He stepped out on the balcony. "Watch."
Closed his hand on the pills and threw them out
over the rail.

Chucky moved a step toward him and Moke
brought out the nickel-plated Mag in a practiced
draw, effortless, a gesture.

"Like the policeman says, freeze, motherfucker . . .
Hey, you know what? I never said that before.
Freeze, motherfucker. Maybe I ought to be a cop. A
narc type, huh? Confiscate the dope"—digging into
his pocket again—"and give it the deep six," fling-
ing out his fist with a handful of caps and tabs, red,
white and blue visible for only a moment, dots
against the dull sky.

Chucky wanted to run. He felt he could run right
through the wall, no problem, pull open his pill
drawer . . . there were some in the kitchen too. No,
he'd eaten them. Ones in the bedroom, eaten. Bathroom, eaten. Down in the car, maybe. No, eaten. If
there were no more in the pill drawer Moke had all
he owned, a pocketful and dropping from between
his fingers on the balcony, couple of red ones, the
bootleg street, 'ludes. He tried to say to Moke as
calmly as he could, as a statement and nothing else,
"What're you picking on me for?" But it didn't
sound at all the way he wanted it to. It sounded like

he was starting to cry. Now Moke was saying it back to him the same way, whining, "What're you picking on me for?" With his ugly mouth curling, his ugliness oozing out of him. "What're you picking on me for?" He didn't want to scream. God, he didn't want to. But Moke's hand was coming out of the pocket again. He could see Moke making a habit of this once he started. Doing it any time he liked. Having fun. Doing it when he wasn't down at the dump shooting gulls. Doing it when he hadn't anything else on. He did *not* want to scream. He wished he could tell somebody, explain how he felt. But as Moke said something looking away—looking at what, it didn't matter—he did scream and rushed at him to grab that hand held in the air . . .

A distraction—and Moke's attention was on Stick coming into the room like he was late for supper, then stopping dead as though he'd found himself in the wrong place or had busted into a surprise party. Look, there was surprise all over his face.

Moke said, "Well, look it here . . ."

Then was instantly inspired, seeing his prize, and said like a happy give-away show emcee, "Well, come on down!" And felt air go out of him . . .

*   *   *

Chucky hit him with his body, arm raised reaching for the fist holding the pills. The force, the impact took them to the iron railing that came to Chucky's navel the times he leaned over it and stared at toy boats down on the Intracoastal. This time his side struck the rail, still reaching to grab the hand. But it was empty now, the hand clawing at his shirt, the other hand hitting at him with the gun barrel. Chucky screamed again or was still screaming without beginning or end, holding this squirming leather smelly thing, lifting Moke up, Moke twisting on him, and got Moke over the rail, his upper body and his head hanging down, hat gone, gun barrel banging on wrought iron now and somebody yelling at him—he heard the voice— somebody yelling to put him down. He had Moke by the legs and would put him down, all right, all the way down. He was between Moke's legs and saw the leather arm with the nickel-plate come through the iron bars, felt it against his shin and he raised his sneaker and brought it down hard to step on the gun, hold it against the floor. He raised the two legs, slippery, greasy jeans, cowboy boots up by his face and said down to Moke behind the bars, "Give me my pills!" Again, so different than he expected to hear it, breathless, on the edge of panic. He saw Moke's hand grope at the pocket, dig inside. He saw Moke's hand come out and saw pills falling in colors, pouring out of the upside-down pocket, Moke opening his hand to hold an iron bar and those pills going too, gone.

Somebody touched him on the shoulder. Chucky felt it. He twisted enough to see Stick on the balcony and yelled at him, "Get away from me!"

He heard Stick say, "Let me help you . . ."

Help him what? He yelled again, "Get away from me or I'll put him over!"

And didn't see Stick again.

He had to get his breath—in and out, in and out, slowly. It didn't do much good. He felt like he was running. He held Moke's ankles, raising them as he went down to his knees and sat back on his sneakers to look at Moke's upside-down face through the bars, Chucky breathing in and out, in and out.

He said, "How you doing, pard?"

Believing he was in control but hearing the words as a raw, breathless sound. It did him good to look at Moke, at Moke's eyes bugged out, face livid, straining, veins coming blue on his forehead. He wanted to tell Moke, "Don't move," and go get his camera. Lighten up the situation. But his shoulders and arms ached and what he wanted was to end it. He said, "You had enough?" He said, "You gonna be a good boy?"

Moke said, straining, but making the words clear enough, "Fuck you."

Chucky stared and began to experience a feeling

of deep sadness, despair creeping over him. He was tired, his arms ached . . . What he should do was jump up, move—let's go!—grab a hat, psych himself, be somebody, *any*body. But with the sad feeling he knew that if he tried even to scream, to lose himself in the effort of emptying his lungs, the sound would come out a moan. He stared at Moke's upside-down face, hair hanging as though electrified. Looked into blunt eyes, unforgiving, that would never change. He thought, oh well. Raised Moke's legs above his head and gave a push.

Moke did it for him. Screamed.

They watched him eat pills he found on the floor of the balcony. They watched him pick up the revolver and come in, closing the glass door, closing out whatever was outside. He sat down in a deep chair, holding the gun in his lap.

Kyle waited. She swallowed to wet the dryness of her mouth; she felt her heart beating. She looked up, surprised, as Stick came over. He didn't say anything. It was like he was checking on her; yes, she was still here. She watched him walk over to Chucky, touch his shoulder, reach to take the revolver. But Chucky came alive for a moment, pointed the gun at him and Stick stepped away. She would remember him talking to Chucky, the quiet tone of his voice.

He said, the first thing he said was, "You have a lawyer?"

Chucky didn't answer. The room was so still.

"You have money to hire a good one?"

Chucky didn't answer.

"I owe you some. Soon as my checks come I'll pay you back. Seventy-two five. Man. Well . . . You want anything? Is there anything I can get you?"

Chucky didn't answer.

"I'd think about dropping the piece over the side. It's his, let the cops find it with him. He assaulted you, didn't he?"

Chucky didn't answer.

"I'll talk to them if you want. I'll talk to Nestor, tell him what happened . . . Let's call nine-eleven and get it over with. What do you say?"

Kyle watched Chucky look up. He said, "I'm not going to jail." He said, "I am not going to jail." She would remember looking at Stick then as he said:

"I don't blame you."

Stick came over to her and said, "Time to go." It was something else she would remember and come to realize how much more he knew than she did. Not, "Let's go." He said, "Time to go."

They were waiting for the elevator . . . The door opened. They heard the single gunshot. She heard her own sharp intake of breath and turned to go back in the apartment. But he held her by the arm.

When they were outside he said, "I'll take us back and get the Rolls later."

"I'm going home," Kyle said.

"All right. I'll drive you."

She said, "I'd rather you didn't. Tell Barry I'll return the car sometime." She paused. "But I should wait for the police . . ."

Stick shook his head. "They'll figure it out."

She said then, "I was right, after all. I'm not ready for you yet." Her eyes, still aware, could look into his and store pictures and feelings, but she would have to decide alone, another time, what to do with them. She walked to the Rolls and opened the door. Before getting in she looked at him again and said, "But call me sometime. Will you?"

"When I'm rich," Stick said.

27

CORNELL WAS TELLING HIM TO look around, man, look out the window at the sights, at the beauty of it, not to mention the food and the fringes, man, the fringes alone you couldn't even find anyplace else. All Stick could think of, he had seventy-three thousand dollars in Florida First National, Biscayne Boulevard and Thirty-Sixth. He told Cornell he was not into fringes.

"I'm not knocking 'em, don't get me wrong. As you say, whatever your imagination allows. This is wonderland, if you like it."

"You learned something," Cornell said, "didn't you?"

"I hope so. I know I can't hang around country clubs with guys that put one hand in their pocket and their foot up on the bumper and think they're smarter than the people they work for," Stick said. "I learned I can't wait around."

"You know where you going?"

"It doesn't matter." Not with seventy-three thousand dollars—Jesus—in the bank.

"Well, you know what direction you going?"

"Straight," Stick said. "I may try Palm Beach."

"You got delusions . . . You give your notice?"

"First thing this morning. He said I'm not going anywhere till they count the silver. We talked it over, he said stop by sometime."

"I got to go take the man some fresh coffee."

"I'll see you before I leave," Stick said, packing his sporty outfits in the canvas bag, leaving the tan and gray and black suits hanging in the closet for the next poor guy.

Barry was at the umbrella table with the *Wall Street Journal* and assorted legal-looking papers. Stick put on his sunglasses, walked down with his bag.

"What's good this morning?"

"Tootsie Roll at thirteen and a quarter and I'm not putting you on. Earnings are up to a buck eighty a share." Barry looked toward the guest house, putting the paper down. "And where's my girl when I need her? Calls me last night, she's home doing her laundry. I said, how can you be home doing your laundry, your clothes're still here? I think she's getting spacey, hanging around with the help. Hey, and the phone in the Cadillac . . . I'm getting some stuff out of there—what happened to the phone, for Christ sake?"

"It broke," Stick said.

"You mean, it broke?"

Cornell was coming with the coffee.

"I don't know," Stick said. "Somebody must've been fooling with it."

"I thought maybe you called your lawyer," Barry said, "and got pissed off and tried to throw the phone out the window."

Stick said, "What? . . . I don't have a lawyer."

"Yeah, well, you better get one, quick . . . Here." Barry lifted the *Journal*, picked up three sheets of white, legal-size paper clipped together. "Here it is."

Cornell said, pouring, "Man come looking for you while you're taking your shower."

"What man?"

"A process server," Barry said.

Why did he seem to be enjoying himself all of a sudden? It tightened Stick up, looking at the legal papers Barry was holding. "What is it?"

"I couldn't help but notice," Barry said. "You've been presented with a motion, a show cause and a hearing date."

"For what?" Not sure he really wanted to know.

Barry held up the papers. "Circuit Court for the County of Broward . . . the plaintiff, Mary Lou Stickley, now comes before the court . . ."

"My ex-*wife*?"

". . . with a motion for immediate payment of child support in arrears etcetera and . . . this one, the court wants you to show cause why you shouldn't be held in contempt, Stickley, for being such a shitty dad and not paying any child support for the past seven years . . ."

"I just gave her three hundred bucks." He sounded amazed now.

"Well, she wants back pay, ten grand a year for the seven years since the divorce, which comes to—"

"Seventy thousand dollars," Stick said, so quietly they barely heard him.

"If you don't have it, you don't have it," Barry said. "I would advise you, though, to seek employment quick and keep mailing in those payments or you'll be going back to you know where . . . Hey! . . . Hey, where you going?" Barry looked at Cornell. "Where's he going?"

"I doubt he knows," Cornell said, and watched him cross the lawn to the driveway and pass from view around the corner of the garage.

There you are, Stick thought.

Coming Up . . .

A sneak preview of

TISHOMINGO BLUES
by ELMORE LEONARD

"America's greatest living crime writer."
The New York Times

Available now in hardcover at a bookseller near you

DENNIS LENAHAN THE HIGH DIVER would tell people that if you put a fifty-cent piece on the floor and looked down at it, that's what the tank looked like from the top of that eighty-foot steel ladder. The tank itself was twenty-two feet across and the water in it never more than nine feet deep. Dennis said from that high up you want to come out of your dive to enter the water feet first, your hands at the last moment protecting your privates and your butt squeezed tight, or it was like getting a 40,000-gallon enema.

When he told this to girls who hung out at amusement parks they'd put a cute look of pain on their faces and say what he did was awesome. But wasn't it like really dangerous? Dennis would tell them you could break your back if you didn't kill yourself, but the rush you got was worth it. These summertime girls loved daredevils, even ones twice their age. It kept Dennis going off that perch eighty feet in the air and going out for beers after to tell stories. Once in a while he'd fall in love for the summer, or part of it.

The past few years Dennis had been putting on one-man shows during the week. Then for Saturday and Sunday he'd bring in a couple of young divers when he could to join him in a repertoire of comedy dives they called "dillies," the three of them acting nutty as they went off from different levels and hit the water at the same time. It meant dirt-cheap motel rooms during the summer and sleeping in the setup truck between gigs, a way of life Dennis the high diver had to accept if he wanted to perform. What he couldn't take anymore, finally, were the amusement parks, the tiresome pizzazz, the smells, the colored lights, rides going round and round to that calliope sound forever.

What he did as a plan of escape was call resort hotels in South Florida and tell whoever would listen he was Dennis Lenahan, a professional exhibition diver who had performed in major diving shows all over the world, including the cliffs of Acapulco. What he proposed was that he'd dive into their swimming pool from the top of the hotel or off his eighty-foot ladder twice a day as a special attraction.

They'd say, "Leave your number" and never call back.

They'd say, "Yeah, right" and hang up.

One of them told him, "The pool's only five feet deep," and Dennis said, no problem, he knew a guy in New Orleans went off from twenty-nine feet into twelve inches of water. A pool five feet deep? Dennis was sure they could work something out.

No, they couldn't.

He happened to see a brochure that advertised Tunica, Mississippi, as "The Casino Capital of the South" with photos of the hotels located along the Mississippi River. One of them caught his eye, the Tishomingo Lodge & Casino. Dennis recognized the manager's name, Billy Darwin, and made the call.

"Mr. Darwin, this is Dennis Lenahan, world champion high diver. We met one time in Atlantic City."

Billy Darwin said, "We did?"

"I remember I thought at first you were Robert Redford, only you're a lot younger. You were running the sports book at Spade's." Dennis waited. When there was no response he said, "How high is your hotel?"

This Billy Darwin was quick. He said, "You want to dive off the roof?"

"Into your swimming pool," Dennis said, "twice a day as a special attraction."

"We go up seven floors."

"That sounds just right."

"But the pool's about a hundred feet away. You'd have to take a good running start, wouldn't you?"

Right there, Dennis knew he could work something out with this Billy Darwin. "I could set my tank right next to the hotel, dive from the roof into nine feet of water. Do a matinee performance and one at night with spotlights on me, seven days a week."

"How much you want?"

Dennis spoke right up, talking to a man who dealt with high rollers. "Five hundred a day."

"How long a run?"

"The rest of the season. Say eight weeks."

"You're worth twenty-eight grand?"

That quick, off the top of his head.

"I have setup expenses—hire a rigger and put in a system to filter the water in the tank. It stands more than a few days it gets scummy."

"You don't perform all year?"

"If I can work six months I'm doing good."

"Then what?"

"I've been a ski instructor, a bartender . . ."

Billy Darwin's quiet voice asked him, "Where are you?"

In a room at the Fiesta Motel, Panama City, Florida, Dennis told him, performing every evening at the Miracle Strip amusement park. "My contract'll keep me here till the end of the month,"

Dennis said, "but that's it. I've reached the point . . . Actually I don't think I can do another amusement park all summer."

There was a silence on the line, Billy Darwin maybe wondering why but not curious enough to ask.

"Mr. Darwin?"

He said, "Can you get away before you finish up there?"

"If I can get back the same night, before show-time."

Something the man would like to hear.

He said, "Fly into Memphis. Take Sixty-one due south and in thirty minutes you're in Tunica, Mississippi."

Dennis said, "Is it a nice town?"

But got no answer. The man had hung up.

This trip Dennis never did see Tunica or even the Mighty Mississippi. He came south through farm-land until he began to spot hotels in the distance rising out of fields of soybeans. He came to signs at crossroads pointing off to Harrah's, Bally's, Sam's Town, the Isle of Capri. A serious-looking Indian on a billboard aimed his bow and arrow down a road that took Dennis to the Tishomingo Lodge & Casino. It featured a tepee-like structure rising a good three stories above the entrance, a precast, concrete tepee with neon tubes running up and around it. Or was it a wigwam?

The place wasn't open yet. They were still landscaping the grounds, putting in shrubs, laying sod on both sides of a stream that ran to a mound of boulders and became a waterfall. Dennis parked his rental among trucks loaded with plants and young trees, got out, and spotted Billy Darwin right away talking to a contractor. Dennis recognized the Robert Redford hair that made him appear younger than his forty or so years, about the same age as Dennis, the same slight build, tan and trim, a couple of cool guys in their sunglasses. One difference, Dennis's hair was dark and longer, almost to his shoulders. Darwin was turning, starting his way as Dennis said, "Mr. Darwin?"

He paused, but only a moment. "You're the diver."

"Yes sir, Dennis Lenahan."

Darwin said, "You've been at it a while, uh?" with sort of a smile, Dennis wasn't sure.

"I turned pro in '79," Dennis said. "The next year I won the world cliff-diving championship in Switzerland, a place called Ticino. You go off from eighty-five feet into the river."

The man didn't seem impressed or in any hurry.

"You ever get hurt?"

"You can crash, enter the water just a speck out

of line, it can hurt like hell. The audience thinks it was a rip, perfect."

"You carry insurance?"

"I sign a release. I break my neck it won't cost you anything. I've only been injured, I mean where I needed attention, was my first time at Acapulco. I broke my nose."

Dennis felt Billy Darwin studying him, showing just a faint smile as he said, "You like to live on the edge, uh?"

"Some of the teams I've performed with I was always the edge guy," Dennis said, feeling he could talk to this man. "I've got eighty dives from different heights and most of 'em I can do hung-over, like a flying reverse somersault, your standard high dive. But I don't know what I'm gonna do till I'm up there. It depends on the crowd, how the show's going. But I'll tell you something, you stand on the perch looking down eighty feet to the water, you know you're alive."

Darwin was nodding. "The girls watching you . . ."

"That's part of it. The crowd holding its breath."

"Come out of the water with your hair slicked back . . ."

Where was he going with this?

"I can see why you do it. But for how long? What will you do after to show off?"

Billy Darwin the man here, confident, saying anything he wanted.

Dennis said, "You think I worry about it?"

"You're not desperate," Darwin said, "but I'll bet you're looking around." He turned saying, "Come on."

Dennis followed him into the hotel, through the lobby where they were laying carpet, and into the casino, gaming tables on one side of the main aisle, a couple of thousand slot machines on the other, like every casino Dennis had ever been in. He said to Darwin's back, "I went to dealer's school in Atlantic City. Got a job at Spade's the same time you were there." It didn't draw a comment. "I didn't like how I had to dress," Dennis said, "so I quit."

Darwin paused, turning enough to look at Dennis.

"But you like to gamble."

"Now and then."

"There's a fella works here as a host," Darwin said. "Charlie Hoke. Chickasaw Charlie, he claims to be part Indian. Spent eighteen years in organized baseball, pitched for Detroit in the '84 World Series. I told Charlie about your call and he said, 'Sign him up.' He said a man that likes high risk is gonna leave his paycheck on one of these tables."

Dennis said, "Chickasaw Charlie, huh? Never heard of him."

They came out back of the hotel to the patio bar

and swimming pool landscaped to look like a pond sitting there among big leafy plants and boulders. Dennis looked up at the hotel, balconies on every floor to the top, saying as his gaze came to the sky, "You're right, I'd have to get shot out of a cannon." He looked at the pool again. "It's not deep enough anyway. What I can do, place the tank fairly close to the building and dive straight down."

Now Darwin looked up at the hotel. "You'd want to miss the balconies."

"I'd go off there at the corner."

"What's the tank look like?"

"The Fourth of July, it's white with red and blue stars. What I could do," Dennis said, deadpan, "paint the tank to look like birchbark and hang animal skins around the rim."

Darwin gave him a look and swung his gaze out across the sweep of lawn that reached to the Mississippi, the river out of sight beyond a low rise. He didn't say anything staring out there, so Dennis prompted him.

"That's the spot for an eighty-foot ladder. Plenty of room for the guy wires. You rig four to every ten-foot section of ladder. It still sways a little when you're up there." He waited for Darwin.

"Thirty-two wires?"

"Nobody's looking at the wires. They're a twelve-gauge soft wire. You barely notice them."

"You bring everything yourself, the tank, the ladder?"

"Everything. I got a Chevy truck with a big van body and a hundred and twenty thousand miles on it."

"How long's it take you to set up?"

"Three days or so, if I can find a rigger."

Dennis told him how you put the tank together first, steel rods connecting the sections, Dennis said, the way you hang a door. Once the tank's put together you wrap a cable around it, tight. Next you spread ten or so bales of hay on the ground inside for a soft floor, then tape your plastic liner to the walls and add water. The water holds the liner in place. Dennis said he'd pump it out of the river. "May as well, it's right there."

Darwin asked him where he was from.

"New Orleans, originally. Some family and my ex-wife's still there. Virginia. We got married too young and I was away most of the time." It was how he always told it. "We're still friends though . . . sorta."

Dennis waited. No more questions, so he continued explaining how you set up. How you put up your ladder, fit the ten-foot sections on to one another and tie each one off with the guy wires as you go up. You use what's called a gin pole you hook on, it's rigged with a pulley and that's how you haul up the sections one after another. Fit them on to each other and tie off with the guy wires before you do the next one.

"What do you call what you dive off from?"

"You mean the perch."

"It's at the top of the highest ladder?"

"It hooks on the fifth rung of the ladder, so you have something to hang on to."

"Then you're actually going off from seventy-five feet," Darwin said, "not eighty."

"But when you're standing on the perch," Dennis said, "your head's above eighty feet, and that's where you are, believe me, in your head. You're no longer thinking about the girl in the thong bikini you were talking to, you're thinking of nothing but the dive. You want to see it in your head before you go off, so you don't have to think and make adjustments when you're dropping thirty-two feet a second."

A breeze came up and Darwin turned to face it, running his hand through his thick hair. Dennis let his blow.

"Do you hit the bottom?"

"Your entry," Dennis said, "is the critical point of the dive. You want your body in the correct attitude, what we call a scoop position, like you're sitting down with your legs extended and it levels you off. Do it clean, that's a rip entry." Dennis was going to add color but saw Darwin about to speak.

"I'll give you two hundred a day for two weeks

guaranteed and we'll see how it goes. I'll pay your rigger and the cost of setting up. How's that sound?"

Dennis dug into the pocket of his jeans for the Kennedy half-dollar he kept there and dropped it on the polished brick surface of the patio. Darwin looked down at it and Dennis said, "That's what the tank looks like from the top of an eighty-foot ladder." He told the rest of it, up to what you did to avoid the 40,000-gallon enema, and said, "How about three hundred a day for the two weeks' trial?"

Billy Darwin, finally raising his gaze from the half-dollar shining in the sun, gave Dennis a nod and said, "Why not."

Nearly two months went by before Dennis got back and had his show set up.

He had to finish the gig in Florida. He had to take the ladder and tank apart, load all the equipment just right to fit in the truck. He had to stop off in Birmingham, Alabama, to pick up another 1,800 feet of soft wire. And when the goddamn truck broke down as he was getting on the Interstate, Dennis had to wait there over a week while they sent for parts and finally did the job. He said to Billy Darwin the last time he called him from the road, "You know it's major work when they have to pull the head off the engine."

Darwin didn't ask what was wrong with it. All he said was "So the life of a daredevil isn't all cute girls and getting laid."

Sounding like a nice guy while putting you in your place, looking down at what you did for a living.

Dennis had never said anything about getting laid. What he should do was ask Billy Darwin if he'd like to climb the ladder. See if he had the nerve to look down from up there.